LANDON

SWANSON COURT SERIES #4

SERENA GREY

SWEET ACACIA PRESS

Copyright © 2019 Serena Grey
All rights reserved.
ISBN-13: 978-1-7336286-4-8
Sweet Acacia Press

To my readers.
You inspire me and encourage me.
Thank you for your support.

PROLOGUE

"Mom?"

I'm shivering, and my teeth are chattering. It's so cold, and there's a weird taste in my mouth.

"Mom?"

I'm lying in the grass, and my foot hurts when I stand. I've lost one of my shoes. My head hurts. My arm hurts. There's mud on my hands and on my shirt.

The road is silent and empty.

"Mom!"

This time, it's not just my voice.

"Mommy!"

Aidan is crying. Looking around for him, I only see smoke rising from near the trees.

I'm already running toward the smoke before I realize it's the car. It's upside down, and the front is

1

smashed and twisted. Through the thick, gray smoke, I can see my mother. She's not moving, and there's blood in her hair.

"Mommy!" Aidan cries again, and I hear the faint sound of his coughing.

It's hot near the car, and there's broken glass on the ground. Something sharp pushes into my bare foot. It hurts. My knees hurt, too. Aidan falls when I unbuckle him from his car seat. He hits his arm and wails. I pull him out through the shattered window. He's still coughing and crying as I carry him away from the smoke.

A few steps from the car, strong arms grab me.

It's a man. He looks concerned. "Are you all right?" he says. "Here, let me take him."

"My mom..." I don't finish the sentence. A whooshing sound comes from the car. I turn and run back to get her, but the man grabs me from behind, pulling me back as heat blasts from the car where my mother is still trapped.

"Mom!"

"It's too late," the man says, lifting me off the ground while I kick and scream. Other cars stop on the highway, and people emerge to watch the flames. I hear sirens. Aidan is still crying as the man carries us both away from the heat.

"Mom," I scream again. "Mom!"

But it's too late.

MR. HAYES COMES TO TAKE US HOME FROM THE hospital. His eyes are red. Beside me, Aidan is whimpering in his sleep.

"Where's Dad?" I ask Mr. Hayes.

"He's on his way."

We're going back to the hotel, our home in the city. I close my eyes, remembering my mother driving, crying.

I don't want to leave. If you're getting a divorce, I want to stay with Dad in the hotel.

I wished we would turn back and go back home.

And now we are, without Mom.

"OH, LANDON!"

Mrs. Hayes—Aunt Betsy—is waiting for us at our apartment in the Swanson Court Hotel. She takes a sleeping Aidan from her husband and clasps him in her arms.

"Your father will be here soon," she tells me in a gentle voice.

"If he hadn't left in the first place, Mom wouldn't be dead!"

My voice wakes Aidan, and he starts to wail again, asking for my mom. I run to my room and shut the door behind me. I'm lying in bed crying when Aunt Betsy comes in and takes me in her arms. I cry until I fall asleep.

AFTER DINNER, AIDAN JOINS ME IN MY BED. WHEN I close my eyes, I see my mother's hair burning behind black smoke. I put my arms around Aidan, and after he stops crying and falls asleep, I do the same.

When I wake up, my dad is slumped in a chair beside my bed, his head in his hands.

"Dad?"

He doesn't reply. He's crying. I want to get up and go to him, but I don't because he's crying so hard. After a while, he leaves the room.

MY DAD DOESN'T COME BACK. MR. HAYES TAKES US to Windbreakers, our house near the beach. Dad is there, but he stays in his room. My grandpa and grandma come from France. They're old, and they stay until after the funeral.

"You have to pull yourself together. Think of the boys," my grandpa tells my dad.

Dad doesn't reply.

"He blames himself," Aunt Betsy tells my grandma, "but he will pull through it, for the boys."

He never does.

My grandma and grandpa go back to France. We go back to the hotel. Aunt Betsy checks on us every day. Mr. Hayes hires more people to look after us. On weekends we go to Windbreakers, where my father remains in his room, shutting himself away from everyone, including Aidan and me.

*a*cross the table from me, Aidan is finishing the last bits of what used to be my salmon. He's silent and focused on his food. I'm frowning in concern, thinking how ravenous he must have been. He wolfed down his food in record time before starting on mine.

The new play he's directing is likely taking a toll on him. As a teenager, when he was intensely focused on anything—exams, a school play, a girl—he'd forget to eat. Chuckling, I shake my head and take a sip of my Pinot Noir. Everybody calls me heartless, and yet here I am, worrying like a mother hen about my twenty-four-year-old brother.

Aidan drops his fork and picks up his glass, taking a long sip as he leans back in his chair. His gaze goes to the wall-to-wall glass of the restaurant, through which the city lights shine like decorations on an endless Christmas tree. He says nothing and neither do I. When we have these dinners, verbal communication is not usually the priority.

My thoughts are interrupted by a waitress—young, with long black hair and honey-toned skin. She's slender as a bone but adequately attractive. She walks toward our table, holding a bottle of wine with a napkin at the base. I watch as she passes by, detached in my assessment of her, but as she crosses Aidan's line of vision, I see his interest is piqued, and he sits up, only a little, but enough to make me smile in amusement.

I don't bother to hide my smirk. "You can't have grown tired of all the talented girls on Broadway."

"That would be impossible," Aidan replies matter-of-factly. "New ones keep arriving every day."

His eyes are still on the waitress. She's behind me now, but right in his line of sight. With obvious reluctance, he turns his gaze back to mine. Looking at him is like looking in a mirror, at a younger, more carefree reflection.

He shrugs. "I'm allowed to appreciate beautiful women, even the ones who can't act, sing, and dance."

"Appreciate away." I chuckle, then add seriously, "I've heard good things about your play."

It's his first time directing a play on Broadway. Off-Broadway he's done, a couple of successful ones, but this is his first big outing, and while I don't doubt that he'll do great, I want to be sure he feels the same way.

"There's only been one viewing. Nobody knows anything yet." He frowns. "I don't want to talk about the play. How's the hotel?"

"Running." I shrug. The Swanson Court is our family legacy. The multi-story hotel was built in the forties, soon after the war ended, under the supervision of my great-grandfather, Gabriel Swanson. A few years later, he almost lost it, but my grandfather, Alexander Court, saved the hotel and used his money to turn it into a world-class name in luxury. He also married Lily Swanson, Gabriel's daughter, and changed the name of the hotel to the Swanson Court.

I own it—most of it, anyway. Aidan has his shares, but it's mostly mine, and I run it, too. In the ten years since my father died, I've expanded the brand across the country and made the Swanson Court name synonymous with luxury living.

"I'm sorry I forgot." Aidan's voice cuts into my thoughts.

I know what he means. "It doesn't matter," I tell him with a slight grimace. "I couldn't care less if it's my birthday."

My mind goes to a headline from one of the news magazines I saw this morning. **Hotel magnate**

turns twenty-nine! it screamed above a picture of me leaving some event.

Hotel magnate.

When did that become my name?

"I'm just glad we're having dinner together." I continue as Aidan empties his glass. "Next week I'll be in San Francisco, and you'll be knee-deep in the murky depths of perfecting your play."

"You'll be here for opening night, though." Suddenly he looks like a child again, hopeful. *Is Daddy coming back?*

I blink then chuckle, banishing the memory. "Of course."

He grins. "If it bombs, at least you'll be there to take me to a place where I can get well and truly wasted."

"Let's hope it doesn't bomb."

"Well if it does, I want to wake up in a suite in Vegas with no memory and at least three call girls who won't care that I've forgotten their names."

Laughing softly, I swirl the wine around in my glass. "If everyone got that after a bad show, we'd see more of them." I watch as Aidan's eyes find the slender waitress again. "Call girls? You must be losing your touch."

He turns back to me and grins. "Maybe I've learned that the only women who understand the term *no strings attached* are those who expect to get paid."

He may have a point. My mind goes to my last, recently ended sexual connection. Cecily Feinstein, a curator at a prominent private gallery. Dedicated to her career, detached, and uninterested in a romantic commitment—just the type of woman I prefer.

That lack of interest only lasted three months before the usual questions began.

Where are we going with this?

Where do you see our relationship going?

And finally, the ultimatum. She asked me to commit to her or lose her, so I went with the second option. I don't like hurting women, and the sheen of tears in her eyes when she told me she hoped she never saw me again still feels like an indictment.

She'll get over it. For women like her, it's not the man that matters, but what he represents—the money, the prestige, the diamond ring. Some other guy will tick those boxes for her soon enough, and I'll find someone else and enjoy what I can get before the demands for commitment get unbearable.

"You have a point," I tell Aidan. "At least with a hooker, everyone gets what they expect."

He chuckles, and when he looks at me, there's a familiar, mischievous glint in his eyes. "I might just get you one as a birthday present," he says. "To make up for forgetting."

I wouldn't put it past him. "Thanks, but I'm sure I can manage."

He only shrugs. "Whatever you say."

My apartment is at the top of the Swanson Court Hotel in Manhattan, a luxurious three thousand square feet of space I don't need, beautifully spread out over two floors. It's vast and silent, and while the sense of solitude it provides can be overwhelming to others, I like it. I've never been the kind of man who's afraid to be alone.

Outside, the city is a mass of shapes and light. Up here, I can't hear the cars and people, but I can hear the wind, whistling and forceful.

Forceful. The word dances around my mind. Forceful, ruthless, single-minded—words the press love to use when they describe me. Cold, heartless, unfeeling—the words the women prefer. Words that reduce me from Landon Alexander Court, brother, friend, and whatever else I am, to just *hotel magnate*.

Do I mind? Not really. I've been too busy planning how to expand the scope of what my father left to me and working to engrave the name of Swanson Court in every mind interested in luxury living—and even those who are not. I have expanded what my great-grandfather built and made it greater than he, my grandfather, or even my father ever dreamed.

So, yes, I am single-minded. I am forceful. I am determined. I rescued Swanson Court from the brink of bankruptcy when my father died, and I am pushing further than even he ever dared to imagine. If ruthlessness is what it takes, I'll be ruthless, with pride.

Taking a sip from the brandy in my hand, I listen to the ice cubes clink against the glass as I lower it from my lips. Against the silence, I can almost hear the sounds from my memories—this now quiet apartment filled with light and laughter. My parents, the way they used to be a long time ago. Aidan, running around and sneaking off to torment hotel staff by showing up in places he wasn't supposed to be. Love and family.

All that's left of that now is me and Aidan, now a man, no longer the reckless rebel he used to be.

Thinking of my parents again, I drain my glass and turn away from the windows, suddenly restless. I need a woman, if only to distract me from the past. Cecily would have been perfect, but I can't call her now. The last thing I want is for her to imagine that her ultimatum is working. I'll have to find someone else, someone who won't be interested in commitment, at least not for a while.

Placing my empty glass on a coffee table, I

retrieve my jacket from the back of a chair where I draped it when I came in earlier. I'll go downstairs to talk to the hotel manager and thank the kitchen staff for the birthday cake that's now chilling in my fridge. That'll distract me from my thoughts for the time being.

I shrug on the jacket and walk to the foyer, toward the elevator. The call button for the penthouse overrides all other instructions. On my floor, the doors don't open unless a special passcode is entered from inside the car or I push the call button from inside my apartment.

Once in the foyer, I hit the button, expecting to wait, but I'm surprised when the doors slide open at once. I glance inside the elevators, surprised, and my surprise turns to a mixture of amazement, appreciation, and something else...something wild and insistent that flares to life inside me with a force I can't quite explain.

Inside the elevator is a girl. She's slender, with pale skin, beautiful red hair flecked with gold, and mossy-green eyes fringed with long dark lashes. She has a good figure, shown off by a flattering green dress the same color as her eyes, which are right now trained on me, her expression a curious mixture of relief and apprehension.

My first thought, before I remember Aidan and his promise to send me a hooker as a birthday present, is, *Who the fuck is she, and what in God's name is she doing here?*

My second thought, after I remember Aidan and allow my eyes to linger on the body under her dress, is, *I'll deal with Aidan later, but right now, this girl is exactly what I need.*

CHAPTER 2

She looks as if she's not entirely sure she wants to enter the apartment. In my imagination, hookers are confident, brassy creatures, but this girl...it's almost like she needs me to put an arm around her and whisper reassurances in her ear.

"Good evening?" Her voice is halting, unsure. Something in the tone makes me want to pause, to ask if everything is okay, but I shut that thought down, focusing instead on the way the fabric of her dress skims over her full breasts. Already, my body is hardening, my fingers tingling with an insistent need to touch and take. Her eyes land on my face again, and beneath the apprehension, I see something familiar. Lust.

"Well..." I let my gaze skim over her body again, "you're not what I would have chosen, but you'll do."

She doesn't reply. Her eyes stay trained on my face, that hint of confusion still lingering in their depths. Stepping aside, I invite her in, and she takes a step forward then stops and looks at me with wondering eyes.

"Come in," I repeat, puzzled at her hesitation. "I won't bite." Then, with a smile to put her at ease, I add, "Unless you want me to."

That does it. I sense her tension easing. I lead her into the quiet living room, shrugging off my jacket before offering her a seat.

"Would you like a drink?" I keep my tone friendly and relaxed. "Brandy, water, wine...?"

"Brandy."

Her voice is whispery soft, a little too hesitant, but I like it. I leave her for a moment and go over to the bar to pour the drinks. I can feel her eyes on me, and I can't shake the sensation that I'm missing something.

But I don't want to delve too deep into it... whatever it is. I want her. I can already imagine how her skin would feel beneath my fingers. I can already imagine those eyes closed in ecstasy as she comes. It's all I can do not to pull that green dress up around her waist and fuck her over the sofa, but I'm not an excited teenager anticipating his first sexual experience, although right now I almost feel like one.

When I turn back to her, she's looking at the

pictures hanging on one wall—an old family portrait, my mother's ballerina picture, and a few others. I admire the slender curve of her neck, and that hair...I want to plunge my fingers into it. I breathe, willing the straining hardness in my pants to hold on a little longer.

I offer her the drink. "Here."

She turns to me, and her eyes focus on the glass before she reaches for it. Her fingers brush mine and I stiffen, taken aback by the jolt from that small touch.

Pulling in a breath, I lower myself beside her on the sofa. Her dress has ridden up, exposing a lot more of her smooth thighs. My nose fills with her scent— peach shampoo and a hint of perfume—and my body responds by hardening some more.

It's not helping that her eyes are lingering on my face in a way that makes me want to take the glass from her and get down to business.

"You like ballet?" I'm trying to stay cool. I'd much rather be discovering what her luscious pink lips taste like.

"Hmm?" Confusion floods her features again.

I tear my eyes from her face and gesture at the picture of my mother on the wall. "You seemed interested in the picture."

"Well, I like ballet as much as any little girl who ever wanted to wear a tutu." She laughs breathily, and

I wonder if she's nervous. It's ridiculous, but somehow, I'm nervous too. "But I was looking at the quote printed on the picture," she continues. "It's from one of my favorite poems."

To His Coy Mistress by Andrew Marvell. My mother loved that poem. I quote the first line then smile. "But you're not coy, are you? That would be inconsistent with your profession."

Her brow furrows. Does she mind being reminded that she's a hooker? Should I apologize? What would be the point?

Why are we still talking, anyway? I'm aching to fuck her. By now, I should be discovering the body under that green dress, working on the wild lust that seems to be growing with every second.

Her voice snaps me out of my thoughts. "The woman in the poem..." she muses. "Was she being coy or careful? Many people toss caution to the wind, surrender to passion, and regret it later."

I couldn't care less about Marvell's mistress. I'm fighting the urge to pick this girl up, carry her over my shoulder to the nearest bed, and bury myself inside her. I can't remember the last time, if ever, a woman got me this hot without even a touch.

Calm down. "You're absolutely right," I reply. "Though only my brother would find a hooker who talks poetry on the job."

As soon as the words are out of my mouth, she

chokes on her drink. Momentarily setting aside my desire, I hurry to the bar and return with a glass of water. "Here." I take her brandy and give her the water. "Drink this."

She takes a few sips without looking at me. Why is she so quiet? I know little about hookers, but the women who usually share my bed go out of their way to show me how intelligent and sophisticated they are. I watch her for a moment as she looks everywhere but at me, then I reach down and take her free hand in mine. It's small and soft, and at the contact, there's that jolt again.

"Are you okay?"

She wets her lips with a quick flick of her tongue, and I can barely stop myself from groaning.

"I'm fine." A small, humorous smile touches her lips. "I drank it too fast, but I'm fine."

"Good." I take the water from her and set it down on the coffee table. "What's your name?"

"Rachel."

Rachel, I repeat in my mind. It suits her. "I'm Landon."

She gives me another smile, and a tiny dimple dances on her right cheek. It's insanely cute, and I resist the urge to brush it with my fingers.

"Did Aidan tell you it was my birthday?"

There's a pause. "Yes."

"What are your rates?"

She hesitates again, and I understand why. It's bad manners to ask the value of a gift, after all, but I'd like to know.

"It's...um, it's already been taken care of."

"Of course, but tell me anyway."

She does, and it's an impressive sum. "My brother is being very generous," I say with a chuckle. My eyes roam over her face, the luminous eyes, full lips, and smooth skin. She's almost too perfect. I breathe. "So...what do I get for that?"

"The whole night," she replies.

My fingertips tingle in anticipation. "Anything I want?"

Her voice is a whisper. "Anything you want."

Perfect. I get to my feet, unable to wait any longer. "Follow me."

I head up the stairs to one of the guest bedrooms. It's not until we're already there that I realize how ill-equipped I am for an encounter with a prostitute. I usually keep my rendezvous with women away from this apartment, mainly because of the memories it holds. What that means, is that if she doesn't have condoms, I'll end up having sex with my hand.

I turn to her. "You have condoms?"

At first, I think she'll say no. Disappointment floods my insides, but then she retrieves a roll from her purse and hands them to me.

I toss them on the bed before lowering myself

into an armchair by the dresser. I'm trying my best to stay cool, but I'm aching to tear off her clothes and fuck her till my lust is sated.

She's still waiting by the door, and I motion for her to come inside. When she's a few feet from me, I raise a hand to stop her.

"Take off your clothes."

Slowly, she unzips her dress while my whole body tightens in anticipation. Under the dress are panties and a black lace bra. Her breasts are full, her belly flat. Her legs in her high heels are long and perfectly shaped, and I can already imagine them wrapped around my waist.

She's looking at me, waiting for more instructions. I'm so turned on I can barely articulate what I want. "All your clothes," I clarify, watching as her chest rises and falls, once, twice, then she unhooks her bra and her beautiful pink-tipped breasts spill out.

My cock is straining in my pants, hard and insistent. My eyes fix on her nipples, which harden under my gaze. She shimmies out of her panties, and when she's done, I can't tear my eyes away from the perfection of her body.

"Get on the bed." My voice is rough.

She walks over to the bed, her breasts swaying with every step. The shapely curve of her ass is an invitation to touch. I want to throw her down on the bed, spread her legs, and taste her. The thought takes me closer to the edge. Rising to my feet, I undo my cuffs.

"Take off your shoes, Rachel." My voice is thick with arousal. "Pull up your legs and spread them. I want to see you touch yourself."

She does as I say, her fingers slipping between her legs, rubbing over every spot I'm aching to cover with my tongue. She moans, and her head falls back.

I tear at my buttons, watching her fingers hungrily and yet also needing to see the look in her eyes. "Open your eyes. Don't close them. Don't do anything unless I tell you to."

She complies, and I rip off the rest of my clothes. Her eyes cloud as she looks at me. She lets out a low moan when I pull off my briefs. My cock is rock hard, tight, and aching with the need to replace the finger she's currently slipping inside herself.

Fuck. I roll on a condom and kneel on the bed between her legs. Her fingers are still moving, and I cover them with mine, taking over with a gentle massage of her slick center before slipping my fingers inside her.

She's wet and hot, tight and soft, and so responsive. Her body tightens around my fingers, communicating her need. I move them in and out of her, and she moves in time with me. She's so hot, so eager, and it's so fucking arousing. "Don't stop," she moans, "Oh please don't stop."

As if I would. My cock is at the point of pain, but I hold on, curling my fingers inside her. Her legs stiffen, and her back arches tightly as she comes with a soft groan.

I can't wait anymore. As soon as the first wave of her orgasm is over, I pull out my fingers and grab hold of her legs, spreading them wider and burying myself deep inside her heat.

Sweet Jesus! She's fucking tight and so, so hot. She feels so fucking good.

I barely feel her legs tightening around my waist. All my senses are focused on the need to thrust into her again and again, relishing the pleasure as her moist heat surrounds my cock—hungry, demanding everything. I hear her moan as her body stiffens again, tightening around me and squeezing everything from me. I soon lose myself, groaning aloud as I come with an intensity I've never felt before.

CHAPTER 3

My heart is pounding against my chest like a sledgehammer. I try to catch my breath, and when I finally do, I release her legs and pull out from inside her. She shudders and lets out a soft sigh, her eyes heavy as she falls back on the pillows. With a languid expression, she watches as I get off the bed to take care of the condom.

After I return, we're both silent. I hand her a tissue from the box on the nightstand, turning away while she wipes herself.

Who knew sex with a hooker could be so mind-blowing?

She's still staring at me, and I have an impulsive, insane urge to stroke her face, to kiss her on the lips and run my hands over her smooth skin.

"I can't feel my legs," she says with a small chuckle.

"If it makes you feel any better, I can't feel mine either."

Her chuckle turns into a laugh, and the cute dimple appears again. Her amusement is beautiful to watch. When the laughter turns into a small smile, my eyes travel down to her nipples, hard and pink. I'm getting hard again.

"Can I ask you a question?" She sounds curious.

Reluctantly, I drag my eyes back to her face. "Go on."

"Why would someone who looks like you ever need a hooker?"

I raise an eyebrow, amused. "Looks like me?"

"You know what I mean." She rolls her eyes. "Someone as hot as you."

I've often been described as good-looking, but hearing her say it makes me grin like a fool. "Not to mention devastating in bed," I add, still smiling.

Her hand goes up. "I didn't say that."

"No," I tease, "but you said you couldn't feel your legs."

She chuckles. "Okay, devastating in bed." There's a pause as she studies my face. "Why would you ever need a hooker?"

I consider the question. It's not one I ever envisioned myself having to answer. "Are all your clients unattractive?" I ask mildly, though the thought of her with other men, other clients...causes a sharp stab of jealousy.

She only hesitates for a moment. "Yes," she replies, "or busy, or just adventurous."

I shrug. "Maybe I'm busy and adventurous."

Her eyes travel over my face, and I wonder what she's thinking. The silence stretches, and I search for a topic, anything so we can keep talking. It's ridiculous. I'm not some average guy on a first date who needs to pull out all the stops to keep a girl interested.

"Do you want another drink?"

She shakes her head. "I'm fine, thanks."

My eyes stay on her face. I have a strange urge to commit her features to memory. Where did I hear that hookers don't kiss? I want to kiss her, to taste her lips. I watch her eyes travel down to my cock and back to my face. A faint blush stains her cheeks.

She is enchanting, and I can't get enough of her.

I have the whole night, after all.

"You're not tired," I ask. "Are you?"

She shakes her head.

"Good." I run my hand down the side of her body, from her shoulder to her thigh. She trembles. My hand moves to her back, sliding over her soft skin until I'm cupping her smooth, firm ass.

Her skin is flushed already, and her breath is

coming in soft pants. I turn her over so she's lying on her stomach, her back to me. I run my hands over her supple skin, and she makes a sound that's somewhere between a moan and a sigh.

Positioning her on her hands and knees, I reach between her legs, pleased to find she's soaked. She moans when I run a finger over her wet clit, and it turns into a groan when I slide my fingers deep inside her.

I move them and she trembles. "You're so wet," I murmur, "so wet and so hot."

Her muscles tighten around my fingers, demanding more. Suddenly, I'm impatient to be inside her again. I reach for the condoms, rolling one on before taking hold of her waist, positioning her so I can slide into her.

This time I take it slow, letting the sensations wash over me. As I move, she whimpers, her fingers gripping the sheets. She's so tight, so hot, and it feels incredible to be inside her. I want it to last as long as possible, so I flex my hips at an almost leisurely pace, sliding in then out again, until she's pulsing uncontrollably around my aching cock. Her body shudders, the hot clenching in her core urging me deeper. I bend over her, plunging faster and deeper. She cries out and I feel the contractions as she comes. I reach for her breasts, teasing her hard nipples as her body continues to convulse around me.

Leaning back up, I grip her thighs and lift her legs off the bed, losing control as I thrust deeper into her pulsing heat. Vaguely, I hear her cry out as she climaxes again, and the pleasure rises in my brain until I can't take it anymore. With a loud groan, I slam into her, almost losing my mind as I come.

I release her legs and collapse on top of her. She's breathing deeply, her skin dewy with sweat. I pull out of her and get rid of the condom before collapsing back on the bed.

"Now I definitely can't feel my legs," she pants.

I surprise myself by pressing a kiss on her shoulder. "Me neither," I admit. She smiles at me, and I smile back.

The silence stretches as our breathing returns to normal. "The elevator doesn't require a code to leave," I inform her, in case she's thinking of leaving. "Just hit the call button." When she doesn't respond, I glance at her face, and she has a strange expression I can't decipher.

Rising from the bed, I retrieve my wallet from my pants and pull out a few bills, leaving them on the nightstand on her side. "I know you've been paid," I tell her, "but consider that a bonus."

She gives me a small smile, but she still doesn't say anything. I imagine she's tired. I know I am.

"You can leave whenever you like. And don't forget to leave your number."

I'm a light sleeper, so I'm surprised I don't hear her leave. When I wake up hours later, she's already gone. The cash is still on the table, and there's no number anywhere.

CHAPTER 4

"He's taking the loss of the hotel very hard," Ava declares. She stirs her coffee delicately then glances at the view from the balcony of my suite at the Rosemont. She invited herself over to join me for breakfast and discuss her brother, Evans Sinclair, who is the only reason I'm in San Francisco right now.

Since I purchased the Gold Dust hotel, built by their father, Evans has been going around accusing me and my business of any baseless offenses he can dream up in his imagination. Ordinarily, I wouldn't be worried. I didn't get to my position without a few loudmouthed detractors. However, consistent negative publicity is not good for any business, even mine.

"I don't care how he's taking it," I reply. Ava sighs

and flicks glossy black hair over her shoulder. Her worried frown somehow manages not to create any lines on her flawless face. She is a friend, an ex-girlfriend, and has at times been my confidant. My regard for her does not extend to her spoiled, irresponsible brother. I don't bother to hide my impatience. "He was running the hotel into the ground."

"Yes, but that doesn't mean he didn't love it or want to hold on to it."

I stare at her across the breakfast table. Her beauty is like classic art, nurtured by years of exquisite and expensive attention. Of course, like with me, the beauty masks decades of pain. In her case, an absent, uncaring father, a mother whose only expectation was for her to be beautiful, a family that never considered that she might be more suited to run the family business than her little brother.

Despite all that, she loves Evans, fiercely, perhaps more than anything else in the world.

"You wanted me to buy the hotel," I remind her.

She shrugs. "I assumed Evans would take the money and go back to living his frat boy life. The hotel bored him. I thought..." She sighs. "He can't get over the fact that it's you, you know. He's always hated you."

I'd never paid much attention to the sullen, resentful teenager who followed Ava around when we first dated, and I couldn't care less how he feels about me now.

"If after this, he keeps trying to spread unfounded rumors about me or my company, we will sue, and he won't like how it turns out."

She grimaces. "He's my brother, Landon. That should mean something. Be gentle with him—for my sake."

I don't reply, and she reaches for my hand across the table. Her palm is soft, and in her eyes, there's a plea, and something else, an invitation to shared intimacy.

There was a time in my early twenties when I was attracted to her, when it seemed like we could join our scars and somehow become whole.

That didn't last long. The Swanson Court hotels were too important to me, and without the constant attention she needed from me, Ava spent the next few years in high-profile relationships, marriages, and divorces from South America to Europe.

We sometimes got back together between her relationships, but it's been years since there's been anything remotely romantic between us.

I pull my hand from hers, and she considers me for a moment, one eyebrow raised.

"Let's have dinner at my place after your meeting," she suggests.

I shake my head. "I'm leaving for New York this afternoon."

"Oh." She looks surprised. "Work?"

An image of red-gold hair flashes in front of my eyes. It's been three days since that night at my apartment. *Rachel.* Even thinking her name transports me back to that unbelievable night. I still don't know what to think about the money she abandoned on the nightstand, or the number she didn't bother to leave.

Rachel.

I can't stop thinking about her.

"Not particularly." I ignore Ava's curious expression and rise from the table. She follows me and I kiss her on her soft, perfumed cheek. "It was great to see you."

"It's always great to see you, Landon." She smiles. "Take care."

A few hours later, I'm sitting across a table from her brother in his lawyer's office. Evans Sinclair is no longer the sullen boy he used to be, but the Sinclair family looks can't mask the petulant sulk on his face.

He signs the papers which restrict him from making any public allusions to the circumstances surrounding the sale of the Gold Dust. As soon as he's out of here, he'll go back to his life of exotic cars, fast women, and the never-ending party that is his life. He's spent the years since his father died paying lip service to his position as the president of the management board of the Gold Dust Hotel, but as soon as the other board members forced him to sell rather than watch the hotel die a painful death, I became the villain, at least to him.

"Mr. Court." His lawyer rises and extends a hand to me as soon as the signatures are on paper.

I rise from my seat, leaving my lawyer, Alex Haven, to retrieve the papers. I shake Sinclair's lawyer's hand. "Thank you," I tell him, then turn to Evans.

He stands and takes my hand in a soft, indecisive grip. "Fuck you, Landon," he says resentfully.

I shrug and redo the button on my jacket, turning away from the table. Before I get to the glass doors, I spy the Gold Dust, soon to be Gold Dust, A Swanson Court Hotel, through the windows. The retention of the old name was the condition of the board members, all members of the extended Sinclair family. I was to take total control but keep the original name of the hotel. I agreed. Before Evans, the Gold Dust name was one to be reckoned with.

Already, my team is working, refurbishing the old hotel and transforming it into an establishment worthy of the Swanson Court name. In a few weeks, we'll open for business.

Downstairs, the hired car is waiting outside the main doors, my chauffeur, Joe, in the driver seat. With graying hair in a crew cut and an ordinary black suit, he looks nondescript, but he's a security expert, deadly with a firearm and a skilled martial artist. With him around, I don't need any other bodyguards.

Not that I can't take care of myself. On good days, I can outshoot Joe, and I still do mixed martial arts, but his job is to make sure I never need to use those skills.

Alex catches up to me before I get into the car. He's a few years older than I am and is a partner at Fincher and Haven. The name of the law firm has changed since they were my grandfather's lawyers back in the day. I've known Alex since he started working there as an associate, and he's one of the people I trust with my business.

"I have a meeting with the interior designer's firm," he tells me, "so I'll be in New York later tonight."

"Fine." I already met with most of the people working on the refurbishment before my meeting with Sinclair, but there are still a few legalities for Alex to resolve. "I want a full report."

"Of course." He nods. "Are you returning right away? You're not staying at least a night?"

I almost smile. Of course he would expect me to have a date ready for my short visit. We've spent the last decade working hard and playing very hard.

"I have some business to attend to in New York,"

I tell him, as the now constant image of gold-red hair and deep green eyes flashes through my mind.

He laughs. "That's a first. I'll let you know when I arrive."

In the car, and Joe starts the engine. "Airport?" he asks, looking at me through the rearview.

I nod.

As we navigate the street, heading for my plane, my mind goes back to Rachel.

It's not that she's so much more beautiful than other women I've been with. She's gorgeous, but it's not just that. In my memory, everything about her feels perfect in every way.

There's a familiar straining in my pants. It's become the norm whenever I think about her or remember that night. Even now, I can still hear her moans, like an aural memory that won't go away.

Get a hold of yourself, Landon. She's a hooker. She's probably been with five more men between then and now.

"Sir?"

I realize I've spoken aloud. "Nothing, Joe," I say. "I'm just thinking."

He turns back to the road.

She didn't leave her card. Why? I retrieve my phone from my jacket pocket and dial Aidan's number. It's time to do something about this...about her. Aidan will tell me how to find her again, and this time, I'll pay for as much of her time as I need to get my fill of her body.

Aidan doesn't pick up at first. I keep trying until he finally does.

"Landon." He sounds exhausted. "Sup."

"I take it you're in rehearsals."

"You have no idea," he sighs. "I have to work with this nineteen-year-old Broadway princess whose dad is producing the show. If she weren't so talented, I'd fire her and tell her dad to go to hell."

I chuckle. "If she's talented, what's the problem?"

"Where do I start!" His groan is dramatic. "Anyway, forget about all that. What's up?"

"Nothing. I'm in San Francisco."

"Sinclair taken care of?"

"Yes."

"And work on the new hotel is going smoothly?"

The questions make me smile, mainly because Aidan has no real interest in hotels or anything that doesn't have to do with performing arts. "Yes, everything went fine."

"Well, congratulations."

"Thanks, but that's not why I called. I need to know more about the girl you sent over to my apartment."

There's a pause. "What girl?"

What girl indeed. "On my birthday," I clarify. "The hooker."

"Umm...I have no idea what you're talking about."

I snort impatiently. "Aidan, the hooker you sent to my apartment as a birthday present."

"Landon, you told me you weren't interested, remember?"

"Since when have you ever listened to me? Stop playing around, Aidan. I need her number."

"I'm not playing around," he insists.

He sounds sincere, and I got enough practice when he was a teenager to know for sure when he's lying. "So...you didn't send a hooker to my apartment."

"No!"

Then who did?

"Let me see if I'm getting this," Aidan says. "Some girl showed up at your apartment, and you had sex with her because you thought she was the hooker I promised?"

"Yes." I grind out the word.

"Woohoo!" he crows, making me want to pull his ears. "I don't even know if that's funny or scary. Was she cute? Did you use protection?"

"Oh, shut up," I growl.

"She could have been a thief...or an assassin." He laughs, his imagination on overdrive, as usual. "This is precious." He laughs some more. "Why do you want to find her, anyway?"

Because I can't stop thinking about her. I catch myself

before I say the words. "I have no idea," I grumble. "Why don't you go back to your Broadway princess and show her who's the director?"

He's still laughing when I cut the connection, but I'm not. If Aidan didn't send her, who is she, and why the fuck was she at my apartment?

IT'S LATE IN THE EVENING WHEN I GET BACK TO New York. I spent most of the five-hour flight trying to work while constantly distracted by thoughts of Rachel. Who is she? Why was she in the elevator? Why didn't she take the money, and why didn't she leave her number?

My mind is churning with possibilities. Was she a thief? Unlikely. Apart from a few paintings and accessories, there aren't many items of immense value in the apartment that can be moved by a single person, and since I didn't notice any pieces missing, I can rule that out.

A corporate spy sent by a competitor to steal information about my business? It's possible, but then her effort would have been in vain. I don't keep sensitive information lying around, and the level of protection on my computer ensures that nobody else can log in.

Now that I think about it, I realize how careless I

was. If Aidan had sent her, someone would have called from the front desk to confirm that I was expecting a guest, but I was too intent on fucking her to consider things like that.

Could she have been lost? If she was, why she didn't tell me instead of...instead of letting me think she was a whore and...

The images of that night fill my head. Her full breasts spilling out of her bra, the soft cloud of gold and red hair, how wet and tight she was around my cock, her response to my touch, her soft moans... As annoyed as I am by all the unexplained questions, my body reacts to the memories. My fingers clench, aching to touch her again, to relive the images in my head. I want to know who she is. I want to know why she was at my apartment, and yes, I want to fuck her again.

As Joe navigates the streets, I wrestle with my impatience to get back to the hotel and find out what really happened on Friday night. I've already called Jed Fray, my head of security, to review the footage from the elevators. I resist the urge to call him again. He'll inform me as soon as he has something.

Almost as if I've communicated my thoughts telepathically, my phone vibrates. It's him.

I take the call. "Yes."

"We reviewed the footage," he informs me. "The subject came into the lobby at a few minutes past eight and attended a birthday party for a photographer named Chadwick Black at the Oyster Restaurant."

The subject.

Rachel.

"And?"

"She seems to have had a heated discussion with a man outside the restaurant. After that, she took the elevator to the ground floor." He pauses. "Then when the elevator opened, she entered the button for the penthouse. We have the footage of her leaving your apartment early in the morning, but she went straight outside and took a taxi."

"The man outside the restaurant—do you know who he is?"

"We're working on it."

"Find out everything you can. I want to know who she is. Check the guest list for the party then do a social media check."

"Already on it."

"Let me know when you have something."

Later, when I'm in my study reviewing the videos the security department sent to me, I watch her argue with a dark-haired man outside the restaurant. When she walks away from him, she enters the elevator, and the footage shows her wiping tears from her cheeks. She didn't even look at the panel when she hit the button for the penthouse, and at my floor, she seems genuinely confused as she vainly taps the buttons on the elevator panel, obviously trying to make it go back to the ground floor.

My desk phone rings. It's Jed.

"I'm coming up."

"Fine."

He lets himself into the apartment and comes to meet me in the study, knocking discreetly before opening the door.

"So?" I barely look at him. I just want answers.

"We've been checking the names on the guest list and hoping to find her from there. We identified the man she spoke to outside the restaurant. He's Jack Weyland, a senior editor at *Gilt Traveler* magazine."

Jed looks at me then continues.

"He's listed on the site as a contributor, along with a headshot." He hands me a printout. "Farther down the page, we have another headshot, which seems to be the subject."

I find it almost immediately. The gleaming hair stands out, as well as the sweet half-smile and the solo dimple. I read the text beside it: *Rachel Foster, Features Associate*.

I tear my eyes away from her face. "Anything else?"

Jed nods and hands me an envelope. "That's all we found on her."

I study the envelope for a moment before I reach for it.

"Thank you." I dismiss him. As he leaves, I have a short moment of sanity when I ask myself why I'm bothering. So what if I slept with some girl whose last name I never bothered to ask? Why can't I let it go and forget about her?

I extract the contents of the envelope, and I have my answer. The first sheet is a picture of her, in color, wearing a t-shirt with her hair in a ponytail. Her arm is around someone, but that part of the image has been cropped out. She's laughing. Carefree and beautiful.

I study the picture for a long time before I go to the next page, where all her information is neatly printed.

Rachel Foster, twenty-four years old, Columbia graduate with a degree in English Literature, features associate at *Gilt Traveler*.

Jed has included her home and work addresses, family information, and printouts of articles she has written for *Gilt*. I stare at the contents of the envelope, confusion slowly giving way to anger.

Rachel Foster is going to have a lot of explaining to do.

CHAPTER 5

"I know it seems packed now, but you should come on a Friday night. We have lines around the block."

I swirl my drink around my glass, watching the amber liquid catch the colors from a thousand strobe lights before turning my gaze back down to the club below. I'm at Insomnia, a club I own in Midtown Manhattan.

Duane Wilson, the manager, watches me as I study the dance floor below us. From his glass-walled circular office right at the top of the club, everything is visible. It's like being on the deck of a large spaceship.

"I can imagine," I say, in response to his earlier comment.

He walks back to his desk, leaving me alone at the

glass. "Do you need anything else," he asks. "A drink? Someone to keep you company?"

I turn around, eyebrow raised, and he shrugs.

"I'm just saying. I know a lot of beautiful women here tonight would love to meet *the* Landon Court."

Chuckling, I shake my head. *The Landon Court.* "Not tonight."

"Whatever you want, boss," he declares. "I'm going down to the VIP for a little meet and greet. Stay as long as you want."

When he leaves, I go back to looking down at the club. Insomnia is one of my many good investments. In the few weeks since the club opened, it has become one of the hottest spots in the city.

Which is profitable, and very convenient now that I need to see Rachel Foster up close and decide...

Decide what exactly? I'm not sure. I'm curious, and slightly confused. I'm not accustomed to being confused. I want to know without a doubt what she was doing in my apartment that night.

I also want to see if the passage of time has dampened my desire for her. I need to see if the madness that drove me to arrange this interview and request her specifically will be dulled when she shows up.

I see her almost as soon as she walks into the club. A hostess leads her and two others to the VIP area. Her companions are obviously together, a slender girl with wavy black hair and a tall guy with a mass of unruly black curls. I know the girl is her cousin and roommate, Laurie, and the guy is Brett, Laurie's long-term boyfriend. Jed's notes were extremely thorough.

They order drinks, and soon, Laurie and Brett go to the dance floor.

Rachel stays seated, sipping her drink. Her beautiful hair falls around her shoulders in soft waves. She is wearing a short black dress, and I can't look at her without remembering what she looks like without her clothes.

Her face lights up when the publicity manager, Marjorie, approaches her. They talk for a while then Marjorie leaves, and she's alone again.

Idly, she looks around, and I have to fight the urge to go straight to her and demand the answers I want then drag her out of the club and back into my bed.

A guy approaches her, and I feel something like jealousy clench in my insides, only releasing when she sends him on his way. It makes no sense—the way I feel about this girl who lied to me, deceived me, and left me feeling like a fool.

Her cousin returns and pulls her to the dance floor.

Watching the soft sway of her hips as she walks, I suppress a groan. I must be crazy. I have better things to do than obsess over a girl after one night of sex.

One night of the best sex of my life.

I take a deep breath and leave Duane's office, shutting the door behind me before I descend to the VIP area. Duane is chatting up a table of football stars and their groupies, and he raises a glass to me as I walk past. I nod in acknowledgment and settle at a table, from which I have a good view of the part of the dance floor where Rachel is moving to the thrumming music like she was born to dance.

A waiter arrives to replace my drink, but my eyes stay on Rachel. An image of her body, flushed and soft beneath mine, flashes through my mind, and my cock hardens.

Go home, Landon. The voice of common sense in my head is not used to being ignored, but I can't bring myself to leave. I watch her dance, pretending she's dancing for me alone. I stare shamelessly, enjoying every movement of her body.

Some hopeful guy tries to dance with her, and she shoos him away. She shimmies and twists until it's all I can do to remain in my seat. Then, as if she can feel me watching, she turns in my direction and her eyes lock on mine.

Everything stops. The music, the dancers, the conversation...everything except that wide green gaze and the shocked expression in their depths.

I'm not above feeling a perverse satisfaction at the puzzlement on her face. She stands frozen, gaping at me, and I stare back, daring her to make the next move...or to run. Not that it would matter. I'd always find her.

I release her from my gaze for long enough to drain my glass then I'm watching her again, watching her walk slowly toward me. I don't make a move until she's standing right in front of me, looking almost as if she's in a daze.

What's the matter, Rachel? Don't you like it when your lies catch up with you?

I give her a careless smile, enjoying it as her confusion intensifies. "You're a great dancer."

Her brow furrows. "Thanks?"

Her voice stokes my memories from our night together and blood rushes toward my groin. I hold out a hand, willing her to take it. I want to feel her skin again. I want to smell her hair, taste her lips... "Come on," I say, like we're old friends. "Join me."

Her hand is soft in mine, and my skin tingles where we touch. I draw her down beside me, still holding her hand as I order more drinks. She smells of peach shampoo and a soft flowery perfume, and the combination is intoxicating.

"What are you doing here?" The curiosity in her voice is tinged with accusation.

I lean toward her, close enough to see her pupils dilate. My voice is silky. "I was in the area."

She pulls back from me. "Really?"

"Really." I'm enjoying her suspicion, and I bring my face close to hers again. She's trembling, and when her lips part on a soft breath, all I want to do is taste that pretty mouth and make it mine.

Something flares in her eyes. I take a deep breath, drawing back just as our drinks arrive. I release her hand and she gulps her cocktail. She's nervous.

"So..." she starts, and I can sense the effort behind the lightness in her voice. "Are you on the prowl or what?"

I hold her gaze. "Are you working tonight?"

That confusion again. "Working?" she repeats.

"Are you working the joint?" My words are deliberate, and I watch with satisfaction as her face shadows with a quiet indignation. I wait for her to come clean, but she doesn't.

"Not tonight." She meets my gaze in a silent challenge. "I'm here with my cousin and her boyfriend."

Her tone makes me want to apologize, but that makes no sense. She should be the one apologizing to me. She should be telling me the truth right about now.

I sip my drink. "Does she know what you do for a living?"

"No."

Tell me the truth, Rachel.

Her eyes search the club. Is she looking for her cousin? Thinking of leaving? She rises from the seat.

I should let her go. Whatever I hoped to achieve here, to make her confess or explain...I haven't achieved it. Yet, I can't bear for her to walk away. I catch her hand in mine. "Don't go."

She loses her balance and falls back on the seat, closer to me than before. She inhales softly, lips parted and as soft as temptation. I'm aching to taste her, to send everyone out of the club so I can bury myself deep inside her, right here and right now.

She licks her bottom lip and my cock presses against my pants.

"Don't do that," I warn.

Her breath catches. "Why not?"

Because I'm in danger of forgetting myself. I want her, and I can feel the arousal like a drug, clouding my senses. My hand is on her thigh, and my fingers are aching to go higher, to explore more, to touch, to possess. I pull in a breath and lift one hand to stroke her cheek. "I think your cousin is looking for you."

She looks a little dazed. At the sound of her name, she turns to face Laurie, who is approaching us with her boyfriend in tow.

"I was looking for you." Laurie frowns in my

direction as if I'm to blame for Rachel's temporary misplacement, which I am. "Why'd you move tables?"

"I... This is Landon," Rachel says, her eyes on Laurie.

Something passes between them, and I realize her cousin knows about that night. I rise from my seat and hold out my hand. "Please join us," I say with a smile. "I'm Landon Court."

Laurie looks suspicious as she takes my hand, and I can see her inner lawyer assessing me. "Laurie," she says.

"And Brett." Brett takes my hand with a warm smile.

"We were just going." Laurie looks from me to Rachel. "Do you want us to wait or..."

"Just wait for me," Rachel says quickly. "I'll be right out."

Brett gives me an appraising glance. "Well, it was nice to meet you." Then to Rachel. "We're right outside, Rach."

They both walk away, and Rachel turns to me. I don't want her to leave, and I'm sensing she feels the same. I can tell that, if I asked her to come home with me, she would.

I'm tempted, but the next time I fuck her, it won't be behind a lie.

She needs to tell me the truth.

"I'm leaving," she tells me.

I take her hand, tracing patterns on her skin with my fingers. "I gathered."

She hesitates. "It was nice to run into you."

"It was nice to run into you Rachel," I reply with a chuckle.

She doesn't move, and I wonder what it feels like for her, knowing, or at least believing if she walks away now, she'd be leaving me with a lie.

Tell me the truth, Rachel.

I release her hand, watching her eyes cloud with something that looks like disappointment.

"Good night," she says, before hurrying away. I take a deep breath. A car is waiting outside to take her home, but I'm not done with her yet. She had a chance to tell me the truth, but she chose not to. Now, I'll have to confront her with it and give her a taste of what it feels like to be played for a fool.

CHAPTER 6

"This has been a great meeting, gentlemen." I walk around the desk to shake hands with Verne Matthews and Alistair Cordwell, co-owners of an online booking service.

"It's a pleasure doing business with you," Verne says.

I smile as they leave then turn back to my desk, tapping my fingers on the polished surface. In less than an hour, I have the one meeting I've been looking forward to attending all day, and I'm oddly nervous.

Rachel.

She's like a fire in my blood, hot and spreading, unquenchable. After that night at Insomnia, my desire for her has only grown and spread until I can't go more than a few minutes without my thoughts going back to her.

Well, I will see her today, and I'll watch her reaction when her lies explode in her face.

Anticipation makes me smile. Just then my assistant, Tony Gillies, opens the door and sticks his head inside my office.

"Joe is waiting," he tells me. "You have the Gilt Building in twenty."

"I'll be right down."

He leaves me alone again, and I see Rachel's face in my head. I imagine her expression when she walks into her boss's office and sees me there. Almost too eagerly, I button up my jacket and head downstairs.

On the ground floor, a low hush descends once I walk out of the elevator into the cavernous marble and glass lobby. I know every marble tile, every stone, every pane of glass in this place almost as if I built it with my own hands. My building, a culmination of years of dreams. Without breaking my stride, I head out the main doors, where Joe is already opening the rear door of my car.

I settle into the back seat, checking my phone for pertinent emails.

"Gilt Building?" Joe asks, his eyes meeting mine in the mirror.

"Yes, Joe."

Silently, we make the short drive to the building

where, right now, Rachel Foster has no idea what's about to hit her.

Me.

~

"THIS IS SUCH A PLEASANT SURPRISE," JESSICA declares, rounding her desk to place kisses on both my cheeks. She's lovely for her age, which is something around the mid-sixties. I've known her for most of my life, first as one of those people who orbited around my parents, and later as part of the whole circle of events and patronages that make up my social life.

"I was in the building and I had to stop by."

She smiles at me, her eyes showing that she's not quite taken in by the lie. She's probably guessed that I want something, and now she's curious.

"Have a seat, Landon." She walks back to her side of the desk. Behind her, the view of Central Park is almost like a painting. "So, tell me, what's going on with the Swanson Court hotels?"

I shrug. "Business is good."

"Oh, don't be modest. What you've achieved in a few short years is simply incredible." She smiles and continues in a softer voice. "Your parents would be proud."

My smile is bitter. "Yes, I suppose they would."

Her voice brightens. "How's your little brother?"

"Aidan...he's fine. Raising hell on Broadway." I pause. "So, the article about Insomnia Lounge."

"Yes, that." She smiles. "It went up on the website today."

"Yes, and it was very well written." She gives me a queer look and I respond with a charming smile. "I've been considering the feature you pitched to me some time ago, about...the new hotel in San Francisco."

"I'm still interested." She sits. "A new Swanson Court hotel rising out of the ashes of the Gold Dust. It's the sort of thing our readers want. Have you changed your mind?"

"I have."

"Well then." She grins. "I'll get a team on it."

That's not what I want, but I don't argue. Instead, I meet her eyes and smile. "As a matter of fact, I'd like to meet the writer who did the article about the lounge. I had a chance to read a few other pieces she has written and I'm curious."

"Oh..." She raises an arched brow as her eyes dig into me. "You were specific about wanting her for the lounge article."

I hold out my hands. "As I said, I read some pieces she wrote, and I was curious."

"Of course. I'm sure she'll be glad to meet you."

She makes the call to her assistant, asking for Rachel to join her in her office. We talk about Aidan's play and how eager she is to see it. It seems like an eternity before the door opens behind me and Rachel enters the room.

I want to see her face, but I force myself to hold on, to give her a moment to approach Jessica's desk. She takes a few steps then stops, and I can feel her eyes on me. That's when I turn around and meet her gaze head on.

Her eyes widen in shock. Her body seems to freeze. Confusion and realization slowly wash across her face.

Yes, Rachel. I know.

"Rachel," Jessica is saying, making Rachel turn her gaze to focus on her boss. "I'm glad you're here. This is Landon Court."

I rise from my chair and take a step toward her. Her throat works and color stains her cheeks. I hold out my hand to her. "It's nice to meet you."

She places her slim, small hand in mine, and I pull in a breath at the buzz from that small contact. No, I won't be satisfied with this. I need more than her confusion and realization. I need her body. I need to lose myself inside her again.

"It's nice to meet you," she stammers before facing Jessica, waiting for an explanation.

"Landon was in the building for a meeting, and he stopped to say hello to an old friend—"

"Definitely not old, Jessica." I'm still holding Rachel's hand, and I don't want to let it go.

Jessica preens at the compliment. "Thank you, Landon." She addresses Rachel again. "He wanted to thank you for that lovely article on Insomnia Lounge."

Rachel looks from me to Jessica, her bewilderment deepening. "I don't understand. Why...?"

"Landon owns the place," Jessica explains. "We had a little discussion earlier in the week and decided an article about it would be the right fit for our website, and Landon requested that you write it. Luckily he'd read a couple of similar articles you've written..."

I'm still watching Rachel, and her expression gives way from confusion to understanding and then to anger. She jerks her hand from mine as if she's been stung. Then, she takes a deep breath and gives me a polite smile that doesn't reach her flashing eyes. "I'm glad you like the article, Mr. Court—"

"Landon," I offer. "Of course I liked it. You're obviously good at what you do."

She can barely hide her scowl. "Mr. Court," she says in a firm voice, "I had a great time at your club, and the article reflected that. If that is all, I have to get back to work." With a smile in Jessica's direction, she turns and heads out the door.

I watch her leave. I haven't gotten what I came for, though I'm not exactly sure what it is I want.

"It was great to see you," I tell Jessica, ignoring her bemusement as I follow Rachel out of the office.

A short hallway leads to the office where Jessica's assistant sits like a bad-tempered guardian. On the wall, portraits of Jessica with a variety of high-profile people announce her importance and achievements. At the end of the hallway, Rachel is about to open the door.

"Wait."

She stops and turns around to face me. Her cheeks are flushed, and her eyes are still blazing with anger. I take a step forward.

"Why the rush, Rachel?"

She glares at me. "I have work to do."

"As you said." I wait for a reaction. "Although this is a strange workplace for a hooker."

She inhales sharply. "Why didn't you tell me you knew?"

She's going to put the blame on me? "Why did you lie to me?"

"I didn't lie to you," she says through gritted teeth. "You made an assumption."

Unbelievable. "And you didn't think you should have corrected my mistake? I spent the weekend wondering why you didn't leave your number, but I thought it didn't matter since I could always get it from my brother. Try to imagine how surprised I was when I called him and he had no idea what I was talking about."

She gives me a defensive glare. "Look, I'm sorry for the inconvenience, but you had no right to get me to your lounge under false pretenses just so you could..." Her glare deepens. "How did you even find out who I was?"

I don't bother to answer the question. Finding out her real identity was easy. What I want to know is why she persisted in the lie and what it will take to get her back into my bed. "You had every chance to tell me you weren't who I thought you were. Why didn't you?"

She ignores the question. "Why are you here, Landon?"

Because I want you. I close the distance between us. I stop when I'm standing right in front of her, so close I can smell the peaches in her hair and see the faint quivering of her lips.

"I'm here because you owe me an explanation." I watch her face as I speak. "That night at my apartment—why did you stay? Did you know who I was?"

She shakes her head, telling me what I already know. "I didn't, and I don't owe you anything. I wanted a one-night stand, and you wanted a hooker."

She shrugs. "We both got what we wanted. Why can't you leave it at that?"

Why can't I leave it at that?

Because I can't get her out of my mind.

Because I want her.

And because I can see she's not as unaffected by me as her words suggest. I move closer, pinning her against the door. She wets her lips, nervous and more. I smile down at her, hearing her breath quicken, watching her skin flush.

My voice is soft and taunting. "I didn't get what I thought I was getting, and in any case, my hooker didn't get paid, did she? That's unacceptable to me, Rachel. I always pay my debts."

"Maybe your *hooker* decided to make it a charity case."

That makes me laugh. "I'm sure I don't strike you as someone who needs charity."

"Well then." Her eyes challenge mine. "Back to my original question: why are you here?"

I inhale, drawing in her sweet scent. "Maybe..." I murmur, bringing my face close to hers. "Maybe I want to fuck you again."

Her chest rises as she sucks in a gulp of air through parted lips. I wanted to shock her, and it's clear I have.

"If that's why you're here," she says evenly, "you're wasting your time. Jessica could walk into this hallway any moment," she continues. "So, if you don't want her to come in and find us like this, I think you'd better let me go."

I smile down at her, knowing she's already mine, despite her words. "I couldn't care less about Jessica finding us," I murmur, "and I never waste my time."

Placing my arm around her waist, I lift her away from the door, ignoring her shocked gasp as I set her down. "I always get what I want, Rachel," I say softly, and then I reach behind her and open the door, walking away without another word.

CHAPTER 7

I'm not naturally inclined to patience, but it's a habit I've learned, for my business and for my life. When you've done your homework and put all the pieces in place, all you can do is wait.

And now I'm waiting.

At the head of the conference table in my office, I listen as Alex argues with two other lawyers from our legal department about the finer points of the agreement we have with Evans Sinclair. I let them hash it out. It's what I pay them for.

"We've got him tied up. If he tries to slander Landon or the company, we'll have him in court before the end of the day."

"If he really wants to slander us, he'll have succeeded, whether or not we tie him up in litigation."

"And he'll pay through the nose for that—"

"He's rich."

"Not nearly rich enough."

I glance at my watch and rise to my feet. "Gentlemen, it's time you took this discussion to your own offices."

They gather their papers. Alex is the last to leave. "I really wouldn't worry about Evans Sinclair," he says.

"I'm not worried." Evans is like a dissatisfied gnat, and once I focus on him, the buzzing will stop. For now, he is harmless. I return to my seat and study the papers in front of me, a few contracts, schedules, correspondence...most of which I already know by heart.

Alex leaves. In a few moments, Rachel will be here. Jessica has offered her the feature on the Gold Dust, and it entails a trip to San Francisco.

With me.

I rise from my seat and walk toward the door, then stop and return to the conference table. I remove my jacket and drape it on my chair, and then I wait.

I hear my fingers tapping on the glass surface and realize I'm nervous.

It makes no sense. She's just one woman.

A woman I can't stop thinking about.

A woman I'm about to offer a very indecent proposition.

Because of how much I want her.

The door opens, and she walks in, clearly hesitant. She's dressed in a pencil skirt that shows off the lush curves of her hips and a silky blouse that makes me want to run my fingers over the soft material. I force a damper on my lust and smile in her direction.

"Come in, Rachel."

At my words, she looks like she will turn around and walk away, as far away as possible from me, but she comes forward, lowering herself gingerly into the seat I pull out for her. My fingers brush against her shoulders and there's that buzz again. I pull in a breath and go over to my chair, waiting as Tony sets up a slideshow.

I leave most of the talking to him. I assume Jessica would have explained the basics of a *Gilt Travel* feature on the Gold Dust to Rachel. Now, Tony does the rest. He describes the project, and she takes notes, directing her inquiries at him. Her questions are sharp and insightful, and I have no doubt she will approach the feature from a very creative angle.

At the end of the presentation, she looks from the screen to me, and for a moment, our eyes hold. I don't want to look away.

"Is that all?" I ask Tony, still looking at her.

"Yes."

"Thank you. You can leave us now." I turn a grateful smile in his direction. "Ms. Foster will communicate any requests for additional information or clarification."

With a nod, he leaves, and Rachel starts to rise from her chair. "I should be going."

No way.

I touch her arm. "No, don't." My voice is firm, but inside, it feels like a plea. I shift my chair close to hers so we're facing each other. "We should talk."

Her eyes flash. "I know what you're doing." There's hurt and accusation in her voice, and I'd feel contrite or ashamed if I still didn't blame her for lying to me. "You engineered this assignment so you can get me to spend time with you. Well, guess what? This time, you're not going to get what you want. You're wasting your time. I'm not going to let you get away with manipulating my job just so you can fuck me."

Her lips quiver on the last few words, reminding me just how much I want to fuck her. I hit a button on my desk and the frosted glass walls of my office darken almost to black, giving us even more privacy.

"Let's see," I say softly, "I generously agreed to a request your boss made a long time ago. How is that manipulating your job?"

It's bull, and she knows it. I am using her job to get close to her.

Her lips curl. "And the article about Insomnia?"

"I brought you there to give you a chance to tell me the truth, which you didn't take, for whatever reason."

"Maybe because I didn't want to," she snaps. "Maybe because I was perfectly fine with you thinking I was a hooker. Maybe because I had no intention of ever seeing you again."

I lean closer to her. The quivering of her lips intensifies. Her skin flushes. I can feel the arousal coming off her in waves, but I don't feel any triumph, not yet. I want so much more than arousal. I want capitulation.

My voice is a low murmur. "Quit lying to yourself."

Her chest rises, and her breath rushes out. "I don't know what you mean."

I ignore the lie. "Tell me the truth, Rachel," I challenge in a low voice. "What do you want?"

She doesn't reply.

I smile, only a little. "You see, I know what I want. I want you. I didn't ask Jessica Layner to give you the feature, but I hoped she would, especially after I told her I was a fan of your work. I'll be in San Francisco for a week, and I want you there with me. I want to fuck you every day we're there. I haven't stopped thinking about it since that night at my hotel. I want to make you come until you beg me to stop, and I know you want the same thing."

She makes a sound in her throat, but I don't take my eyes off hers.

"But if you'd prefer not to..." I shrug and back away from her. "Then we won't see each other in San Francisco. You'll do your work, return to New York, and probably never see me again. Is that what you want?"

Her chest is rising and falling. Her eyes are glazed. Her arousal in like a drug to me. I want to cover her lips with mine, to taste the desire that so closely reflects my own, but I can wait a little longer—though only a little.

"What do you want?" I ask again.

Her eyes dip to my mouth, and her lips part. I hold back only for a moment then I'm closing in, unable to wait any more. I cover her mouth with mine, tasting the heat and sweetness that is her, drowning in a nectar that's more addictive than anything I've ever tasted.

It takes all my willpower to pull away, to tear my mouth from hers. She moans, her eyes unfocused as they roam over my face.

"This is what you want," I say, my calmness belying the raging arousal in my blood, the hardness of desire straining in my pants. I want her so badly. I want to devour every inch of her.

"Your nipples are hard, Rachel," I tell her, brushing my thumb over one hardened nub peeking through her silky blouse. She lets out a soft moan and I continue. "Between your legs, you're wet and aching for me, aren't you?" I hold her gaze, watching desire cloud her eyes. "I know you want me to fuck you, right here, in this office, on the floor, on my desk, against the wall—anywhere. You wouldn't care. You just want me inside you, right now."

She reaches for me, pulling my face to hers. Triumph merges with desire and I claim her with a hunger that verges on madness. I rise from my chair, still kissing her as I lift her off the ground, one hand pushing up her skirt to expose creamy thighs and perfectly curved hips. She wraps her legs around me, and I move toward my desk, carrying her.

She tastes like desire and heat, and I can't get enough. I find her breasts through the material of her blouse, letting the soft weight fill my hands. Heaven. Her hands explore my body, almost frenzied. She loosens my tie and tosses it away then starts on my buttons.

I take her hands, needing her to slow down. I need this, but not so fast. I lower my head to her breast, and through her shirt, I take one nipple between my teeth.

She lets out a groan and pulls her hands from mine, arching and lifting her breasts closer to my mouth. Her fingers thread in my hair, not even close to gentle. I seize her lips again, plunging my tongue deep into her mouth, and push her skirt up around her waist at the same time.

She spreads her legs for me, and my fingers find her clit through the damp lace of her panties. I stroke her gently and she cries out.

I can't get enough of her glazed eyes. "Do you like it when I touch you like this?"

"Yes." Her voice is hoarse. Her hips move in time to my fingers, rubbing shamelessly against my touch.

Capitulation.

With a triumphant smile, I push her panties aside and slide my fingers inside her. She makes a strangled sound and spreads her legs wider, giving me a wide view of her perfection. I drop to my knees, wanting more than anything to taste that sweetness.

She shudders when my tongue touches her. Impatient with her underwear, I rip it away and dive deep into her moist heat, tasting every inch as she squirms and moans on my desk.

"Landon." My name is like heaven on her lips. "Oh God, Landon."

I join my fingers to my tongue, bringing her closer and closer to the brink. Her hips undulate with a mad urgency, her entire body trembling as she screams my name, begging for more. I plunge my fingers deeper and find the tiny mass of nerves inside her, stroking her there and watching in satisfaction as she explodes in a rocking orgasm.

I don't let her catch her breath before I rise and take her face in my hands. "I love the way you taste, Rachel." I kiss her gently, sucking on her full bottom lip. "I want to taste every inch of you. Tell me you'll come with me."

She doesn't reply, and I kiss her again. Her body is soft and pliant against mine. Her nipples are poking through her blouse. I rip the fabric open, pulling down her bra to free her beautiful breasts. I take a swollen nipple in my mouth, and a wordless cry escapes her lips.

Aching to be inside her, I free my straining erection, releasing her long enough to reach for the condoms I placed in my desk this morning, just in case. I don't miss the way her eyes devour my cock. I don't miss the hunger in those green depths.

Baby, I feel it too.

I roll on the condom, my eyes on her face.

"I want to fuck you without one of these," I tell her, wanting more than anything to feel her flesh against mine. "Will you let me once I prove I'm clean?" She nods, and I touch the tip of my cock to her quivering entrance. "Tell me you'll come with me to San Francisco."

Her hips move, urging me to slide inside her heat. "Yes." Her voice is a whisper. "Yes."

I grip her waist, my fingers digging into her soft skin. I draw her forward and push into her at the same time.

She's tight, hot, and sweet. My breath leaves me as her exquisite sweetness envelopes me. I could never ever get enough of this.

Her body pulses around me, tightening, squeezing. It takes me a moment to realize she's coming again. I start to move, fucking her as her body comes apart. I lower my mouth to her breast and suck hard on one swollen nipple.

The spasms of her body pass, and she lifts her hands to my shoulders, gripping me tightly as I move inside her. I can't stop looking at her. Her hair, her eyes, her parted lips, the flush in her skin...everything about her turns me on. I could do this forever and not get tired.

When she climaxes again, her body tightens around my cock, and my control slips. I plunge into her, wild in my need for her. A hoarse sound tears from my throat as I slam into her one last time and come so hard, I feel like I'll explode.

When I catch my breath, I'm holding her close, and her face is buried in my neck. Slowly, I pull out of her, feeling her body tremble. I want to kiss her again. I want to hold her close until she falls asleep in my arms.

Instead, I adjust her skirt, smoothing it over her hips. Her panties, I put in my pocket. I fix her bra, but a couple of buttons are missing from her blouse, and there's nothing I can do about that at the moment.

Leaving her for a moment, I discard the condom and fix my clothes. She's still on the desk, looking languid with sex, but also a little pissed. I take her arms and gently pull her to her feet. "Come on," I tell her. "Let's get you decent."

"Unless you have a blouse exactly like mine somewhere in this office, I don't see how you can manage that."

The primness in her tone amuses me. Smoothing a finger over the fabric, I meet her eyes and give an unapologetic smile. "I doubt a blouse like that would look as good on me as it did on you."

She doesn't reply, and I hit a button on my desk.

"Mr. Court?" Tony says through the speakers.

"I'm going out. Reschedule the Clifton meeting." I end the conversation and usher Rachel out of the office through a rear door. There's a small waiting room then stairs leading up to the apartment I use when I'm too swamped with work to go back to my apartment at the Swanson Court.

Rachel glances from the stairs to my face. "Don't tell me you have an apartment here as well."

I lead her up. "I do."

"How many apartments do you have?"

"A few." I give her a reassuring smile. "The apartment at the hotel belongs to my family, and I spent some of my childhood there. This is where I mostly live these days, especially when I'm busy with work."

She follows me inside, looking around. The apartment is much smaller than the one at the Swanson Court, but it works for me.

"This is convenient," she says, lips pursed. "Every workaholic's dream. Why leave work when you can live at work?"

I hold her gaze. "One more dig at me, and I'm going to have to fuck you again just to keep your mouth otherwise occupied." I ignore her scandalized expression. "Make yourself comfortable. There're drinks in the fridge, over there." I show her. "I'll be right back."

In my bedroom, I pause in front of the closet, surprised by how calm I am. I can still hear Rachel's moans in the back of my head. I want her again, almost as if I haven't just made love to her. Now that I know I'll have her for a week, I'm eager to use that time to quench this wild desire that's slowly driving me insane.

I retrieve a sweater from the closet. It's green, like her eyes. I emerge from the bedroom and find her in the kitchen drinking from a bottle of sparkling water.

I hand her the sweater. "You can wear this."

She accepts it then shrugs off her ruined blouse. My eyes linger on her bare skin, the creamy rise of her breasts, but only for a moment before she pulls the sweater on.

I fold the blouse and hand it back to her. "It looks better on you than it ever did on me," I say, referring to the sweater.

She snorts. "Somehow, I doubt that."

I can't help smiling. "I love it when you pay me compliments."

She shrugs, resistant to my teasing. "I was only making an observation."

"I love your complimentary observations."

She chuckles. Not so resistant after all. Her eyes meet mine, and for a second, there's a startling vulnerability in their depths.

"So, what now?"

I reach out and curl a strand of her silky hair around my finger. The mixture of red and gold is entrancing. "Now that there's no question of how good we are together, I hope you'll finally agree to spend more time with me."

"You mean sex."

"Lots of it."

She shakes her head. "Actually, I meant, what happens right now?"

I chuckle and release her hair. "Now, I take you home."

She follows me down to one of the underground parking floors and to my Jaguar. I don't drive often, but when I do, I love a beautiful car. I drive through the busy streets, stopping in front of her four-story walk-up. There's something I need to say to her, and I spill it out before I change my mind.

"About San Francisco," I start. "I want us to go together. I want you to stay with me, spend the whole time with me when you're not working. But, if that's not what you want, you don't have to do it because of what happened today."

She nods slowly. "What happens after it's over? When we come back?"

I don't know. I have made no plans beyond that one week, but when I recall the sight of her spread out on my desk, I have a feeling a week will not be nearly enough.

"What do you want to happen?"

My question makes her pause, as if it's not what she was expecting. "I don't want a relationship," she says firmly. "This is just sex. I don't want to pretend it's anything more."

I've never wanted a romantic relationship either,

so I don't expect the words to sting so much, but they do.

"I also want exclusivity," she continues. "For as long as it lasts."

I haven't even thought about another woman since I touched her. I shrug. "Not a problem."

She looks at me, and there's that vulnerability in her eyes again. I'm still smarting from being rejected for a relationship, which is comical, but now I want to ask her if everything is all right.

Her next words are decisive. "And it only lasts as long as we're in San Francisco."

"A week." I can almost hear a door close on something ephemeral I haven't quite grasped yet. "Are you sure that's what you want?"

"Yes."

"All right." The wide neck of my sweater has fallen over one of her shoulders, exposing the smooth curve. I have an incredible urge to place my lips on her skin, to kiss her with tenderness and extreme care, to love, and not to bruise. I put a damper on those thoughts and glance at my watch. "Why don't you go up and change? I'll take you back to your office."

She shakes her head. "It's almost five. I'm done for the day."

She doesn't make any move to leave the car, and I raise an eyebrow. "So, are you going to invite me up?"

She smirks. "Don't push your luck. I don't even like you."

For now. She will like me. I'll make sure of that.

"But you will." I flash her a grin and she rolls her eyes before climbing out of the car. "Tony will let you know the travel details," I tell her, starting the engine. "See you soon."

I pull off the curb. In the rearview mirror, I see her walk into the building. I want to feel more confident about what the next few days hold for us, but I know she's going to surprise me. Nothing about being with her will be as uncomplicated as it should be.

CHAPTER 8

I spend most of the next day on the phone with my team in San Francisco. The refurbishment is progressing fast, but not fast enough for me. I want everything to be impeccable before the grand opening.

I force thoughts of Rachel from my mind as I work. I've left the travel arrangements to Tony. Thinking about her and the things I'd love to do to her once I get her alone in a suite with me...well, that's one way to make sure I don't get any work done.

As evening comes, however, I can barely keep the thoughts at bay. Idly, I wonder if she has received the replacement blouse and lingerie I sent to her apartment. I picked them out myself, with help from a bemused salesperson at an exclusive department store.

Does she like them?

Will she let me tear the lingerie off her body and trail my lips over every inch of her skin?

Tony pokes his head through my door. "The plane is ready whenever you are," he tells me

I nod my acknowledgment, and he leaves. Joe is already on his way to pick Rachel up, and I don't want to keep her waiting. I hit the button on my desk and Tony returns.

"I'm ready to leave now."

Tony follows me down to the entrance, where a car is waiting for me. His voice is a constant stream of reminders about notes and emails and meetings. There's no need—he'll join me in San Francisco tomorrow—but I'm sure he's OCDing a little about not coming with me now.

My plane is a sleek gray jet with *Swanson Court International* painted along the sides. The interior is custom designed with soft carpets and plush leather seating, although the convenience of seamless travel is much more important to me than the comfort.

After a short conversation with the crew, I settle in to read news reports on my tablet.

And wait for Rachel.

I don't wait long. Soon, she arrives, and the part

of me that has been waiting to see her all day looks up eagerly.

I find her gazing at me with a strange expression on her face.

She looks lovely in soft pastel pants and a white shirt. Her hair frames her face in soft waves, and I wonder if she knows just how pretty she is.

I should be wooing her with well-planned dates and focused attention, not using her sexual attraction to me to pull her into my bed.

I should be making her fall in love with me.

I shake the strange idea out of my head.

Why on earth would I want that?

"Hey." I give her a smile.

"Hey." She smiles back, walking toward me. There's something edgy and nervous about her demeanor. Has she changed her mind?

"Come sit." I pat the seat next to me. "We should be leaving in a few minutes, so buckle up."

She does just that, staying silent as the plane ascends. I close my eyes and let my mind relax. I can feel her gaze on me, and when I hear her chuckle, I open my eyes.

"What's funny?"

"Nothing." She shrugs.

Deciding not to push it, I go back to my news reports.

"I thought Tony would be here," she says, retrieving a laptop computer from her handbag.

"He'll arrive tomorrow." For entirely selfish reasons, I wanted tonight to be just us.

She opens the tiny laptop and starts typing. I don't ask her what she's working on. I continue reading my reports then abandon them to focus on her. She has a small frown on her face, and as she works, she chews on the corner of her lower lip. When she catches me staring, I don't look away, but she does, turning her gaze back to her screen.

Did something change between yesterday and now? I don't want to consider that possibility, but if something has changed, I can't very well force her to adhere to our agreement.

She's typing again, chewing furiously on her lip.

"If you need anything—a drink, food—there's a button right there." I show her. "If you'd like to lie down, there's a bedroom through the doors at the back."

Something flashes in her eyes, something I recognize. Lust. Then as fast as it came, it's gone again.

"You're the one who looks in need of a bed," she says, a teasing note in her voice.

She's right. I am exhausted. "Yes, but I have no intention of going in there without you." I give her a slow smile. "And if I get you in there, neither of us will be getting any sleep."

Her eyes skitter back to her screen, nervousness coming off her in waves. Now, I'm more convinced than ever that she has changed her mind. I'm about to ask her if that's the case, but she starts to talk about the Gold Dust, and we discuss that instead.

When she's satisfied with my answers, she goes back to looking at her screen. I order fresh juices for the both of us then go back to reading the news on my tablet.

Soon, she's asleep. I make sure she's comfortable, trying to focus on work even when she curls up at my side with her head on my shoulder. She sighs in her sleep, and at one point, she mumbles my name.

It's a few hours before she wakes. She straightens, blinking. "I fell asleep."

"So you did." I give her a reassuring smile. "I hope you enjoyed using me as a pillow."

"I'm sorry," she says self-consciously.

"I didn't mind." I shrug. "I think we've established that my body is here for you any time you want it."

Her face flushes, and like the last time I alluded to sex, she changes the subject. "Are we almost there?"

"We're about to land."

We talk little during the drive to the hotel. When

I ask, she tells me it's her first time in the city. She takes in the sights, avoiding looking at me, and I let her be.

We are staying at the Rosemont Royal, where the manager is waiting. He leads us through the luxurious hotel, up to the penthouse suite. Once he leaves us, I again consider asking if she's changed her mind, but I decide against it. I won't put any pressure on her. If she wants to go on with our arrangement, she will come to me.

Having made that decision, I focus on settling in and showing her around while efficient hotel staff bring up our things.

"Service elevator and fire escape are through that door."

Her eyes follow my directions, but she stays silent.

I gesture around the suite. "Do you like it?"

She gives me a look that suggests I might be insane to ask. "I think it's gorgeous."

Good. "There's a library too. I'm sure you can find a poetry book or two."

She responds to my teasing with a smile. "Thanks." She looks around. "So, I take it you've stayed here before."

"Whenever I'm in the city, yes." I open the doors that lead out to the terrace. The view from there is exceptional. It's not lost on me that soon, the

Rosemont Royal won't be my preferred accommodation anymore. It will be competition.

Rachel comes out to join me on the terrace. "It's a lovely view," she murmurs.

The slight wind is playing with her hair, making tendrils dance around her face. Out here, she's almost breathtaking in her loveliness. I want to kiss her. I want to tease the sensitive spots I've already discovered on her body and maybe find a few more. I step toward her then stop myself. Reaching out, I stroke her cheek with my finger.

"I'm sure they're done unpacking," I murmur, referring to our luggage. "Let me show you to your room."

Her face registers bewilderment, but only for a moment. I lead her through the suite, now empty but for the two of us, to a bedroom with a beautiful four-poster bed.

"Wow," she says breathlessly, stepping past me into the room. She walks over to the bed and runs her fingers over the soft sheets then turns back to the door and gives me a suggestive glance that sends all my blood rushing into my cock.

"Aren't you going to come in?" Her voice is soft and inviting.

I want to. I want to do things to her on that bed that will leave her panting for more, but I won't. If she is considering changing her mind, I will not be the pushy bastard who gets in the way.

Even so, I can't resist going to her and placing a kiss on her lips. Just one.

"You must be tired," I murmur, savoring the taste of her lips on mine. "And you have a lot of work to do tomorrow. I'll see you in the morning, Rachel. Good night."

I can feel her eyes on me as I walk away, and I almost say what the hell and turn back, but I've already decided to wait, and I know, when she comes to me, her capitulation will be so much sweeter.

CHAPTER 9

I sleep little. My dreams make sure of that. The second time I'm awoken from seeing my mother's face and hair catch on fire, I abandon any hope of sleep and spend the next few hours working instead. Some nights are worse than others, and this seems to be one of the bad ones.

I try not to think about Rachel, asleep, a few feet from me. Holding back has its costs. I'm in a restless state of semi-arousal, tortured by the expectation I saw in her eyes last night and the surprise when I left her alone.

Now, it doesn't seem like the best decision to wait until she comes to me. What if she never does?

It's entirely possible I've overestimated the intensity of her desire for me. I can live with that. It would be hard, but hard things are doable.

As it gets light outside, I hear the faint sounds of the city waking. I take a shower before going out to the balcony. It's lovely outside, and I order a jug of fresh orange juice, waiting for the sun to come up before I order breakfast.

Rachel emerges from her room soon after. She looks beautiful in cream pants, a blue cotton shirt, and a light jacket. Her face is free of makeup and her hair hangs loose around her face.

It's a pleasure to look at her, and not only because of how beautiful she is. There's a light that radiates from inside her, a light that has never seen the kind of darkness or pain I have.

I cover my thoughts with a smile. "Good morning. Did you have a good night?"

"Perfect." She smiles, a little too brightly, and joins me at the table.

I gesture toward the jug in front of me. "Juice?"

She nods, and I pour her a glass. The food arrives, a simple breakfast, but Rachel insists she doesn't want anything else.

I butter a piece of toast while she watches silently, accepting it when I hand it to her.

"Tony is arriving this morning," I inform her. "He's going to be staying a floor below us for a few days before he returns to New York."

"Okay." She sounds as if Tony is the last thing on her mind.

"We'll leave for the Gold Dust after breakfast," I continue. "You've discussed your itinerary with him?"

"Yes. I meet with the hotel manager today, tomorrow the designers, and the photographers after that."

She'll be busy, and I'll be busy too. I don't let myself think what that means for the survival of our arrangement. I force a smile. "I'll be in meetings all day."

I can feel her eyes on me, but she says nothing.

I leave her to eat. Tony arrives just as we finish breakfast. "Tony's here," I tell Rachel. "Are you ready?"

"Yes." We both get up at the same time. Her eyes are wide as they focus on mine. She is irresistible, and the next couple of days will be excruciating if things continue like this. A tiny speck of butter stains one corner of her lip, and I have an insane urge to lick it.

I know if I touch her, I'm gone. In fact, the whole morning will be gone.

Carefully, I touch my finger to her mouth and wipe the butter off. As she watches me, I put the finger in my mouth and lick it.

Her breath quickens. No, I haven't overestimated the intensity of her desire for me.

"I'll wait in the living room," I tell her.

She leaves me standing there then joins me in the

living room a few moments later, carrying her bag. We go down together, silent in the elevator.

Oh well.

Tony is waiting in the lobby, and we all head to the Gold Dust. Something tightens in my chest as we near my new hotel. It's a beautiful building with cream walls and exquisite detailing on the facade. It's set back from the street, and even with the work still ongoing, it's already showing the promise of coming perfection.

Inside, I try to see the large lobby through Rachel's eyes. She's looking around, taking in the covered floors and newly refinished walls. Her eyes go to the domed ceiling and she sighs.

"It's lovely," she exclaims in a rapt voice.

There is something gratifying in her appreciation, almost as if I've been waiting, eager and hopeful for just that.

"I'm glad you think so." I say the words close to her ear, and she turns to look at me, green eyes wide. I have to fight an urge to kiss here right there, in front of everyone working on my fucking hotel.

"I'll see you later." There's a brusqueness in my voice that I don't intend. I touch her arm before walking away, leaving her with Tony.

For the next few hours, there's no time to ponder my situation with Rachel, though she seeps into my thoughts without warning. I have meetings with local suppliers, labor providers, service vendors, and a few local groups. By lunchtime, I take a break, and even though there are a lot of other things I could do, I go to find Rachel. My plan is to take her to lunch. That's time I can spend with her without there being any pressure.

I find her in the temporary office that was set up for her work. She's frowning into her screen when I open the door. At the sight of me, her face relaxes, but only a little.

"How're you getting on?"

There's a pause. "Okay," she says. "Claude was very helpful."

"Good." Claude is the hotel manager, an efficient, flamboyant man—exactly what I need for this hotel. "We'll go out to lunch. Afterward, if you're done with Claude, you can return to the Rosemont. I'm going to be here for a while."

"That's fine." She rises from the chair and gets her things together, then she stops and meets my eyes. "Did you change your mind about this trip? Did you decide you don't want to fuck me anymore?"

The words are like a thunderclap in my head. *Did you?* I want to counter. Have I imagined her hesitance in the last couple of hours, her skittishness? She holds my gaze with a challenge that makes me realize I probably have. She wants this as much as I do, and God help me, I'm not prepared to wait anymore.

The door—I make sure it's locked before facing Rachel again. I'm sure she can see my intention clear on my face. Her eyes follow me as I close the distance between us. Pushing her chair out of the way, I stand behind her and, with one hand on her belly, pull her flush against my front.

Her soft curves mold to my body. I'm hard, straining against my pants, pressing into her backside. She gasps and moves a bit, rubbing against me.

My breath escapes me. "Does this feel like I don't want to fuck you?"

She releases a trembling breath. "No."

Still pressing her body to mine with one hand, I undo the buttons of her blouse. I need to touch her skin, and it's all I can do to stop myself from tearing the fabric right off of her. I undo the clasp of her bra, and when it's good and loose, I cup one of her breasts, rolling a hard nipple between my fingers.

A sound escapes her throat. Pleasure and desire. I want to tear her clothes off and be as deep inside her as it's possible to be. "I want you so much it fucking hurts. I can hardly keep my mind on anything else." My lips are close to her ear, and with each word, her breathing quickens. "I've never wanted anyone so much."

She rubs her ass against my cock and I almost lose my mind. Her voice is weak. "But last night...why?"

"Why did I stay away? Why did I try to give you a chance to change your mind? I have no fucking idea. I must have been crazy." I'm crazy now...with lust. I undo her pants and slide my fingers between her legs, into the slick, wet heat that's waiting there.

Her back arches. She's so wet, so sweet. Unable to wait, I tug her pants down then do the same with her underwear, exposing the soft curves of her hips and thighs. Sliding one hand down her front, I cup the soft folds of her pussy and slide my fingers over her clit, again and again, spreading the slickness of her arousal. From behind, I slide two fingers into her tight heat.

Trapped between my body, my hands, and the desk, she can barely move. All she can do is feel, and she does. She's moaning, panting, swearing, and crying out my name. Her hips jerk as she strains toward release.

"Let it go," I whisper, aching to see her fall apart. She lets out a wild sound and her body arches, throbbing as she falls forward on the desk.

Almost satisfied, I watch as she tries to catch her breath. I'm still stroking her, leisurely, enjoying the light shudders that work their way through her. She's captivating, and I've never wanted to fuck anyone so much.

Making short work of my zipper and briefs, I position my cock at the parting of her thighs. She pushes backward, rubbing herself against me. It's the sweetest torture.

I reach for the condoms in my wallet, then stop.

"Are you on the pill?"

She nods impatiently and rubs on me again. "Yes."

"I'm clean," I tell her, wanting more than anything to feel her around me, hot and sweet. I've always been careful, and with regular tests, I know I'm fine. "I want to fuck you like this, with my skin against yours. I want to feel your heat. I want to come inside you."

"Please," she sighs. "Please now."

It's the only invitation I need. I enter her, and she closes around me like a hot fist. She's tight, and being inside her is incredible. She lets out a moan as I withdraw and thrust deep again.

So sweet.

Fucking her is like a mind-altering drug. Each moan that escapes her chips away at my control until there's nothing left, only her skin beneath my fingers, her heat throbbing around me, her body and mine. She arches and shudders, and I push deeper, harder, losing parts of myself inside her with each thrust. Her cry of pleasure comes out the same time as mine, as I spill myself inside her.

My weight finds the chair behind me, and I pull her down with me. I bury my face in her hair, stroking her shoulders. I'm still inside her, and I know I could fuck her again. I could go all day if she made herself available.

I run my fingers over her shoulders and back, stroking her gently, drawing slow patterns on her smooth skin.

She's breathing slowly, trembling as I explore more of her skin. When I cup her breasts, she squirms on my lap then moves more deliberately, until she's riding me up and down, slick, wet, beautiful.

I let out a breath. "You're so hot."

She moans. "You're so hard."

No fantasy was ever this good, this sweet. I grip her waist and move her hips up and down my length. I could do this forever, I realize, groaning as her slick walls pulse and tighten around my cock. It feels so good to be inside her.

So good.

When her body starts to shake and shudder, I'm almost there too. I hold her in place and rock my hips, sliding deep into her until she's gasping and crying out, and I'm coming again, releasing my whole being into her sweet pulsing heat.

I keep her on my lap, holding her close as her eyes flutter into drowsiness.

"You said something about lunch," she reminds me after a while. Her voice is soft and full of content.

I chuckle. Food has been the furthest thing from my mind for the past half-hour. "Yes, I did."

"I'm sleepy," she murmurs, "but I'm also unbelievably hungry."

"Me too...for some reason." I lift her to her feet then do my best to clean us both up with a handkerchief from my pocket. When I'm done, I push it back in my pocket, looking up to see her watching me with a teasing grin.

"You're not going to keep that as some sort of weird memento, are you?"

I could. "I don't need a memento when I have you," I say confidently. *For a week only*, a voice reminds me, but I ignore it.

I help her adjust her clothes before starting on mine. She doesn't say much as we pack up her stuff to leave. When she picks her phone up off the desk, whatever she sees on the screen makes her face cloud, but she doesn't tell me what it is, and though I'm curious, I don't ask.

CHAPTER 10

"W e're not flouting any city ordinances."

Claude smirks. "Just skirting close—"

"And ensuring that we don't have to push the opening back by a month or more."

"We can expand the delivery bay without having to delay the opening."

"Then they'll find another obscure regulation—"

I let them argue, Claude and one of the engineers. We'd found a relatively quiet spot for the meeting, but there's still construction noise.

My mind goes to Rachel, back in our suite, waiting for me.

After lunch together, she returned to our hotel, and even though I've spoken to her on the phone since then, I miss her.

I can't wait to devour her again.

And I will, tonight, after we have dinner at the famous chef Cameron McDaniel's newly opened restaurant. I don't have many friends, and Cameron, one of the most talented chefs I know, is one of the few I'm proud to include in the limited number.

I interrupt the argument and face the engineer. "Get the permits for the expansion. I'm sure you can fast-track that if you put your mind to it."

He accepts with a nod. "Fine."

After my final meeting, I return to the Rosemont. Rachel is in her room and doesn't hear me arrive. Resisting the temptation to go straight to her, I get ready for dinner. By the time I emerge a few minutes later, she's coming out of her room, wearing a blue dress, her hair in a messy bun at the base of her neck.

Damn.

I cross the room as if drawn by a magnet, taking her hand and placing a kiss on her cheek. "You look amazing."

Her lips curve in an appreciative smile. "You don't look too bad yourself."

"I aim to please."

"And you never miss."

We're flirting. I like it. "Not if I can help it."

She's laughing softly as we go down to the entrance, where our ride is waiting. It's a cool, foggy night, and outside the car, the city is full of light and vibrance. Already, bookings are coming in for the Gold Dust, and I wonder how long the excitement will last. Months? Years? A lifetime if I can help it. Every hotel that bears my name will always be the first name in luxury accommodations. That's my goal.

The car stops in front of Cameron's restaurant and Rachel is looking at me. She has been silent through the ride, deep in thought. I turn in her direction, and she looks away. I reach over to stroke her hand, and she lifts her eyes to mine. There's an uncertainty in her gaze I don't understand.

Leaning across the seat, I place a kiss on her lips. It's supposed to be quick and gentle, but she doesn't let me pull away. She deepens the kiss, seeking more. I oblige her without hesitation, pushing past her lips to taste the sweetness of her mouth.

She lets out a soft moan, and I let her go, barely stopping myself from fucking her in the car.

"I can't imagine why I thought I could make it through the evening without wanting to tear off your clothes," I say with a rueful smile.

She slides a small hand along my thigh then lets her fingers tease the ridge in my pants. She wets her lips in a gesture that goes straight to my cock. "I'm not very hungry," she whispers, her face inviting me to turn the car around and go back to our hotel.

I take a deep breath, sorely tempted. "I wish we could go back, but there's someone expecting us."

Cameron's restaurant is on the hill by the waterfront and the views are spectacular. Inside, a waiter leads us to our table, and just as we sit, Cameron arrives.

He's like a vibrating ball of energy with twinkly blue eyes and bright red hair, and I'm glad to see him. After we hug, he turns his attention to Rachel.

"You must be an angel," he proclaims, gazing deep into her eyes.

I shake my head, resisting the urge to roll my eyes. "Rachel, this is Cameron McDaniel. Cameron, Rachel Foster."

She smiles up at him. "Pleased to meet you."

"Delighted." He places a kiss on her hand, and I glare at him. There's only so much I can take.

"Cameron is an old friend," I tell Rachel. "And he only recently opened this restaurant, so he's dying to hear you say it's awesome."

She gives him a charming smile. "Definitely awesome."

"Definitely—I like you already." He takes a seat at our table. "What are you doing with this handsome devil, anyway?" He gives her a serious stare. "We reds should stick together. I know all the dirt on him, known him for years. I could tell you things that'll make him squirm."

Rachel is smiling. She glances at me, her eyes warm in a way I haven't noticed before. This is the first time she's seen me outside of work and sex, I reason. *Yes, I am a human being, Rachel, one who can't wait to peel your clothes off and make you melt with pleasure.*

She turns back to Cameron. "I look forward to hearing the worst."

Cameron can't hide his excitement. He summons a waiter and orders wine. "For my friend, who I haven't seen in ages, and his lovely girlfriend, I have prepared something special." He looks at Rachel. "You don't mind seafood, do you?"

I see Rachel's eyebrows go up when she hears the word girlfriend. Apart from a small headshake, she doesn't give any other reaction. She doesn't seem flattered, either. She's clearly not hanging on to the hope that being with me in that way will become a possibility.

I don't want a relationship.

Well, neither do I.

Cameron charms Rachel with his bottomless well of stories, making her laugh almost to the point of tears. While I'm glad Cameron is running his own restaurants now, some of his stories make me nostalgic for the days when we were both flying by the seats of our pants in New York, me trying to run a hotel that was much larger than anyone thought I could manage, and Cameron learning the ropes in restaurant management and trying to make his way in the world.

The food is delicious, as is the wine. Hours later, after much laughter—much of it at my expense—we leave. Cameron follows us to the car, giving Rachel a warm hug before turning to me. "Take good care of her."

"I believe I'm already doing that," I reply with a chuckle. My eyes find Rachel's, and she flushes. She knows what I mean.

There's a sudden flash from across the street and I curse, one hand going to pull Rachel close to me and shield her from the camera.

"They always come here hoping to catch the movie stars leaving," Cameron says dismissively. He grins at me. "You can blame yourself for looking too much like a movie star."

Rachel giggles. "I agree."

My arm tightens around her. *This guy, movie star looks or not, can't wait to get you in bed, baby.*

As soon as we're inside the car, I reach for her, pulling her into my arms and covering her lips with mine.

She's like an explosive cocktail that goes right to my head. She kisses me back, small sounds spilling from her as her hands roam over my body.

Jesus!

Pulling away, I try to get some control of my

desires. I'm panting and so is she. "I've been thinking about this all evening," My voice is hoarse. "No, since we spoke on the phone earlier. I need to fuck you."

She sighs. "Me too."

"You're going to give yourself to me. Every part of you." I trail my lips down to her neck and her head falls back. I inhale the sweet scent of her skin and kiss the pulse beating in her throat. *Mine.* "I want you so much, Rachel, and I'm going to make you mine."

Her eyes stay closed as I continue to trail my lips over her body. When the car stops outside the Rosemont Royal, I want to fly up to our floor. I maintain my composure until we're inside our suite. Once there, I don't wait a moment more. I mold her body to the wall and cover her lips with mine. She tastes like sex and desire, like everything I need.

She tears at her dress and it falls open. I toss my jacket away then my shirt, my lips still on hers.

She reaches for my waistband, fumbling with my pants as I slide her dress off her shoulders. Next is her bra. I free her breasts and they spill out, pink-tipped and beautiful.

Fuck.

I tug her panties down, and when the tiny bit of lace falls to her ankles, she is completely, totally naked.

And glorious.

I feast my eyes, barely noticing when she

unfastens my pants. She strokes me through my briefs, and I can hardly take it.

Sliding one hand between her thighs, I can feel just how wet she is. I lift her off her feet and spread her legs around my waist, her back to the wall. She moves against me, rubbing her wet core on me, and I almost lose my mind.

"Landon," she moans.

"Shh, baby." I free my cock, and she squirms, her hips straining.

"Fuck me, Landon," she says, breathless. "Fuck me now."

With pleasure. I drive deep inside her. She tightens around me and my mind fractures. My whole being is centered on that point where our bodies are joined, and for as long as I'm inside her, there's nothing else, only us, only sex, only this.

I take one nipple in my mouth, then the other. She makes a tortured sound, and I rock into her, deeper, harder, fucking her until she screams, coming hard and loud. I follow almost immediately, my climax hitting me harder than a speeding truck.

My legs are shaking, and I fall to my knees, still bearing her weight. She buries her face in my hair, breathing hard. I rise to my feet and carry her to my bedroom. I'm still inside her, still hard, and once I lay her on the bed, I start to pull away.

"Don't." Her arms tighten around me. "Don't go."

Truth is, I don't want to. I don't want to leave her side, ever. I slide my lips over hers, caressing her tongue with mine before placing kisses on her throat. After a few moments, I start to move, gazing at her face, watching her green eyes widen and dilate as I make love to her.

This is heaven. The thought comes as her moans fill my senses. We move together, perfectly joined, until she shudders and comes with a long, soft cry. My arms tighten around her, and soon, I'm coming too, letting go of everything except the pleasure she gives me.

I collapse on the bed beside her and pull her close, holding her in my arms until we both fall asleep.

CHAPTER 11

"*H elp me, Landon.*"

I wake up with a start, an image of a burning car in my head, my mother's voice distinct in my memories. Beside me, Rachel is still asleep, her hair spilling out on the pillows like a silk curtain. I place a kiss on her temple. She stirs but doesn't awaken.

Just a few more days. I don't want to think about after, when we return to New York. If I do, I will be tempted to beg, and that's something I've never considered doing, for any reason.

I find my phone near the foyer, along with our discarded clothes. I take care of the clothes, and in the closet, I pull on a pair of pajama bottoms before going out to the terrace.

There's a text on my phone from Cameron.

I like her.

Yeah, me too. I set the phone down and stare out at the city. A cold breeze blows past me, and I close my eyes. I don't mind the cold. It's more bearable than the flames in my nightmares.

I'm not sure how long I stand there before Rachel comes. A sound behind me alerts me to her presence, and I turn around to find her watching me. She's wearing a white robe drawn tightly around her, concern shadowing her green eyes.

I straighten. "You should be asleep."

"So should you." She cocks her head to one side and looks me over. "What are you doing out here?"

I shrug. I can't tell her about the images and memories that plague my sleep. "Just thinking."

She comes to stand beside me. "What about?"

"Work."

Another breeze slides across the terrace and I notice she's shivering.

"You're cold." I put my arm around her, glad for the excuse to breathe in her scent and her warmth. "Come on. Let's go back inside."

I lead her back to my bed and soon, she falls asleep. When I'm sure my movements won't disturb her, I leave, going to the library inside the suite where I work till morning. Rachel stir when I return to bed and melts easily into my arms. Once again, I lose myself in her body, and the experience is more exquisite than I can put into words.

My morning at the Gold Dust is uneventful, at least until Jed calls me from New York.

Jed is not one for social calls, so I know there's a serious issue that requires my attention. "What's going on?"

"It's Aidan," he says.

My body seizes with something like fear. My brother is talented, artistic, clever, intense, but he has also struggled with depression for most of his life. I live with a barely contained fear of something happening to him, and at times like this, it paralyzes me.

"Where is he?"

"I'm not sure. Nobody is." Jed's voice is grave. "He hasn't shown up for rehearsals in a couple of days and nobody can reach him."

"Have you checked his apartment?"

"His and yours, and I've checked with the Hayes. They haven't seen him at Windbreakers."

I close my eyes. If Aidan is not at his place or mine, if he isn't at Windbreakers either...where can he be?

Memories of past destructive behaviors threaten

my composure. *He's past all that*, I tell myself. *He's grown so much.*

"What about the cabin?" It's a long shot, but Aidan purchased a remote cabin far upstate. He wanted it for solitude, according to him. To my knowledge, he has never actually spent a day there.

"I'll get on it," Jed says.

"No," I reply. "I'll go." This is Aidan. "I'll be there as soon as I can."

Jed is quiet for a moment. "Okay. Joe will pick you up at the airport."

After I ask Tony to arrange for the plane and the car to take me to the airport, I realize I haven't told Rachel I'm leaving.

"Where's Rachel?"

He frowns and looks up from his phone. "She's just finished talking to the interior designer."

I dismiss him, already dialing Rachel's number. I'm paralyzed with worry about Aidan, but I'm also seized with a deep hesitation to leave her, even for a day.

She takes the call. "Hey." I can tell from her voice that she's smiling.

Happy to hear from me.

We've come a long way from when she was mad at me for showing up in her office.

"I have to go to New York." I tell her, regretful. "I'll leave in about an hour. I'll be back tomorrow."

"Oh." She sounds so disappointed it causes an ache in my chest.

"It's very important, or else I wouldn't leave..." I stop myself. "Or else I wouldn't go."

She is quiet. "I'll be here when you get back."

I let out a breath. "You'd better be."

In the car, on the way to the plane, I reflect on the words I'd been about to say. *Or else I wouldn't leave you.*

I stopped myself from saying them, because they'd have communicated much more than I am supposed to feel, and yet exactly what I already do.

ON THE PLANE, I SNATCH A FEW HOURS OF SLEEP. In my dreams, my parents are happy. My father, home from one of his many trips, is teaching Aidan to ride a bike while I show off the skills I've already mastered, luxuriating in my mother's praise. Later, they go out to dinner and return in time to tuck us in bed.

I wake up with an intense sensation of nostalgia and sadness, and the questions no therapist could ever answer. Why did everything go wrong so fast?

There were no external factors. My parents were in love. They were happy. We were happy, and without warning our lives fell to pieces, leaving us broken, wounded souls, unable to deal with memories of pain.

Perhaps if my mother had been a less passionate creature, she wouldn't have tried to leave my father based on unsubstantiated rumors from a busybody. If she'd loved him less, she wouldn't have been speeding that day, barely able to control the car. Perhaps if my father had been more considerate of her feelings and spent less time on business trips, she'd still be alive. Maybe if he loved her less, he wouldn't have died when he lost her. Because that's what happened—he died too, and only a shell remained, a shell that couldn't bear to live, even for his sons.

Beside me, the screen of my tablet shows a picture taken outside Cameron's restaurant last night. In the picture, Rachel's face is turned away from the camera. An accompanying article speculates about the *mystery woman* with me and Cameron.

Off the market? the headline screams.

I grimace as another headline squeezes in through the walls I've constructed around my memories.

Ballerina Alicia Creighton dies in fiery auto inferno.

Almost as if it's happening right now, I can hear my brother crying, asking for our dad, my mother's voice as she loses her temper and then loses control of the car. I remember carrying Aidan out of the wreck, and the hands, strong hands, holding me back from the burning car, forcing me to watch my mother burn...and do nothing.

My soul is tearing all over again. "Let me go," I mutter under my breath.

"Do you need anything, Mr. Court?"

I shake my head, and the stewardess retreats.

Calming myself, I direct my mind to Aidan. Wherever he is, it's my job to make sure he's okay.

He's all that matters now.

And Rachel.

I close my eyes as she slips into my mind.

Rachel.

Thinking about her lights me up inside, and for the rest of the flight, I allow myself the luxury and the pleasure.

IT'S RAINING WHEN I ARRIVE AT AIDAN'S CABIN. There's a spare key hidden under a window ledge, and I let myself in.

The small living room is empty. In fact the whole place is bare and clean, very spartan. There's a fire in the grate, telling me Aidan has been here. That's not the only sign. On an end table in front of the worn leather couch, there are three unopened bottles of scotch.

In his short life, Aidan has tried almost every

harmful vice. Alcohol addiction, gambling, and even drugs...every path that presented itself as a means to forget the one thing for which he's always blamed himself, he's tried.

He discovered from experience that those things don't work, and that suppressed memories always return.

Now he's returned to considering the forgetfulness he can find in a bottle.

I consider dumping the contents of the bottles in the sink, but I stop myself. If he has been here for days and isn't passed out drunk by now, it's likely he has a handle on the situation and whatever he's dealing with.

The door opens, and my brother walks in, soaking wet. He's not surprised to see me. The car outside would have told him I was in here.

He shrugs off his dripping jacket. "Hey man."

Everyone always forgets how young he is, but I never do. I try not to hover, not to worry or control, but he is still my little brother, the only thing left from an idyllic past only the two of us can remember.

I study him with a raised eyebrow. "You're running around in the rain now?"

"I needed some time." He smiles and joins me at the fireplace, warming his hands over the grate. "I thought you were in San Francisco."

"I was, but...here I am." I eye his wet clothes.

"You should change out of those clothes before you catch your death of cold."

It's the wrong thing to say. His eyes harden and I can see the memories of that cold morning in their depths. Wilson's voice, grave and pained. *"It's your father. He's dead."* Aidan, a teenager, screaming *"I killed him!"* over and over, crying until he had to be sedated.

"How's that for poetic justice?" he says now.

"Don't be ridiculous." I sound harsher than I intended.

Aidan doesn't reply.

I take a deep breath, hating my role of the scolding big brother. "You skipped out on work, didn't tell anybody where you were, switched off your phone...is there something you want to tell me, Aidan?"

A shadow of hurt crosses his features. After a moment, he shakes his head. "Not really."

"Aidan—"

"Landon, I'm fine. I needed some time off to clear my head."

My eyes go to the bottles on the table. "So it's the pressure from the play?"

"Something like that."

There's more, but he's not ready to share. "Aidan." My voice is firm. "You've taken on a lot of responsibilities for someone your age. I know you're committed to the production, but if you want to pull out and start seeing a professional again, I'd understand."

He doesn't like what I'm saying. A stubborn frown deepens on his face. "You've always had a lot of responsibilities," he retorts. "Even when you were much younger than I am now."

I sigh. "That's different. I had to—"

"Take care of me? Be the responsible one?"

"Maybe. Yes."

He scoffs. "Maybe now it's time for me to be responsible for myself."

I study him for a moment then smile. "So, what are you doing hiding so far out here?"

He glares at me, trying to hide the smile tugging at his mouth. "I painted myself into that corner, didn't I?"

I'm just happy to see him smile. "You know I've always been smarter than you."

He snorts. "Erm, who was it that mistook some girl trapped in an elevator for a hooker again?"

Even now, thinking of Rachel makes me miss her with an intensity that should be impossible. We barely know each other, and yet, it feels as if she has always been a part of my life, waiting just outside for me to open the door and let her soothe me.

"Rachel isn't some girl," I say quietly. Aidan's eyebrows go up, but I don't explain. "Are you ready to leave now, or do you need a few more days of staring into those bottles? I could give you a ride."

"I brought my bike," he tells me with a snicker.

I hate his bike. The thought of him on that monstrosity gives me panic attacks. "Not in this rain," I tell him. "Stow the bike. I'm giving you a ride."

I SPEND THE NIGHT IN NEW YORK, IN AIDAN'S apartment. He doesn't need a nursemaid, but it feels good to talk and play video games and forget about the demands of my life.

The next day, I stop by the office for a few hours before heading back across the country.

It's evening when I arrive in San Francisco. I'm eager to see Rachel, almost too eager. When I enter the suite, though, I can tell at once that it's empty.

She probably went out for dinner. I should order something for myself and wait for her, but I'm too impatient. I call Ralph, the manager of the Rosemont, to find out if Rachel made any reservations at any of the in-house restaurants, and he says no, she left in the chauffeured car with a friend.

With a friend.

Which friend?

Alarm bells go off in my head. I'm not usually a jealous person, but the thought of anybody else having any claim to her time, or to her body...

It's unbearable.

Calm down, Landon.

No.

She doesn't belong to you.

For this week, she does.

My next call is the hired driver. He works for me, so in a few minutes, I have Rachel's location.

She's at a lounge.

With a man.

Stay calm. I take a deep breath and go out to the balcony. Wherever she is, she'll return after a few hours at the most.

But I want to know who she's with. I want to know if the exclusivity rules she set for our arrangement mean anything to her.

Probably not.

The only reason she ever landed in my apartment that first night was that she was distressed over another man. She's not mine. Sexually, I may have some hold on her, but she's not mine, and she never has been.

The thought cuts me with a white-hot edge of jealousy.

Unable to bear waiting, I dial her number on my phone and wait for her to answer.

"Hello." *God! I've missed her.*

I don't bother with any pleasantries. "Where are you?"

There's a pause. "Have you returned?"

"I have. I landed about half an hour ago."

"You could have let me know you were on your way."

"Why?" I sound like a jerk, but I'm too jealous to care. "I told you I would return today."

"Yes, but..." I hear her take a breath. "I went out."

"I gathered." She doesn't say more. At least she's not lying to me. "Are you alone?" I know the answer, yet I dread hearing her say it.

There's a pause. "No, I'm not, but I'm about to leave."

"Where are you?"

She tells me where they are.

"I'm on my way."

"You don't have to—"

"I'm on my way," I repeat firmly. Maybe I'm not thinking straight. Maybe I'm jealous, but while she's with me, any *friend* will be made aware of the fact that she is mine.

CHAPTER 12

I arrive at the lounge a few minutes later. It's a nice place. A chanteuse on a stage is singing soulful music accompanied by a talented band. At a table by the windows, Rachel sits opposite a guy I recognize instantly.

The ex.

The one who made her cry.

I suppose I have him to thank for pushing Rachel straight into my arms.

But right now, the last thing I want to do is thank him for anything.

He's saying something to her, smiling, his hand placed over hers on the table. He's trying to get her attention, but she's looking in my direction. Does she hate that I interrupted her date?

I should turn back and end our arrangement. Maybe she won't mind that. Maybe it would be for the best if I left her to continue...whatever she has with him.

I don't, of course. I want her too much.

Rachel's eyes follow me as I approach their table. I ignore her companion, taking her face in my hands and covering her lips with mine. She tastes of wine and sweetness, and for a moment, I almost lose my head. Finally, I release her, noting with satisfaction that she's flushed and breathless.

That's when I turn to her companion. I hold out my hand. "Landon Court."

There is comprehension and jealousy in his eyes as he rises to take my outstretched hand. "Jack Weyland."

I already knew that. "Pleased to meet you." My voice is blank. "You write for *Gilt*, don't you? Are you here for work?"

He gives Rachel a look then faces me again, chin raised. "No, I'm here to see Rachel."

Well, he has...and now it's time to go. I turn to Rachel. "You ready?" If she chooses not to come with me, I'll let her go. I'll let this all go. It will be hard, but I'll manage it.

"You're leaving?" Weyland frowns, his eyes on Rachel. Did he assume the evening would end with

Rachel in his bed somewhere? Well, fuck him. That's not happening.

"Yes." Rachel rises to her feet, and I feel something like joy in my chest. "I had a great time."

"Yeah," Weyland replies drily. "Me too."

I curl my arm around her and lead her outside, leaving Weyland at the table. Once we're inside the elevator, she whirls around to face me.

"What was that about?"

I know what she means. "What exactly?" I ask in a silky voice.

"Coming here. Kissing me in front of Jack." She scowls. "Acting as if I did something wrong by going out—"

She looks flustered. She has since I kissed her. The words spill out of her, and I let her talk, only interrupting when she's almost out of steam.

"I wasn't aware my actions were so out of place. I came here because I wanted to see you and I was tired of waiting. I kissed you because I wanted to." I study her face. "What exactly is the problem? That I interrupted your reunion with your boyfriend?"

Her eyes skip away from mine. Is she shocked? Did she think I wouldn't know who he was? The elevator doors slide open and she follows me to the entrance.

"I came in one of the Rosemont cars," she

declares stubbornly, as if she would rather not share a ride with me.

I open the door for her. "Your driver has already returned."

She enters the car with a sigh. When I join her, her arms are folded over her chest. "First of all," she tells me, "Jack's not my boyfriend. Secondly, I don't think it was necessary for you to flaunt our... arrangement in his face like that."

Because she's still in love with him? Because there's a limit to how jealous she's willing to make him? How far she's ready to push him?

Because she loves him?

I pull in a breath to soothe the wild flare of jealousy in my chest. "Why do you care so much? What is he to you?"

"It's not about him."

"Isn't it?" I don't want to talk about her ex, or to acknowledge his existence and his hold on her emotions. I hate the way it makes me feel. "I seem to recall that exclusivity was one of your conditions for agreeing to this arrangement. Did that particular condition apply only to me? Am I supposed to sit back and accept the fact that you went out with him, the same man with whom you had a fight in my hotel the day we met? He's the reason you were crying in the elevator, and he came all the way here to see you." My lips curl. "Talk about a grand gesture."

Her shocked expression is almost comical. *That's right. I know everything.*

"Security cameras, Rachel." I shrug. "How do you think I found you? I had dinner with my brother that night. He was trying to convince me that hookers were a better deal than relationships, and he offered to send me one. I refused. When you appeared in the elevator, I thought he'd ignored me, as usual. You didn't leave your number, and I couldn't get you out of my mind. So, I called him, and it turned out he had no idea what I was talking about. I had the security team at the hotel review the tapes to find out who you were, and I saw them too. I saw your argument with Jack Weyland, and I saw how distressed you were afterward."

She's quiet.

"Did he come here to apologize?" I continue, a taunting edge to my voice. "Am I standing in the way of some romantic reunion?"

"Would you care?" she snaps.

Isn't it obvious that I do? I care, much more than I should. "No," I lie. "Let's just be clear, for as long as this arrangement lasts, I have every right to be extremely selfish when it comes to you. I don't give a fuck about what he wants, because right now, you belong to me."

"I don't belong to anyone," she replies. "I sure as hell don't belong to you."

The surge of possessiveness that kicked in when I saw her with Weyland rises again. I place a finger under her chin and lift her face to mine. "Unless you're telling me you want to stop this, to end this... arrangement right now, then you belong to me." I hold her gaze. "Is that what you want?"

She's silent. Have I read her wrong? Is she going to throw my blasted arrangement back in my face?

Her eyes fall from mine and she shakes her head.

I taste the sweetness of triumph, but it's not as satisfactory as I want it to be.

"Say it," I demand.

"No," she whispers. "That's not what I want."

I know she's mine before I take her lips in a gentle kiss. There is no resistance from her. She melts into me, offering her mouth, her body.

I pull her onto my lap, my fingers exploring. I'm aching to expose every inch of her skin so I can touch every part of her.

The car stops, and I release her, smoothing her hair. Her eyes stare languidly back at me, cloudy with arousal.

That's right, baby.

"We're here."

She nods, still looking dazed. I place my hand on the door handle then stop and face her. "I'm sorry I didn't call," I say softly. "I wasn't sure..." I swallow. *I missed you, but I didn't want to stretch our arrangement to a level of intimacy we didn't plan.*

I don't say that. Instead, I choose a half-truth that's far easier. "I was very busy, but I should have called."

"Okay."

Outside the car, I place my hand on her waist, needing even that small touch as we cross the lobby. Inside the privacy of the elevator, hunger wins out and I'm kissing her again, my senses igniting with a wild possessive desire.

She responds perfectly, moaning into my mouth and matching my need with hers.

"I couldn't stop thinking about you," I whisper in her ear. "Every single minute I had you in my head."

Once the elevator arrives, and I carry her all the way into my bedroom, laying her down on the soft bed. I tear off my clothes, and she does the same with hers.

When we're both naked, I join her on the bed. Starting from her lips, I tease her with my tongue, tracing soft licks from her mouth to her throat, then to her lovely breasts. Her skin flushes wherever I touch. I trace a path of kisses over her belly, and when I reach the juncture of her thighs, I spread her legs, eagerly tasting the sweetest parts of her.

Her helpless sounds of pleasure are like a melody

I want to enjoy forever. I join my fingers to my tongue, sliding them into her. Inside, she's hot and slick. Stroking her inner walls, I roll my tongue around her clit, intent only on her pleasure.

It doesn't take long before she shatters in a shuddering climax.

I pull my fingers out of her body, and she starts to curl up, still shuddering, but I spread her legs, rubbing my cock against the slick entrance to her body. She looks up at me, her eyes glazed and wanting.

In a moment, babe.

I slide into her tightness and my breath leaves me. She feels so good. So fucking good. With a sigh, she reaches up to stroke my chest as I surge deep into her.

The feeling is incredible.

Her muscles clench around me as I move, and she wraps her legs around me, urging me deeper.

I can still taste her on my lips, but I want more. I want so much more. She's moaning softly, her body arching as pleasure overtakes her. I rock into her, losing more of myself with every thrust.

We climax at the same time. Her name escapes my lips as I come. It takes a moment to catch my breath, and I cover her body with kisses before lying down beside her.

She falls asleep in my arms, and after a while I drift off too, waking up a few hours later in the middle of a nightmare. I leave Rachel in bed, careful not to wake her, and spend the rest of the night focusing my mind and my thoughts in the familiar demands of my work.

CHAPTER 13

"What's the plan for today?" It's late in the morning, and after a very interesting hour together in the shower, Rachel is cuddled against me in bed, wrapped only in a towel.

I could get used to being like this with her.

I only have a few more days.

Smiling, I drop a quick kiss on her nose. "I already said I was going to spend all day fucking you."

She giggles, and the tiny dimple on her right cheek dances in the bedroom light. "I'd probably be dead by lunchtime—though it wouldn't be so bad, dying of pleasure."

"I'd probably be the one dying from trying to keep up with you." I've already arranged to spend the day alone with her. I owe her that after my disappearance and the whole fiasco with Weyland last night. "After breakfast, I have a few calls to make, then we're going out."

Her interest perks. "Out to where?"

My mind goes to the boat waiting for us in the bay. "It's a surprise."

She pouts prettily. "I hate surprises."

"I'm sure you'll like this one," I say confidently.

We get dressed and have breakfast together out on the balcony. It's a beautiful day, and it's pleasant, just being with her. I have an unbidden image of the two of us, together in my apartment in New York. It feels inevitable, and desirable. Arresting the thought, I look up to find her gazing at me, a strange expression on her face.

I raise an eyebrow. "You want to tell me something?"

She shakes her head slowly. "No."

"Then stop looking at me like that, or else I won't be able to get anything done this morning."

She turns back to her phone, making me wonder what she was thinking. I want to flatter myself that she was thinking along the same lines as me, imagining a future for us beyond this one week.

It's a foolish line of thought. Impractical, too. There's no room in my life for anyone permanent.

There isn't.

I leave her after breakfast and work for a few hours. When I emerge from the library, I find her on the sofa, hard at work on her computer. Her hair is piled in a loose ponytail on top of her head as she frowns in concentration at her screen.

Standing at the doorway, I watch her silently. She's not just beauty, she's light, and for the first time in my life, I'm aware that if I fall any deeper for her, I'll be lost.

As if she can feel my gaze, she turns in my direction. Her fingers hover over the keyboards, her cheeks stained with a barely visible flush.

"Are you going to say something?" Her voice is teasing and light. "Or are you going to keep looking at me like that?"

I cross my arms and lean against the wall behind me. "Looking at you how?"

She shrugs. "I don't know, like you can see inside me."

I chuckle. "Believe me, I wish I could."

She looks puzzled, and her eyes follow me as I push off the wall and go to stand behind her, behind the sofa. Gently, I stroke her hair, undoing her ponytail and watching as it falls around her shoulders in a mass of soft silk.

She sighs and sets her work down.

"I love your hair." It's true. I do. "Sometimes it's red, sometimes gold, and sometimes it's both."

She turns around to face me, her eyes searching my face. "Is that the only thing you love?"

No. Not at all. "You have no idea," I say softly. If I give her a hint of how I feel, how reluctant I am to let her go, she'll probably run screaming to Jack-Whatshisname. I straighten and step away from the sofa. "You should pack an overnight bag. We're leaving in about an hour."

Her eyes dance with excitement. "You still won't tell me where we're going?"

I grin. "You'll see soon enough."

A car takes us from the hotel to an exclusive clubhouse that boasts a golf course and a dock. As we approach the large boat waiting in the water, Rachel turns to face me, eyebrows raised in a silent question.

My lips quirk. "Do you like sailing?"

"I don't know." She smiles. "I've never done it."

I take her hand, loving the feel of her fingers wrapped in mine. "Well, come on, then."

Once in the boat, she changes into a bikini that shows off her exquisite curves. We have lunch on the deck, enjoying the view as the boat sails across the bay.

Rachel glows in the afternoon sun, relaxed and laughing. She's also fun, making me realize how long it's been since I've hung out with a woman whose company I actually enjoy.

I've spent most of my life emotionally closed off and remote, but she makes me wish I could surrender the barriers I've built around myself, even if only for a while.

Near evening, we dock at a tiny island with a flight of carved stone steps leading up to a spacious bungalow.

Rachel loves the house. I watch, amused as she runs from room to room, looking at the views. I own the house, though I can't remember ever enjoying it as much as I am right now, through her eyes.

She makes everything better.

Slow down, Landon.

"I'm famished," she declares in the kitchen when I open the fridge to confirm that the groceries I requested were delivered. When I offer to make dinner, she can't hide her surprise. She insists on watching me throughout, like I'm a magician doing tricks. I don't mind. I'm a good cook—growing up with access to hotel kitchens has some advantages.

After dinner, she lies with her head on my lap while I screen *Sunset Boulevard* in the den. Once she gets past her reservations about the movie being in black and white, she enjoys it almost as much as I do.

"That was tragic," she complains when the movie ends.

"But," I insist, "a classic."

She makes a face then turns to me, her eyes softening. "I had a great day today."

I stroke her hair. "Me too."

Rising to her feet, she holds out a hand. "Come on. Let's go to bed. I've been thinking about jumping your bones since you made me dinner."

I follow her, chuckling. "You don't think you could have told me that two hours ago?"

"And skip the movie?" She gives me a teasing smile. "No way."

"Fuck the movie." I grab her waist and carry her into the master bedroom, where we make love until we both fall asleep.

On the drive back to the city the next day, Rachel is animated on the phone with Laurie. I'm luxuriating in the sound of her voice, unable to stop smiling. It's a strange feeling.

It's happiness.

Even the knowledge that the feeling is temporary does nothing to dampen it. She's like an angel of light, making the days and nights more bearable.

In her arms last night, even though the dreams were there, I slept all night and woke up feeling like a new man.

She ends the call and faces me, her eyes shining, and for a moment, all I want to do is look at her.

How did this happen?

"Your cousin?" I ask, referring to the phone call.

She nods. "Yup."

"She must miss you."

Rachel grins. "Nah, she just misses having someone to torture with her teasing." I raise an eyebrow and she chuckles. "I'm joking. I miss her too."

"Maybe I can cheer you up," I offer. "How would you like to go to a party tonight?"

"A party?"

"Well, not really a party per se. It's the opening night gala for the San Francisco Ballet."

She frowns. "Isn't that a big deal?"

You are a big deal, I want to say, but I keep the words to myself. "I wasn't planning to go, but I thought you might want to. My mother used to be part of the company before she was hired away to New York. I've always been a sponsor."

She makes a face. "Well, thanks for telling me now instead of when I could have actually packed a dress to wear to a ball."

I'm smiling. "Don't worry about what to wear— that's what fairy godmothers are for."

She laughs. "If you were the fairy godmother, Cinderella would never have made it to the ball." I raise an eyebrow, and she continues, her lips lifting in a teasing smile. "She wouldn't even want to, not with the multiple orgasms she'd be getting in the pumpkin carriage."

I can't help smirking. "I wouldn't ruin a children's fairy tale just for sex, but thanks for letting me know you think I'm more desirable than Prince Charming."

She laughs softly. "I love how humble you are."

That word in there makes me catch my breath, whether in desire or fear, I'm not sure. I hold her gaze. "Is that all you love?"

Her smile gives nothing away. "You have no idea."

BACK IN THE SUITE, I SEQUESTER MYSELF IN THE library while a couple of people from the spa help Rachel get ready for the gala. I don't want to be anywhere near the primping and pampering, but I can't wait to see how beautiful she'll look when she's ready.

Not that she isn't always beautiful.

Just thinking of her makes me smile.

And I have only one more day with her.

The thought is almost unbearable. We're only playing pretend. She's not really mine. For all I know, she's still pining for her ex, and judging from his trip to see her, he hasn't let her go either.

It shouldn't sting so much that I'm probably just a footnote in their story, but it does. Selfishly, I want to be the main part of *her* story.

And what will you offer her, Landon? Sex and a pretty face? Is that all she deserves?

Pushing the thoughts from my mind, I make a few calls and study an expense report for a resort I own. Close to an hour later, I go to change, steering clear of Rachel's room, where the spa treatment is still ongoing. It only takes me a few minutes to get ready, and by the time Rachel emerges from her room, I'm waiting.

She's wearing a dress I chose, in bold purple silk, but it's not the dress that takes my breath away. It's her. It's almost as if every time I see her, she looks infinitely more beautiful. She stands at the other side of the room from me, her eyes on mine, looking almost shy as she waits for me to say something.

I cross the room without taking my eyes from her. "You look ravishing."

She gives me a small smile. "I had help."

"No." I shake my head. "This is all you."

She places her hand in mine, and I lead her down to the waiting limo. In there, as we navigate the streets of the city, I reveal one more surprise for her. The marquise-cut stones of an exquisite choker and earring set gleam in the interior of the car. They're stunning, but they'll look even better on her.

Her eyes widen. "God, it's perfect." Her voice is an awed whisper.

You are perfect, I reply internally. "I'm glad you

think so," I say out loud. I take the choker out of the box. "May I?"

"I don't..." She looks uncertain. "I don't think I can take this."

"Why not? It's just jewelry." If she lets me, there's so much more I can give her, so much more I want to give her.

She still looks unconvinced. "Very expensive jewelry."

Why would that be a problem? "You wouldn't feel better about it if it were cheap."

She gives me an impatient frown. "That's not the point."

Okay. So what is?

"How many women have you given jewelry?" she continues.

I don't want to think about any other women right now, but I answer her truthfully. "A few."

She pulls in a sharp breath. "Well, this makes me feel like one of *your* women, and I don't want to feel like I'm being given expensive gifts for spending time with you."

The thought of her as one of *my women* is amusing, not only because I don't have a harem of women like the words suggest, but also because being with her makes even the thought of other women impossible. "Even if I had any *women*, I'd never consider you as *one of them*." I clasp the choker around her neck, and she doesn't resist. "Consider it a loan then, just for tonight. It looks wonderful on you."

Inside the venue, I politely navigate through clusters of people eager to talk to me. Rachel is stunning, and her appreciation of her surroundings translates into a beautiful glow that makes it almost impossible to take my eyes off her.

I'm glad she's enjoying herself, but selfishly, I'd much rather be alone with her.

For the short time I have left.

My depressing thoughts take a turn toward annoyance when I see Evans Sinclair approaching me.

I haven't spoken to Ava in a while, haven't thought about her brother either, but I don't need to look twice to see he's drunk already and spoiling for a fight.

"I suppose now you have more reason to be in San Francisco," he sneers at me, and then his eyes rake over Rachel with lewd sexual interest that makes me want to break his jaw. "Something else you've bought, I presume."

I put a dam on my anger. He's not worth it. "You need to learn to control your tongue if you don't want to get your nose broken," I warn. "You've already lost too much to risk losing that pretty face of yours too, haven't you, Sinclair?"

He runs away like the coward he is.

"Well, that's one person who doesn't like you," Rachel quips, uncowed by his petulance.

I snort. "He happens to be one person whose good opinion I can do without."

"Hey, Red." Cameron is with Jules, his wife, who is visibly pregnant and glowing. "Don't tell me you're still hanging out with this one," he teases Rachel.

Her lips curve. "I hate to disappoint you, but I am indeed."

"More's the pity," he declares with fake sorrow.

I want to elbow him. "Shut up and stop badmouthing me." I hug him before kissing Jules on both cheeks. "Hey, Jules. How are you?"

"Knocked up." She grins and turns to Rachel. "I'm Jules McDaniel, Cameron's wife."

"Rachel Foster. I'm here with Landon."

Jules takes Rachel's hand. "Where's our table?" she asks, turning an arched eyebrow to me and Cameron. "Or are you two planning to keep a pregnant woman standing all night?"

We find the table, though my mind is on Rachel's words. *I'm here with Landon.* They are so lacking in anything real. So empty of a connection. So bland.

You only have one more day, I remind myself, *and then you'll have even less of a connection.*

At the empty table, we are joined by Nelson Bledsoe, the cosmetics billionaire, and a young girl I don't recognize, though she's staring at me like I should know who she is.

"I'm sure you don't remember my daughter, Davina," Nelson tells me. "You only met her once."

I vaguely remember a serious little girl in black shaking my hand at my father's funeral. I pull my memories back from that dark place and give the girl a friendly smile.

"At my father's funeral ten years ago," I tell her. "You've changed."

She blushes. "So have you."

"Davina served on the board for the gala this year," Nelson says, glowing with pride. "She's now a swan in her own right."

"In San Francisco at least," Davina adds.

Nelson grins. "Let's sit," he says. I pull out a chair for Rachel, letting my fingers brush her shoulders as she takes her seat. Again, I find myself wishing we were alone.

When I'm seated, Davina is on my other side. I say something vague and complimentary to her before turning my attention to Nelson and enquiring about some investments he made. Mingling with the sounds from the orchestra, I can hear Rachel and Jules talking and laughing, and idly, I wonder what they're discussing.

"I can't wait for the performances," Cameron says from across the table. He's studying the program.

"Did you know there was a time I wanted to dance ballet?"

At the thought of my big friend in tights, I burst into laughter. "You'd have made a spectacular dancer."

His shoulders are shaking. "I have no doubt."

Just then, I turn in Rachel's direction and find her watching me, an odd look in her eyes. I reach for her hand under the table, squeezing it gently.

Her eyes flare, but only for a few seconds before clouding with a sadness I don't understand. She turns her face away from me but leaves her hand in mine.

"How would you compare the new San Francisco version to the Swanson Court in New York?" Nelson is addressing Rachel.

She considers the question for a moment. "I haven't visited the New York hotel extensively, but from what I've seen, I'd say San Francisco tends more toward modern luxury, while New York is timeless elegance."

Her choice of words makes me want to preen. When did her approval and good opinion become so important to me?

"Well put." Nelson nods.

"Modern luxury is the exact concept we had in mind for the refurbishment," I add. "It's very gratifying that Rachel thinks we succeeded."

She meets my eyes and we share a smile. The sadness is gone. "Your team did an excellent job bringing out the concept in their design," she says, her eyes on mine.

And I will do an excellent job making you come tonight.

"Landon lives at the Swanson Court." Davina's voice pipes up, interrupting my thoughts. "If you haven't spent a lot of time there, then you two are not very close."

Rachel looks amused. "We're as close as we need to be," she replies with a smile. "I'm only writing a feature on his hotel."

"Landon here has a knack for building hotels people can't resist," Nelson says. "His father would be so proud of him. Preston had all these dreams for expanding the Swanson Court hotels, and Landon is bringing them to life."

I try to hide my grimace. There's nothing I hate more than when people bring up my parents, especially at events like these.

"You knew Landon's father?" Rachel asks, curiosity lighting her face.

Nelson nods. "Yes, I did. Preston and Alicia were close friends of mine, and they were spectacular, I tell you. Alicia was the pride of the New York City Ballet, and Preston...well, he was Preston. I remember when Alicia danced Odette in *Swan Lake*. It was phenomenal. I believe *Gilt Style* did a feature on her, called her the Swan of New York."

I tune out the conversation, forcing my mind

away from the vortex of memories threatening to erupt.

He also let his work take him away from her again and again until she started to believe rumors he was cheating on her, and then she let her jealousy drive her to her death.

Nelson doesn't go close to that part of the story. Nobody ever does. Finally, Rachel changes the subject and I can try to relax again.

After dinner is served, we move to the opera house across the street for the performances. Even though my mother was a famous dancer, or perhaps because she was, my interest in ballet is mild, but I love watching Rachel's face. She doesn't bother to hide her pleasure. There's no mask of sophistication or forced disinterest. She's just who she is.

And it's particularly charming.

Later, on the dance floor, we move together to a slow ballad. I close my eyes and let her closeness fill all my senses.

How will I ever let you go, Rachel?

As if she can hear my thoughts, she sets her head on my chest, and I pull in a breath.

"Enjoying yourself?" I ask.

"I am." She lifts her head and cocks it to one side. "Are *you* enjoying yourself?"

My lips curve in a slow smile. "I have a lot to look forward to." First of which is peeling that dress off her.

She doesn't miss my meaning, and her eyes darken. Her tongue flicks over her top lip and I resist the urge to cover her mouth with mine. Her desire sears me, and I want to dive into it headfirst.

"When Nelson was talking about your parents earlier..." she murmurs. "I just...I read about you on the internet, so obviously, I found some news stories. I noticed that you were upset. I don't know how it feels to lose someone, but I'm sorry."

"I wasn't upset." The last thing I want to talk about is my parents. "I would just rather not think about it."

"I can imagine."

I chuckle bitterly. "You can't. Not really." Painful memories from my childhood take over, and everything good about the moment fades away. "They were all in love with her, you know, every single man in their circle—including Nelson Bledsoe—but she was crazy about my father. The rumors made her crazy. No matter how often he told her they were lies, if he wasn't right in front of her, she drove herself to jealousy imagining he was with someone else."

Rachel's brow furrows. Is she surprised I'm sharing all this with her?

I continue. "The day we had the accident, some busybody called her about yet another rumor..." It hurts to describe the events of that day, watching my mother crying, getting our things packed, bundling us in the car...

I want Daddy.

I hear Aidan's plaintive voice like the four-year-old version of him is right beside me. I take a deep breath. "We never found out where she meant to take us. Car crashed. She died. End of story."

Rachel's eyes are glistening with unshed tears. Somehow, her pain, so many years later, compounds the memories, making them almost unbearable. Her voice breaks on my name. "Landon..."

"Aidan didn't utter a word for the next five years," I shake my head. "My father was never the same. People like to say he became a recluse..." This part hurts even worse because of how much older I was, how much I needed the man who chose instead to drink himself to death. "One winter, he left the house in the middle of the night and went out into the water. By the time they found him in the morning, it was too late. He died of hypothermia, at forty-nine, a few feet away from a warm house."

Your father...he's dead.

I killed him. I killed him.

"I'm so sorry," Rachel says. She's going to cry, and I feel a pang of regret for causing her any pain at all, even if the pain is on my behalf. Her arms tighten around me, and I want to lose myself in her embrace.

I want to believe she will take my pain away, even though I know I don't deserve that.

"I don't know why I told you all that," I say with a light chuckle. "You shouldn't think too much about it. It's all ancient history."

She meets my eyes again, and when she speaks, her voice is tender. "But you dream about it."

I stop moving. "What?"

She pulls in a nervous breath, as if she knows I don't want to share that part of me with anyone. "Last night, you were dreaming, and you said a few things. I didn't want to wake you because I was afraid you wouldn't go back to sleep." She swallows. "It's why you hardly sleep, isn't it? Because you still dream about it."

I don't reply.

"Have you talked to anyone about it?"

I want to laugh at the ridiculous question, and at how quickly she's gone from naked sexual desire to wanting to help me, to cure me. "Let it go," I snap.

"I'm just trying to help."

My temper stretches. "I don't need your help... and just to be clear, it's really none of your business."

Her eyes cloud with hurt, and immediately, I'm contrite. Then she gives me a tight smile. "You're right, it isn't."

We talk little for the rest of the dance. When Bledsoe cuts in to dance with her, I take Jules and her belly for a spin then return to our table, chatting with her and Cameron and the people who find reasons to stop by. Throughout, I can see Rachel dancing, laughing, having fun.

I hurt her, and as much as I regret it. I can't... won't open that part of me to anyone, even her.

And I don't want her pity.

I miss the moment Rachel disappears from the dance floor. It makes me nervous, not knowing where she is. I'm trying to find her when Davina Bledsoe waylays me with random questions about moving to New York. I suspect she's flirting, but because she's so young, I try not to be cruel in my dismissal. By the time I finally excuse myself, I see Rachel pushing past Evans Sinclair, who's sneering at her as she marches out of the ballroom.

Hurrying toward her, I shove Evans out of my way and follow her through the lobby to the main entrance. When I reach her, she's standing alone under the awning, looking angry and lost.

"Where're you going?"

"What do you care?" she snaps.

Her tone is unexpectedly irate. "What's that supposed to mean?"

"You should go back in there," she says, waving me away. "I'm sure Davina is waiting, and you seemed to enjoy flirting with her." She gives me an accusing look. "I don't mind. I just don't want to sit there and endure being harassed by someone who hates your guts."

Damn Sinclair. "What did Sinclair say to you?"

"Who cares? I've already forgotten." There's hurt in her eyes when she looks at me. "Like everything else about you, it's really none of my business."

So that's what she's mad about. Well, I'm not going to apologize for keeping some things to myself. "Fine," I tell her. "You want to leave, let's go." I call for the limo, and on the drive back to the Rosemont, she remains on her side of the car, silent.

This is not how I planned our evening, but she has no right to be angry with me for keeping my problems to myself.

I'm not going to apologize for that.

Even though, for some reason I can't explain, I want to. I want to apologize and open myself up to her.

Which makes no sense. Soon, she'll walk right out of my life into whatever she has waiting for her.

In fact, she seems almost ready to do that right now.

Once we're inside the suite, she ignores me, heading straight for her room.

My voice stops her. "Rachel."

She turns to face me. "What?"

"Look, whatever Sinclair said to you...I'm sorry.

I'm the one he hates, not you, and he really doesn't matter."

That's not the apology she wants, and I know it. She glares at me. "Yeah...and neither do I, neither does this...whatever it is we're doing. It doesn't matter, because soon, we'll be back home and it'll be over. Which is for the best, anyway."

My temper snaps. "If you're so eager for it to end, we don't have to wait until tomorrow."

"Is that what you want?" Her eyes flash with anger. "Is that why you told me so bluntly how your nightmares are none of my business and then spent the rest of the night flirting with every single socialite in San Francisco?"

I take a patient breath. "First of all, yes, I believe my nightmares are my problem. I've dealt with them for twenty years, and to answer your question, I have spoken with people—therapists, doctors, you name it—and they haven't helped at all. I didn't ask for your pity, Rachel, and I don't need it." She flinches at my words, but I continue. "And I wasn't *flirting* with anyone, so there's no reason for you to be jealous."

"There's no reason for me to be jealous," she throws back at me. "Why would I be? You're just some guy I'm having sex with, for now."

Something freezes inside me. "Thanks for clearing that up."

She shrugs. "It should never have been in doubt," she shoots back.

"Of course not." I'm pissed now, angry and jealous, irrationally afraid of losing her and knowing I already have, knowing I never actually had her. "After all, only a few days ago, you were entertaining your ex-boyfriend." The words are bitter on my tongue. "Were you ironing out your issues? Deciding you'd made a mistake agreeing to come here with me? Arranging how to get back together once this pesky little situation with me was out of the way?"

"Maybe we were."

"Then you must be a glutton for punishment," I say cruelly. "Why don't you go to him now? Pack your bags. My plane will take you to join him wherever he is. You might have to compete with another woman for his attention, but it wouldn't be the first time, would it?"

Her eyes fill. "Fuck you, Landon," she hisses then starts to walk away.

I can't—won't let her go. With one hand around her waist, I pull her back to me, molding her body to mine.

"I have and I will." There's a desperate madness to my actions. I should let her go. I know I should, but I can't, not when I know how little time we have. "You're not going anywhere, Rachel. You're going to stay here and I'm going to make you come, over and over, with my hands and my mouth, and then I'll fuck you properly just to remind you that when you're with me, there's no room for him."

"Why are you so concerned about him?" Her voice is tinged with frustration and anger, and the first signs of arousal. "Why do you care so much?"

"Why?" I lift her face to mine so she can see the determination in my eyes. With my free hand, I gather her dress up and slide my fingers between her thighs. "Because right now, you're mine."

Her legs spread for me. In this one thing, we speak the exact same language. I stroke her through her panties and her hips grind softly.

"I'm not yours," she hisses through her teeth.

"Aren't you?" Moving the lace aside, I slide my fingers slide between her smooth folds. "You're so turned on," I whisper. For me. All for me. I push my fingers into her, and she makes a soft sound of pleasure.

Impatiently, I unfasten her dress and tug it down with my free hand. Her strapless bra follows, and her breasts spring free. At the sight of her hard, pink nipples, acute desire almost blinds me.

Her slick muscles clasp hotly around my fingers, demanding more. "Does he make you feel like this?" I take her nipple in my mouth and she lets out a moan. "Does he make you so hungry to fuck even when you know you should be angry?"

"Maybe he does." Her voice is breathless. "Maybe I'm thinking about him right now."

She's lying. I can see that, but the knowledge doesn't stop the possessive anger from rising inside me.

"You don't mean that." My voice is a warning.

"Don't I?" Her mocking laughter rings in my ears. "Maybe you think you're the only one who's allowed to be an ass."

A measure of sanity returns. I release her and put some distance between us. She hates me now, and she has every right to. Even I hate myself for ruining any chance we may have had for something more than a temporary week of meaningless sex.

She's glaring at me, making no move to cover her naked breasts, which are heaving with every furious breath. She's flushed with a mixture of anger and arousal, but I can't touch her, not now. Not after everything we've said to each other.

With a few jerky movements, she tears off her dress, bundling it into a huge ball before hurling it at my face.

"Fuck you," she spits.

Something snaps inside me, and I know without a doubt that I will regret whatever I do from here on, but there's only one way this argument can end, and I'm sure we both know it. Barely thinking, I grab hold of her waist and bend her over the back of the sofa. "I already said I was going to," I snarl, close to her ear.

It only takes me a moment to free my cock, and then I'm entering her. Her body opens smoothly to give me access. I don't try to be gentle. It's not what I need, and it's not what she wants either.

I fuck her hard, and her moans stoke the fire of lust, anger, and frustration that's already burning inside me. My fingers twine in her hair, and I nudge her head to face me.

"Look at me," I growl. "I want you to be sure who's fucking you right now."

A soft cry escapes her parted lips. Her eyes glaze further with each thrust of my hips. I'm done fighting, and so is she, and I can feel it when she surrenders.

Her voice is a soft moan. "Don't stop."

Like I could. When I'm with her, I can barely function. All I want is to lose myself in her body.

I run my hands down her back, cupping one of her breasts, squeezing. "You like it." My voice is a plea. "Don't you?"

"I love it."

My fingers dig into her skin. I lose control over my movements as I plunge deep inside her, over and over. Pleasure seizes my brain. I hear her scream out her climax. I feel her body pulsing around me, tight and sweet, and I surrender everything just as the world explodes.

I don't want to let her go. I hold her trembling body close to mine, burying my face in her hair. I feel humble. I want to cry, to beg. Surely, it's only an effect of the sex. It must be.

"Rachel. God, Rachel." Her name is a plea on my lips. "You have no idea how you make me feel...no idea how crazy you make me." The memory of all the rough words I said to her earlier makes me cringe. That's not a part of me I ever want her to see. "I'm sorry."

Her eyes meet mine, wary and hurt, but she doesn't reply.

"I lost my head for a moment." I'm trying to explain the inexcusable. This fight should never have happened. I close my eyes. "Thinking about you with him...remembering you two having that cozy moment at the lounge the day I returned from New York...it makes me feel..." I search for the right words.

Her eyes close, and she places her head on my chest. I breathe. When she faces me again, there's a light of understanding in her gaze. "Jealous? Possessive?" She supplies the words I'm seeking.

"Crazy...enraged?" I add with a bitter chuckle.

She rests her head on my chest again, breathing slowly. I stroke her naked back, tempted to pretend everything is all right and our arrangement hasn't turned out to be a disaster.

"Landon." She meets my eyes again. "You weren't...we weren't supposed to feel anything at all."

"No." I take a deep breath. "We weren't."

I don't want to let her go, but after a few moments, she pulls away. She's naked, with only her bra hanging below her breasts. Without thinking, I unfasten it and let it join her dress on the floor.

We both stand in silence facing each other. There are things I want to say, but I don't know how.

I don't want us to end like this.

Neither does she.

She comes to me and links her arms around my neck. There is a determination in her eyes, and tenderness. She pulls my face down toward hers, bringing her lips to mine.

Ah, Rachel.

My arms tighten around her.

She's mine.

For now.

Carrying her to her room, I make love to her with a gentleness that comes from deep inside, with a desire I can't articulate. Later, I wait until she's asleep then I leave, saying a silent goodbye to our time together, and to her.

CHAPTER 14

"*J*'m calling to see how you are. Friends do that, you know. Check on each other occasionally."

"Hmm." I'm in my office in New York, listening to Ava's voice on speaker, but my attention is on the black velvet box on my desk, containing the jewelry I gave Rachel in San Francisco, which she just had delivered to my office.

"How are you, Landon?"

"I'm fine, Ava."

There's a pause. "Are you seeing anyone?"

I frown. Knowing Ava, it's not a blind question. She heard something. "Why do you ask?"

She chuckles. It's a breezy, tinkling sound. "Maybe I heard something."

"Maybe you should stop keeping tabs on me."

"I don't have to. You know that. People make it their business to tell me things about you."

"Then maybe don't listen."

"How could I not? I care about you."

"How's Henri? Or is it Pierre? Or John? Notice my lack of knowledge about the details of your love life, Ava?"

She laughs. "If you want to know who I'm sleeping with, you can always ask me."

"I don't want to know."

She sighs. "Won't you tell me about her, Landon?"

Rachel. Rachel. Rachel. Her name dances through my mind, as well as the green flash of her exquisite eyes, her sweet voice, her smile, her laugh... I want her, and I don't want to share her with anyone, much less Ava.

Rachel.

It feels as if when I left her outside her apartment on our return to New York, I left a part of myself with her.

Goodbye, Landon!

There was so much I wanted to say to her, and yet so little I felt I could say.

Why was it so hard?

Why did it feel like she was shutting me down and pushing me away whenever I tried to risk... opening a door to something more than just sex?

"Landon?" Ava prompts.

"I've got to go, Ava. I have work to do."

"Landon!" There's a pout in her voice.

"Talk later," I say firmly, ending the call. Then I place the box back in its package and call for Tony, giving him instructions to send it back to Rachel.

As soon as he confirms the package has been delivered, I place a call to her, waiting—almost nervously—for her to answer.

When her voice comes on the phone, it's distant and impersonal, yet it fills me with an acute longing.

I want you.

I focus on the topic I've chosen for this conversation, the jewelry. "Don't even think of returning them," I say without preamble. "I'll just send them back, and I can do this all year."

Fight me, Rachel. Give me a reason to prolong this interaction, because I can't bear for it to end.

"Are you there?" I ask when she says nothing.

"Landon." Her tone is patient, but all I hear is her voice, and all I can think is how I want to hear it up close again. "I can't keep them," she says. "We agreed they were a loan."

"And now I want you to have them."

"It's not enough that you want me to keep them," she says. "Maybe you always get what you want, but this time—"

There's a wavering in her voice that I can't bear, a ghost of hurt that somehow comes through the phone. I want to reach across the space between us and fix it.

If she'll let me.

"Rachel..." I sigh. "Stop. I don't carry expensive jewelry around in case I need to give gifts to random women. I bought them for *you*, because I thought they would look great on *you*." It's the truth. I also want to know she has something of mine, a reason to think about me, no matter what happens. I pull in a breath. "And contrary to what I said to you a long time ago, I don't always get what I want."

Her reply, when it comes, is characteristically stubborn. "I'm not going to keep them Landon."

"Okay," I concede, though it's not okay at all. I'm not willing to accept defeat, not on this as well as losing her. "Why don't we talk about it then, face to face?"

"I don't think..."

"Let's have lunch," I persist. "I'll come to you. Is that okay?"

There's a long silence. "It's fine," she says finally. "I'm free at one."

"Perfect."

I feel as if I've won something, taken one step forward, and I intend to keep advancing. I'm not ready to let her go.

Not now.

Not yet.

But what if she doesn't want to be with me?

Something tightens in my stomach and I force the thought away.

At a few minutes to one, Joe parks outside the front entrance of the Gilt building. The doors slide open and closed as people walk in and out.

Where is she?

I shouldn't feel so much tension. It's new and unfamiliar, and somehow, I can't reason it away.

Unable to wait in the car, I get out and wait on the curb then lean back on the car, tapping impatient fingers on the smooth body. A moment later, she emerges from the building and my jaw nearly drops.

She's wearing a silky top and a skirt that shows off her long legs. Her beautiful hair sways in the breeze as she walks, and for a moment, I'm unable to breathe.

What on earth is this feeling?

I stand upright, resisting the urge to go to her, to take her in my arms and promise her the world, promise her all the things I know I can't give.

I shouldn't have come.

Yet nothing could have kept me away.

I must be mad.

She approaches me, cautiously, like a curious fawn approaching a predator.

"Hey." Her voice is breathy.

"Hey Rachel."

There's a short silence, and I open the door for her. When she's seated, I go around the car to join her in the back. I don't say anything as Joe pulls into the street, but I can feel her eyes on me.

I want to kiss her, to propose skipping lunch to go somewhere we can be alone, but I don't want to scare her away. She looks nervous enough as it is.

"How's your day been?" The trite question spills out from my lips and I almost cringe. *Good job, Landon.*

She shrugs. "Okay, just...work."

I nod. Our eyes meet, and for a moment, I'm pulled to her with a force that leaves me unable to think.

What have you done to me, Rachel?

The restaurant is on one of the top floors of a building overlooking the Hudson. Once seated, we stay silent as a waiter comes to take our order, but I'm aware of her, the way her eyes flit over me when she thinks I'm not looking. What is she thinking? What does she want?

Does she want me?

"You said you wanted to talk," she reminds me.

"I did."

"There was no need for us to come here because of your jewelry." The stubborn expression is back. I've missed that, so fucking much.

"Your jewelry, Rachel," I reply smoothly. "I gave

them to you, but that's not why we're here. I wanted to see you."

She doesn't respond, but I can tell the words have an effect on her. Her throat works as she swallows, and her lips quiver visibly.

"I wanted to see you," I repeat. And God knows I want much more.

"Why?" The word is barely louder than a whisper.

"Why?" I laugh ruefully. Because I can't stop thinking about her. Because our arrangement had the opposite effect from what I intended. I haven't gotten her out of my system. I am more addicted to her than I ever was.

I run a hand through my hair. I'm too tense, too nervous. "Because," I say in a measured tone, "you've gotten under my skin in a way I didn't think was possible." She's silent, so I continue. "I want to keep seeing you. I haven't been able to stop thinking about you."

She starts to say something, but our food arrives.

I wait until we're alone again. "When I asked you to take the trip with me to San Francisco, you insisted you only wanted our arrangement to last for a week. I want to know why."

This is the part I fear the most. The part where I fear she'll tell me it could only be temporary because of the other man who already has a hold on her heart.

"I was in a bad place," she replies, looking at me.

"I thought a short physical relationship would help to get me back on track."

And did it? Is she ready to move on from Whatshisname? "You thought?"

She looks down at the table. "What are you asking, Landon?"

I might as well just put it all on the table. "I want to know if..." I exhale, searching for the right words. "What I'm saying is, I want you. I have from the moment I saw you, and I still do. I can't let you go."

I can see her hesitation, and in there with it, longing. She feels something too, even if, for whatever reason, she's not sure how she wants this... us...to go.

"You don't have to let me go," she murmurs. "I don't want you to."

Tension loosens in my belly, and I relax for the first time since I saw her outside her building. I keep a handle on the desire to sweep her into my arms and kiss her till I lose my breath.

"The food is getting cold," I say, my tone belying the intensity of my relief. "We should eat."

The change of subject amuses her, and her lips lift in a small, perfect smile. She's so beautiful it makes me catch my breath, and I can barely take my eyes off her as we eat.

If she notices, she doesn't seem to mind.

"What are you doing tonight?" I ask her later.

She shrugs. "Nothing. Why?"

"Aidan, my brother, has been working on a play. It's still in the preview stage, but tonight is a press night, and I'm going to lend my support. Will you come?"

She sucks in a corner of her lower lip. "I'd love to."

"Good." My eyes follow the smooth sway of her lips, and arousal stirs in my pants. I want to taste those lips, suck on them, hear her moans... I exhale. "Now, I'm going to take you back to your office, because if I don't, I'm going to have to find a place to fuck you."

Her eyebrows rise, and her eyes darken with a lush invitation that goes straight to my cock. "I can get away with another hour or so."

I need no more encouragement. I take her hand and lead her out of the restaurant. In the elevator, I grab her face in my hands and cover her lips with mine, tasting her with a hunger that has been building to a peak since the moment I set my eyes on her.

She melts into my kiss, her body igniting with my touch. Her fingers dig into my hair and she strokes my tongue with hers, driving me to the verge of insanity. I can barely tear my mouth from hers, but I have to, or else we'll end up fucking right here, right now.

She moans in protest when I put some space between us. Her lips are swollen, her eyes glazed. "My place is closer than your hotel or your office," she offers.

Oh Rachel. "Your place it is."

The drive is much too long. Once we reach her apartment, I can barely wait to close the door before I'm devouring her again. Her passion is intoxicating, and desire is like a raging fire inside me. I barely notice anything around us as she leads the way to her bedroom. I just want to peel off her clothes and renew my acquaintance with her beautiful body.

She has the same idea. Inside her bedroom, she hurriedly does away with my pants and briefs then gets on her knees and takes me in her mouth.

Oh God!

I can't take it. "Fuck, Rachel. I need to be inside you right now."

Pulling her to her feet, I carry her to the bed, laying her gently on the soft mattress. Her skirt is in the way, so I push it up around her waist then tug down her lacy panties, tossing them on the floor. I position myself between her legs, kissing her lips as I enter her.

She's crying out and saying my name, and it's the sweetest sound I've ever heard. It feels incredible to be making love to her again, to feel her body spasm around me. Her breasts graze my chest and her nails scratch my back. She wraps her legs around me, pulling me deeper, and the air leaves my chest in a groan.

I never want to stop.

When she comes, it feels like an earthquake, the way her body shatters. I gather her up in my arms, rising to my knees. Her legs are still around my waist and she braces her arms around my neck. With my arms around her, I keep going, fucking her even as the pulses of her climax continue. She cries out my name, over and over, her eyes closed, her body totally mine. I seize her lips in a deep kiss, swallowing her scream as she comes one more time and I spill myself deep inside her.

CHAPTER 15

"*I*s she your girlfriend now?"

I left a message for Aidan earlier, and surprisingly, given how frantic it must be at the theater, he called me back.

"I wouldn't say it's as defined as that," I reply.

"She sounds fun," he says. "I think I like her already from what you've told me."

I chuckle. That would be a new one. Aidan has never liked any girl I introduced to him. "How's it going over there?"

He groans. "Madhouse."

"Don't worry. Everything will come out great."

"I know," he says quietly. "See you later."

I try not to worry about him as evening nears. *Maybe now it's time for me to be responsible for myself*, he said back at his cabin, but old habits take a long time to die.

Is she your girlfriend now?

I take a deep breath. That's not a word that has played a significant part in my life. I've never considered a long-term commitment to any woman, and my short-term affairs have always been devoid of any emotional elements.

It's different with Rachel, but I'm at a loss as to how to define what we have at this point.

It's definitely more than a temporary arrangement for meaningless sex.

We're together. We're exclusive.

I want all of her.

And I'm ready to give her...what exactly?

My tortuous memories? My pain? The emptiness of my life colored with little spots of great sex?

Don't overthink it, Landon.

When I go to pick Rachel up, Brett opens the door for me. His grin is friendly. "Hey man." He steps back to let me in. "How's it going?"

"Okay."

"Rachel's getting ready," he offers, going back to the couch where Laurie is waiting and peering at me with a suspicious expression that's almost comical. She's one moment away from deposing me, obviously.

"Hi, Landon." She places her head on Brett's lap when he sits. "Good to see you."

"It's good to see you too, Laurie."

She gives me a side-eye and I wonder how much of what occurred in San Francisco Rachel has shared with her.

Just then, Rachel walks into the living room, and I stop wondering anything.

Something tender and unfamiliar wells up inside me. God, she is lovely. Almost unbelievably so.

I take a deep breath, wondering how I'll keep my hands off her all night. "Hey baby."

Her cheeks warm. "Hey."

I go over to her and drop a light kiss on her lips. She smells like peaches and sweetness. *Oh Rachel.* "You ready?"

"Almost." She disappears for a moment and returns with a purse.

"Have fun," Laurie calls out before fixing me with a warning look. "Take care of her."

My eyes find Rachel's and I grin. "I fully intend to."

AIDAN'S PLAY IS SPECTACULAR, AND DESPITE HIS reservations about Liz McKay, his star, she makes the story come to life. Throughout the performance, Aidan sits pensively in one corner of the gallery, and I wonder if he's even aware of how appreciative the audience is.

When the final curtain falls, I take Rachel to meet him. After talking to a few theater critics, he looks almost cheerful.

"You must be Rachel." He gives her the smile that charmed all the nannies when he was little. "I'm Aidan."

"It's great to meet you," she replies with a sweet smile. "And your play was very enjoyable."

"I hope the critics think so." He laughs. "But let's forget about work. What's a nice girl like you doing with my brother?"

"None of your business," I grunt.

They both laugh merrily at my expense.

"How're you coping with your ingénue?" I ask Aidan.

He shudders. "Don't ask."

"I thought she was wonderful," Rachel says. She has an idea that Aidan's dislike of his star might be attraction in disguise. Now, watching Aidan, I wonder if she's right.

"She was spellbinding, actually," Aidan says, his expression clouding. "But as I said, let's forget about the play. Landon promised to take me out for a drink." He holds out a hand to Rachel. "I hope you're coming?"

Aidan chooses a bar near the theater, where he entertains Rachel with stories about me. I glare and threaten, but as they are both having fun and hitting it off, I don't really mind.

I leave them together at the table and take a call about work. From the edge of the bar, I watch them talk and laugh. I'm glad about the success of the play, but more than that, I'm just so thankful to see Aidan happy. I still worry about him. It's always after it looks like he's started to soar that he crashes right back to the ground.

Maybe now it's time for me to be responsible for myself.

I won't hover and fret. I'm going to trust that he will be all right.

I took care of your baby, Mom.

I'm slightly emotional when I return to the table. Aidan is still revealing my secrets to Rachel, and I watch her laugh, her eyes shining as she looks at me.

She's mine.

And I'm the luckiest man in the world.

After a few more drinks, I walk with Rachel to the car. I hate to send her home on her own, but I don't want to leave Aidan without talking to him alone.

Beside the car, I take her face in my hands and touch my lips to hers, licking the seam of her lips before sliding my tongue inside her mouth. Sensation explodes, heady, sweet, and so addictive.

"I have to stay," I tell her when I release her. "Aidan and I have some things to discuss, but Joe will take you home." My regret intensifies at the disappointment in her eyes.

She doesn't argue. "Okay."

I open the door for her. When she's inside, I resist the urge to kiss her again. "See you soon."

"Yeah," she replies softly. "See you soon."

AIDAN ASSURES ME HE'S FINE.

"Stop fretting," he groans, but then his eyes light up. "Let's talk about Rachel. I like her."

"Good," I say wryly. "I like her too."

He studies me with raised eyebrows, and his eyes dance with a familiar mischief. "But...she's not your girlfriend, and it's not as *defined* as that?"

"Pretty much. We're good together. That's really all it is."

"It's hard to believe you're okay with that," he says. "You seem really into her."

I am really into her. I'm more than into her, and thankfully, she's mine.

For now.

I ignore the voice and change the subject. "Liz was great tonight."

Aidan looks down at his glass. "She's a talented actress."

I wonder again if Rachel is right about his feelings

for Liz. What would that mean for the play? Has anything happened between them already? I remember the cabin, and the problem he wouldn't share with me. Did it have anything to do with her?

Stop hovering.

"If today is any indication, on opening night, we'll be talking about the Tony Awards."

His chest rises. "Yeah...we'll see how it goes."

After I leave Aidan hours later, I go home to my empty apartment. My mind goes to Rachel, and I can still feel her disappointment from earlier.

I'm not the only one who would have liked the night to end some other way—namely, with us in bed, together.

As the image fixes itself in my mind, it becomes impossible to think of anything else. I pour myself a drink and try to focus on other things, but it's no use.

I'm halfway to her apartment before I even realize what I'm doing.

She'll think I'm crazy.

She'll think I'm obsessed with her. Which I totally am.

Regardless, I park outside her building and call her phone.

"Hey." The sound of her voice chases away all my reservations.

"Did I wake you?"

"No, I wasn't asleep."

"What are you doing?"

"Nothing. I'm just lying in bed."

"Alone?" I'm only half joking.

"Very funny."

I chuckle. "Were you thinking of me?"

"What if I were?"

"I'd tell you I was thinking about you too. I haven't been able to stop thinking about you all night."

I hear her inhale. "You should stop." She exhales. "You're in danger of starting to sound romantic."

Would that be so bad? "Do you have anything against romance?"

"Not really." Her voice is a whisper. "Do you?"

I shake my head. "I cannot be opposed to anything that would bring you pleasure."

"My world is officially rocked," she says with a chuckle.

I laugh softly. "Did you have a good time tonight?"

"Mmhmm. I loved the play, and Aidan is really great."

"I think he may have fallen in love with you. He's usually more reserved with women."

She's laughing again. "That's ridiculous."

"It is. I'd have to challenge him to a duel or something."

"You wouldn't!"

"I'd have to." I let out a deep breath. "I want to see you."

There's a pause. "Now?"

"I know it's late, and you should be asleep, but I'm outside your building looking up at your window, wondering what the fuck is wrong with me."

"You're here?" In a matter of moments, she's at the window.

I climb out of the car. "Can I come up?"

"Yes!"

She buzzes me in, and I hurry up the stairs. I'm halfway up when she opens the door, dressed in a loose tank top and shorts. Her face is scrubbed clean of makeup, and she looks as fresh as a spring blossom. Grabbing her, I kiss her soundly, the way I've been aching to do all night.

She melts into my arms. Still kissing her, I nudge her inside and close the door behind us.

I finally release her to catch my breath. "Thanks for letting me up. I'd have felt very much like a fool if I had to drive back home."

She laughs softly, amused. "I doubt you've ever felt like a fool."

"No, but around you, it's hard to know how I feel."

Her eyes search my face, for what, I'm not sure. "I'm glad I have such an effect on you."

"I kept thinking about San Francisco, about

falling asleep with you in my arms." I stroke her cheek. "What were you thinking earlier? When you were thinking about me."

"I was wondering what you were doing."

"Only that?" I trail gentle kisses along her neck. "You weren't thinking about my lips on your skin, like this?" She lets out a soft moan and I keep going, retracing the path of my kisses. "Were you thinking about me kissing you, my fingers touching you?" I slide my fingers over her smooth thighs.

"Is that what *you* were thinking?"

I grin. "Always. All the time. Everywhere." I slide my hand inside her loose shorts and cup her between her legs. She's wet, and my fingers slide easily between her folds, stroking gently.

Her responsiveness is incredibly arousing. I find a nipple through the fabric of her top and pull it with my teeth. She moans, and I lift her off the ground and carry her to her bed.

I strip off my clothes while she watches me, waiting. Impatiently, I join her, kissing her all over as I pull off her top.

Her breasts are enchanting, and I give them the attention they deserve. At the same time, I tug her shorts aside and stroke her slickness with my fingers, and when she spreads her legs wider, I slide my fingers inside.

Her eyes flutter closed, her hips moving in time

with my fingers. I'm aching to taste her, so I get rid of her shorts then bury my head between her legs.

Her reaction is exquisite. She cries out, her hips undulating, her fingers clutching at my hair. I don't stop until she's screaming, her body jerking uncontrollably. I keep working her with my fingers and mouth until the tremors stop. Then, spreading her legs a little more, I position myself and enter her.

I hold her tight, reveling in the sound of my name dropping from her lips in soft moans. Her pleasure is like a drug, egging me on, and I bring her to climax after climax until I can't hold back anymore. I let go of all my control, losing myself in her heat until my mind shuts down in a shattering release.

Then I hold her in my arms like the treasure she is until we both fall asleep.

CHAPTER 16

a few weeks ago, having lunch with a beautiful woman on the terrace of a five-star restaurant in Geneva with panoramic views of Lake Geneva spread out below us would likely have ended only one way.

Now, though, even as Madeleine Fortrand, newly widowed and perfectly groomed, makes her availability clear to me across the table, all I can think about is Rachel.

Sweet, beautiful Rachel.

I'm obsessed with her, and she's mine.

It should make me happy, should give me some sort of satisfaction, but I want something more, something even I can't define.

"You must think I'm fickle," Madeline purrs in French, pulling me out of my thoughts. "Changing my mind about selling the hotel. It's just...it meant so much to my late husband."

Stifling my snort, I give her a charming smile. Her much older, recently dead husband is very likely the last thing on her mind right now. I want to buy the hotel he left to her. She agreed to sell weeks ago, and now, for some reason, she has changed her mind. "Do you want more money?" I ask in the same language.

She gives me a wounded look. "I've already told your lawyer it's not about the money."

I smile to mask my impatience. I got sick of her giving Alex the runaround and decided to come to her myself. "So what is it you want, Madeleine?"

"It's not every day a man like you flies across the Atlantic just to change my mind." She holds my gaze. "Don't ruin it by talking business."

I raise an eyebrow. "What would you rather I talked about?"

There's no mistaking the invitation in her eyes. "I'm sure you can think of something."

Only slightly amused, I humor her. I want her hotel, and she—she is a bored socialite who wants to be persuaded, charmed, and convinced. I can give her that, but what would she want after? A night or two at the home that's been scrubbed clean of every memory of her late husband?

Not long ago, depending on my mood, I would have taken her up on her unspoken offer without giving her a single thought afterward. Now, I just want to get my contracts signed so I can leave.

Still, I indulge her throughout lunch. She does most of the talking, and I play the part of a patient, attentive listener.

I'm not in the least bit surprised when she dabs her mouth daintily halfway through dessert.

"It's been so great talking to you, Landon Court." She starts to rise. "We should have dinner tonight at my place and talk a bit more. I will rethink your offer and have an answer by then."

I narrow my eyes, all the charm of earlier replaced by a cold demeanor that causes her to stop in her tracks.

"Sit, Madeleine."

Shocked at my tone, she does as I say.

"We're not having dinner." My voice is cold. "You will take my offer, which, in case you have forgotten, is the best you've got. Our lawyers are here with the contracts. I can see you have no real objections to the deal. So, no more games. You can either sign right now, or you'll never hear from us again."

She stares at me. "I don't—"

"I'm a busy man, Mrs. Fortrand, and I don't take kindly to people wasting my time, believe me. I want those contracts signed. I didn't come all the way here just for the pleasure of your company."

She flinches at my tone. "Fine."

I make a call and Alex shows up, her lawyer close behind. With a sulky expression, Madeleine signs the papers.

"It's all granite underneath the charm, I see." She gives me a tight smile.

My shrug communicates that I don't care what she thinks about me. "You can have more wine if you like."

She shakes her head. "All this business has given me a headache. I'm going home." She rises, then stops. "Ava led me to believe this would be more enjoyable. Apparently, she doesn't know you as well as she thinks."

I don't react to Ava's name, or even ask her to clarify. I watch her walk away, scowling internally.

Ava.

What is she trying to achieve?

A waiter comes to offer me a dark coffee, and I take it, contemplating calling Ava. I should ignore her, but I want to know what game she's playing.

Her cell rings for a few moments before I hear her voice.

"Landon! What a surprise, and a coincidence. I've just been talking about you."

"No need to guess with whom, I suppose."

Her tinkling laugh fills my ears. "Don't be grumpy."

"What did you hope to gain?"

She sighs. "I set the stage for you to loosen up a little. A beautiful widow, an exotic location, good wine. The Landon I know would have left poor Madeleine a few good memories."

There's a pause. A long time ago, I might have been amused. Now, I'm just annoyed.

"So...this girl in New York..." she continues. "You're serious about her?"

I close my eyes in disbelief. "You could have asked."

"I did, and you didn't give me an answer."

"Because, Ava, what's going on in my life is none of your business."

"Anymore," she adds. "There was a time when it was."

"Maybe somewhere between your numerous marriages, things changed."

"Between my marriages, we made many good memories, Landon." She stops. "Are you still angry that I left you?"

"If I remember correctly, you proposed, I refused, and a week later you were married to some second-rate driver."

"Rafe." She giggles. "He nearly killed himself trying to make it to Formula One. Anyway, I want to meet this girl. How well does she know you? Or is she one of those girls carried away by the pretty face and bags of money?"

I'm missing Rachel too much to listen to Ava even allude to her. "Good night, Ava."

"It's morning where I am. I'm in Colombia."

"Okay."

"Don't you want to know who I'm with?"

"No."

"His name is Jorge, and he's a stud rancher. Also, a stud."

I don't have time to hear about her idle pursuits and entertain her manipulative tendencies. "Goodbye," I say firmly.

Why does she care so much about Rachel and me?

Knowing Ava, she's likely just bored and playing games, and I have better things to do than to indulge her.

My coffee is getting cold, and I take a sip. My phone is still in my hand, and I hit Rachel's number. In a moment, her voice pulls me all the way back to her side.

"Hey."

Closing my eyes, I let the sound wash over me. She calms me and soothes me without trying, without even being aware. "I thought you might be asleep," I whisper. "What's up?"

"Nothing. What're you doing?"

"Having an early lunch."

"How was your flight?"

"Uneventful." I shrug. "I spent the whole afternoon trying to convince someone who suddenly changed her mind about selling me a property."

"Did you succeed?"

I remember Madeleine's face as she walked away from our table. "Barely."

Rachel doesn't reply. I want to ask her what she's thinking. I wish I were right there, beside her.

"The next issue of *Gilt Traveler* will be out soon," she tells me, "with the article about your hotel."

"I'm looking forward to reading it."

The waiter returns to refill my coffee and ask me if I want anything else. I ask for the bill instead. On the other side of the call, Rachel is quiet.

"Baby, are you there?"

"I'm here," she whispers.

Something in her tone sets off alarm bells in my head. "Are you okay?"

"Yes." She sighs. "Brett and Laurie... He told her they needed a break. She's been crying all night."

I'm shocked. I'd started to think of Rachel's cousin and her boyfriend as a solid unit. I've even envied them their closeness. "Did he say why?"

"Long story," Rachel replies. "He says she has trust issues...thinks if she's not happy then what's the point? But she's miserable without him, and he knew she would be. Why would you hurt someone purposely when you're supposed to love them?"

Trust issues—two words that are easy to dismiss when you have no experience of where they can lead. Two little kids watching their mom die, for example.

I push my memories away. "I wouldn't know, but if she doesn't trust him, maybe it's for the best."

Rachel doesn't like that answer, and I don't blame her. "You're not here, Landon. She's miserable."

Better to be miserable now than do something irrational later. "She'll get over it."

Rachel makes a sound of frustration. "You don't understand. They've been together for four years! You can't just get over someone you've loved for so long. It's not that easy."

She would know, of course. An unbidden image of Rachel crying in an elevator flashes in my mind. Rachel across from a table with Weyland in San Francisco.

Jealousy flares, poisoning my insides.

"Well...you are speaking from experience."

She doesn't reply or try to deny that she still has feelings for Weyland. Of course she does, I think bitterly. She loves him, and me? I'm just the poor sucker who provides the sex in the meantime.

I close my eyes, ashamed of the meanness of my thoughts. "Give Laurie my best."

"I will." There's a pause. "Do you know when you'll be back?"

"Weekend, at the latest. Why don't you try to get

some rest before you have to go to work? We'll talk some other time."

She does as I say.

I SPEND THE NEXT FEW DAYS TAKING ADVANTAGE OF my presence in Europe to resolve a few business interests. I talk to Rachel every night and send a gift to cheer Laurie up.

Rachel doesn't mention my comment implying she is still hung up on Weyland.

I don't mention it either.

But I'm still thinking about it and torturing myself with the idea that Jack is waiting in the wings for Rachel.

It's not like I want to keep her forever, I tell myself. It's just...he's an asshole, and she deserves better.

As soon as I land in New York on Saturday, I call Rachel.

"Hello, hotness," she purrs into the phone.

"Mmm, hotness—I like that."

I imagine the smile on her face, the dimple dancing on her cheek.

I've missed you, Rachel.

"Are you back?"

"Just arrived." *And I'm dying to devour you.* "Where are you?"

"At my parents' place."

"Where is that?"

She laughs. "I thought you knew everything about me."

"It's probably in a file somewhere," I admit, "but you can tell me."

"Why?"

"Because I want to see you."

"I'll be back by evening."

Evening feels like forever. "I can't wait that long," I tell her. "I want to come over."

"To my parents' house?" She sounds not only surprised, but hesitant.

"Is that a problem?"

"I don't think you want to meet my parents."

Because we're not in a real relationship? Because we're only each other's booty calls? Because I'm not Jack? *Don't assume, Landon.* I take a breath. "Why not?"

"Because they're parents!" She exclaims. "My mom will probably start planning our wedding."

"Really?" If that's what she's worried about, I can live with it. "Sounds interesting. Just tell them we're friends." I find her parents' address somewhere in my phone and continue. "Tell them I'm in the area, and

I'm picking you up or something. I really want to see you."

She sighs. "Fine."

"I'm already on my way."

I arrive at the charming brick house less than an hour later. The drive is lined with flowers and shrubs, and more flowers line the paved path to the front door.

I'm slightly nervous as I ring the bell, like I assume a teenager would feel arriving to take his girlfriend out for a first date.

The door opens and Rachel is standing there. Her eyes light up when they land on me, but the hesitation I sensed earlier is still there.

She looks as if she's not sure whether to kiss me or turn me away.

"Your security guys obviously know what they're doing," she quips. "Did they unearth a copy of my birth certificate too?"

"I only hire people who know what they're doing," I say before pulling her into my arms and kissing her full on the lips. It's a short kiss, not nearly satisfactory. I release her just as an older man walks into the foyer.

He's either Trent or Taylor Foster. Her dad and her uncle, Laurie's dad, are identical twins, and the duo behind Trent & Taylor, a successful ready-to-wear fashion brand, which they sold a few years ago. I doubt I could tell them apart, though I'd guess this is Trent, Rachel's dad.

I smile politely, meeting his eyes as he sizes me up. "Good afternoon, Mr. Foster. I'm Landon Court."

"Good afternoon," he says pleasantly. "Don't just stand there. Come in."

He takes my hand in a firm handshake, leading me to the living room, where Rachel's mom and her Aunt Jacie are waiting with questions. Rachel abandons me to their interrogation, and I have no choice but to turn on the charm.

They're both remarkable women. Lynn Foster is a well-known painter with exhibitions in some major galleries, and Jacie, originally from Barbados, was a famous international model in her day.

Lunch is lively. Laurie and Rachel's little brother, a tall boy who looks to be barely twenty, join us downstairs. Laurie looks miserable, and I rethink my statement that she'll get over it.

Maybe she won't.

And maybe Rachel won't get over Jack Weyland either.

Where would that leave me?

Right where I was before she came into my apartment, and into my life, alone.

The thought is sobering, so I focus instead on the conversation and the laughter. It's impossible to miss the love and affection that fills the house. I've missed my family all my adult life, but I've never really felt what it would have been like if things hadn't fallen apart. Now I have an idea.

It's hours later when Rachel and I decide it's time to leave. Laurie is staying behind, so Rachel says her goodbyes and joins me for the long drive back to the city.

In the car, she's quiet, deep in thought. Does she have regrets about letting me meet her family?

"Do you come home often?" I ask, my eyes on the road.

"About once a month." She sighs. "My mom's very pushy."

"Is she? I thought she was sweet, and your aunt too."

Rachel snorts. "Don't be deceived."

She's joking. Beneath her words are a deep affection I can only envy. "Are you eager to get back to the city?"

She gives me a teasing glance. "Why? Do you have plans for me?"

"Actually, I do." My childhood home is less than an hour's drive away, and I want her to see it. I'm not sure why I'm taking her there—to show her some part of my life too, maybe, but my home is not a place of light and laughter. It's a place of sad memories.

Memories I haven't even shared with her.

We soon arrive. A long gravel drive leads to the house from the gates. The house itself, a Greek revival style mansion, is set on a bluff, and behind it, there are miles of sandy beach.

Wilson Hayes meets us outside. He used to be the manager of the Swanson Court in New York, but after my mother died and my father became a shadow of himself, he practically became a parent to Aidan and me. He managed the property and arranged for my father's care, as well as the summer trips to France to visit our grandparents. He's retired now, but he still manages this house and lives in a spacious apartment on the property with his wife, Betsy.

"Good evening Wilson." I smile apologetically. "Sorry to disturb you on such short notice."

Wilson waves a hand. "It's your home, Landon, and we're always happy to see you."

Too bad I'm not always happy to see the house and be reminded of the memories it holds of my father drinking himself to death. I introduce Rachel, and Wilson looks from me to her, grinning.

"Welcome Ms. Foster. It's great to see a new face at Windbreakers."

Rachel smiles back, and Wilson leads us inside.

"I ordered dinner from town," he informs me in the hallway.

"Thanks. We'll eat upstairs at eight. How's Betsy?"

He laughs. "My wife is coping with me as best she can."

Upstairs, Rachel looks transfixed by the sight of the beach and the Long Island sound. "The view is lovely."

She's my view, and she's lovely. "I agree."

She turns around and catches me looking at her. I'm sure my face communicates exactly what I'm thinking, because her cheeks stain.

Her reaction turns me on even more. "Come. I want to show you the bedroom."

"You're supposed to show me around the house," she scolds. "It's the polite thing to do."

"I'm not very polite," I say with a chuckle, leading her to my bedroom and closing the door behind us. "What I am is very aroused." I nudge her so her back is against the door, and I drop to my knees, tugging up her dress before dragging her panties down and out of the way.

Faced with her bared flesh, I can hardly wait to cover her with my lips and draw in the taste of her. Once I touch her, there's no doubt that her body is mine. She arches back, thrusting her hips forward.

Nice. With my mouth still on her, I tug her panties down the rest of the way and free one leg, hooking it over my shoulder, opening her up to the onslaught of my tongue.

She trembles and moans and calls out my name,

her body arching and jerking with every touch of my tongue. *It's not my fault you taste so good, baby. It's not my fault I want to devour every part of you.*

I don't let her go until she screams my name, her body seizing with the force of her climax.

Licking my lips, I rise to my feet, satisfied. She's trembling, leaning on me for support.

"Tell me that wasn't better than showing you around the house," I say with a grin.

"What house?" She grabs me and covers my lips with hers, sliding her tongue inside my mouth as she presses against me. My cock strains against my pants. I'm about to carry her over to the bed when she slides down the length of my body. As soon as she's on her knees, she frees my cock, making a sound of approval as her fingers curl around me.

Her hand feels great, but it's nothing close to her mouth. When she slides her lips over me, my breath leaves my body.

I surrender to her touch, my eyes closing as she works her lips and tongue around me until my brain stops functioning. I support my weight on the door behind her, rocking into her mouth, trying and failing to hold back.

She cups my balls, stroking gently, and I can't take it anymore. I barely manage to warn her before I explode in her mouth.

She meets my gaze, licking her lips. *Jesus!*

Everything she does turns me on. Drawing her to her feet, I dispense with her dress and bra then get rid of my clothes.

My bed is a king-size four-poster. I scoop Rachel by her waist and carry her over to one of the posts. Wordlessly, she curls her fingers around the polished wood, grabbing hold as I tug her hips backward, toward me, and enter her from behind.

Christ she feels good.

She backs her hips up to meet my thrusts, moaning without reservation. I want to fuck her forever, to feel her fall to pieces again and again. I stroke my fingers across her back then find her breasts, squeezing gently and teasing the hard nubs of her nipples. I change my pace, going slow then fast, feeling her orgasm over and over until she's spent.

My release, when it finally comes, wrecks me. I barely keep myself from collapsing on the floor. We both make it onto the bed and lie in a tangled heap. Her head is on my chest, her eyes closed. Gently, I stroke her hair.

Her eyes open and she lifts her gaze to mine. She studies me silently without saying a word.

My hand stills on her hair. "What are you thinking?"

She shrugs. "How good this feels, just lying here with you."

I pull her closer to me. "I know what you mean. There's nowhere in the world I'd rather be."

She sighs and moves closer still, her body burrowing into mine. It feels incredible to be so close to her, to feel her warm, smooth skin sliding against mine.

What did I do before this? Before her?

I kiss her hair. "Are you hungry?"

She nods. "Starving."

"It's eight." I get up, regretting the moment her body slides away from mine. "Dinner's probably waiting for us." In the closet, I find two robes and return to the bed to hand her one. A dinner tray is waiting in the private sitting room outside my bedroom, along with a chilled bottle of wine.

"Wilson seems to know what you want when you have guests over," Rachel says, watching as I uncover the dishes. Her voice is deceptively light. "Does he have a lot of practice?"

I give her a teasing grin. "You can ask if I've brought a lot of women here. Your jealousy flatters me, actually."

"So?" She's smiling. "Have you?"

"No," I say truthfully. "Never." The house is not a place of good memories. I still can't explain why I brought her here. It felt almost like I needed to, but I've never had that feeling with another woman.

She doesn't look convinced. Her eyebrows go up. "Not one?"

"I'm not the playboy the gossip magazines make me out to be. I've had a few relationships, all with women who knew what the terms were." I only use *relationships* for want of a better word. There was never any emotional connection, and there were never any promises.

A shadow crosses her face. "Like me?"

I hand her a glass of wine. "There has never been anyone like you."

She doesn't reply, and I wonder if she even believes me, or cares. I set out the food, waiting for her to say something.

"What exactly were the terms?" she asks finally.

Every woman who came before her now seems like a vague memory. "Exclusivity," I tell her, "but no commitment in the long-term."

With a delicate movement, she tugs her robe tighter around her. "And you never felt tempted to make an exception with any of the women you've been with?"

"No, never." I shake my head. "I've felt pressured, but usually as soon as a woman starts to demand more than I can give, I walk away."

"Oh." Her face is expressionless. "Lucky for me I never asked you for a long-term commitment," she says blandly.

Is she offended? Joking? Mocking me? I can't tell. I hold her gaze. "This is just sex, and I don't want to pretend it's anything more," I say softly, repeating what she said to me before we left for San Francisco. "Those were your exact words."

"Yes." She smiles and turns away from my gaze. "I remember."

She wanted nothing more than a temporary sexual arrangement from me at the time. We might have prolonged that arrangement for a few more weeks, but the specter of an ending is still here, hovering over us.

It's not what I want.

But what does she want?

I refill her wine. "Do you like the food?"

"Yes. It's great."

Our conversation turns to other things as we eat, and after, I finally show her around the house, which is empty. The Hayes are in their apartment, and the staff that help maintain the mostly empty house have left for the night. In one of the balconies on the upper floor, we settle on an outdoor divan and watch the sun set.

We talk late into the night, about her family, Aidan, Laurie and Brett, even work, but we don't talk about us. Finally, she falls asleep, and I carry her to my room, to my bed. When I join her there, she snuggles against me, staying there until I fall asleep.

"IT'S YOUR FATHER." WILSON'S VOICE IS BREAKING. "Come back to the house."

The dread is like bile in my throat. "What happened?"

"Why don't you come back, and we'll talk."

I'm driving down a gray highway. "Dammit Wilson, what's going on? Where's Aidan?

"Just come back."

"Wilson..."

A truck brakes in front of me and I swerve, barely in time to avoid it. I veer off the road, stopping with a screech half off the shoulder.

I see my mother's hair burning. "Let me go! Mom!"

I'm back in the house and Aidan is screaming. "I killed him. I killed him. I killed him." Then he's asleep, sedated.

"Your father's dead," Wilson says.

My mother is driving and I'm in the back, wishing anything would happen to make us turn back, go back home and wait for my dad.

The car swerves off the road.

My mother turns her face to me as the car burns. "Landon, help me."

"Mom!"

My own scream wakes me. Beside me, Rachel is still asleep, oblivious to the ghosts of the house. I swing my legs off the bed and place my head in my hands. A moment later, I feel her hand on my shoulder.

"Are you okay?"

I shrink from her touch, bolting up from the bed. "Yes, I'm fine. Go back to sleep."

She follows me, and her expression is a stubborn one with which I'm familiar. "No." She frowns. "Not when you're going to stay awake the rest of the night." Her voice gentles. "Why don't you tell me about it?"

Never! "Why? Because you're curious?"

Her face shadows with hurt. "Because I care!"

"Forget about it, Rachel. You've already helped more than you know. These past two weeks with you have been the most peaceful I've had in a very long time."

She cups my face in her hands. "Come back to bed."

Surrendering, I let her lead me back to bed. She lays my head on her chest, stroking my hair as I fall asleep.

IN THE MORNING, LEAVING RACHEL STILL ASLEEP in bed, I take a quick shower before going for a walk.

I can't stop thinking about our conversation

during dinner and my fear that soon, I'll have no choice but to let her go.

This is just sex.

That won't be enough to keep her.

And I want to keep her.

I let the fresh air do its work before returning to the house. Betsy, Wilson's wife, is in the kitchen making breakfast, and Rachel is with her, fresh from a shower with her hair pulled back in a ponytail.

I drop a kiss on her lips. "You're finally awake. I thought I was going to have to transport you back to Manhattan unconscious."

Her smile is endearingly self-conscious. "I was tired."

"Understandably." Color stains her cheeks, and I grin.

"Take a seat," Betsy fusses. "It's been a while since I had young people around to feed. Eat up."

"Yes ma'am." I do as she says. Breakfast smells good and tastes even better. Wilson soon joins us, and as family breakfasts go, it's not that bad, despite the memories.

After breakfast, Rachel wants to explore the beach. She runs barefoot in the sand, laughing and letting the waves chase her.

"You should come here more often," she tells me. "It will relax you."

"Aren't I usually relaxed?"

"Not like this." She takes my face between her hands and kisses me softly on the lips. "Wilson and Betsy bring out a nicer side of you."

"Or maybe it's you."

She chuckles, shaking her head as she moves away. "I don't think so."

Later, on the drive back to the city, after a long phone call with Laurie, she puts on classical music, sighing as she leans back in her seat. Helplessly entranced, I keep stealing glances at her as I drive.

"What?" she exclaims after catching me for the umpteenth time.

"Nothing."

She swats my arm playfully. "Tell me what you were thinking."

I take a deep breath. "That I love to look at you. I enjoy the way you enjoy little things."

Her face softens.

I don't want to lose you.

The words are hovering on my tongue, but just then, her phone rings. She looks at the screen and her expression changes, a small frown clouding her brow.

She takes the call and I try not to listen to her end of the conversation, but from what I hear, somebody wants to meet up tomorrow, and it's easy for me to guess who.

I drive silently the rest of the way. I don't own her, and I have no right to be jealous, to feel a sense of loss because the man who has a hold on her heart will always come into the picture.

The call ends, but for the rest of the drive, she looks uncomfortable, her eyes skipping to me and then back to the road ahead.

Do you have something to say to me, Rachel?

"That was Jack Weyland on the phone," I state, not sure why I'm bothering. It's obvious from her body language the effect he still has on her. Now that he has reminded her of his presence, does she feel guilty about being with me?

Does she wish she was with him instead?

She turns to the window. "Yes. It was."

I already knew, yet jealousy seizes my limbs. "And you're going to see him tomorrow."

"Yes."

She doesn't offer more, and I don't ask. At her building, I stop the car. "We're here."

"I had a great time." She sounds as stilted as I feel.

"I'm glad I could be of service."

She sighs at my tone. "I'm just going to have a drink with him."

"It's fine." I shrug. "You said yourself that you can't just get over someone you've loved for years."

"I was talking about Laurie."

"So it doesn't apply to you and Jack?" I sound like

an insecure, jealous lover—which maybe I am. "You're completely over him?"

She makes a frustrated sound. "Yes."

"So why do you need to go out with him?"

She folds her arms and gives me a stubborn glare. "Because he's also been a friend. Not every relationship is built completely on sex."

Unlike ours. She doesn't say it, but that's what she means. "You were the one who demanded that this thing we have had to be based on sex alone."

She swallows. "Maybe now I want more."

From me or from Weyland? "Do you?"

She draws in a breath. "You can't give me what I want," she whispers.

Something freezes inside me. If she'd rather be with Jack Weyland and whatever kind of love and friendship he gives her, it's fine by me.

I will not beg.

Even though I want to.

"I find it very enlightening that we're having this conversation right after you spoke to *him*." My voice is tight and accusing, but I don't care. "If you'd rather be with your ex, you don't have to conjure vague reasons why we shouldn't be together. Just let me know, and I won't stop you."

Her eyes cloud, and a small line forms between her eyebrows. "This has absolutely nothing to do with Jack."

I hate the sound of his name on her lips. I hate that I'm losing her, and that maybe I deserve to.

This is the end.

I reach for her, pulling her to me and covering her lips with mine. I kiss her hard, drinking in the taste of her, the heady feeling of desire and acute want. When I release her, her breaths are quick and sharp, and her eyes are wet with tears.

Jesus.

"I'm sorry." I start the engine, needing to put some space between us. "I had a great weekend too. Goodbye, Rachel."

"Yeah," I hear her say, but I don't turn to look at her. She walks away, and I watch her go, hating her ex, and most of all, myself.

ou can't give me what I want.
I wish I could stop obsessing about those words.

You can't give me what I want.

What does she want that I can't give her?

Because I'm damn sure whatever it is, I can do a lot better than the clown who left her crying in an elevator and pushed her straight into my arms.

At my apartment, I pour myself a drink, letting the soothing sounds of Mozart calm me as I observe the city through the living room windows.

You can't give me what I want.

My phone rings. It's Aidan.

"Just checking on you," he says, sounding cheerful. "Haven't spoken in a while. How was Europe?"

"It was okay," I say with a sigh. "I mostly worked."

"Do you ever stop?"

I snort. "You're one to talk."

I hear him chuckle. "Give Rachel my best."

Rachel.

You can't give me what I want.

I mutter something under my breath.

"What?" Aidan asks.

"Nothing," I lie. "I'll give her your best."

There's a pause on his side. "Ookay."

I'm not usually the kind of person who needs to unburden about my love life, and I don't plan to start now. "I was about to go to bed. Let's talk tomorrow."

I realize after the call that I didn't ask him about his work on the play.

Too focused on your own misery, Landon.

Abandoning my half-finished drink, I undress and get into bed. In the silence of the apartment, I realize I never brought Rachel here after our first night together. It makes her absence from my life seem so much more final.

Leaving my bed, I walk over to the guest room where I first spent the night with her.

Memories of mind-blowing sex mingle with the lingering pain of her rejection, and I curse under my breath.

You can't give me what I want.

I can give her pleasure, but obviously that's not

enough.

I can treat her with all the care and respect she deserves. I can put a fucking smile on her face every single day.

But all that won't matter if she's still in love with Weyland.

I stretch out across the bed, aching to make the memories real. It's one thing if she's in love with him, but if there's any chance that she isn't, well...I've never been a man who gives up easily. I want her, and I'm going to make her see I'm the one she wants to be with.

BY THE NEXT MORNING, MOST OF MY CONFIDENCE has evaporated. Joe drives me over to Rachel's apartment. I wait in the car for her, counting the minutes till she emerges on her way to work.

I should go up, steal a few minutes with her in the privacy of her apartment, and apologize for my abruptness yesterday

Will she listen?

Will she want to listen?

I've never been so unsure of myself in my life.

I wait for almost half an hour before I see her come down the front steps.

She looks unhappy.

And I know it's my fault.

Yesterday, I was too harsh, too abrupt, too impatient. I knew even before I first approached her with my proposition that she had an emotional connection to Weyland, yet I berated her for it as if I had an exclusive right to her emotions.

She reaches the sidewalk and stops when she sees my car. At the same time, I open the door and step out into the morning sun, watching as an array of emotions crosses her face.

Let's forget about yesterday evening.

Let's start all over again.

I take a step toward her. "Hello."

At first, she doesn't respond. Her eyes rake over me, and the raw emotions that were evident on her face before she saw me retreat behind an expressionless mask. "What are you doing here?" she asks in a level voice.

"I wanted to talk."

She shakes her head, dismissive. "I'm late for work."

That works for me. "I'll take you to your office. We can talk in the car."

She gives me a look like that's the last thing she would ever consider. "No. Thanks."

I only want to talk, to apologize. Surely she can give me that. "Rachel, why are you making this so hard?"

Something in my voice gets to her. With a resigned shrug, she walks past me and slides into the car.

I join her inside, and Joe drives toward her office. Her body is stiff and turned away from mine, as if she can't even stand to look at me.

"You're still going out with Weyland tonight?" The words are out of my mouth before I can stop myself. I sound jealous and resentful. Not exactly the right opening for the apology she deserves.

She turns to look at me. "Is that what you wanted to talk about?" She shakes her head and turns back to the window. "I don't know," she continues, answering my question. "I already told him I would."

So she's going. "What did he say to you at the Swanson Court, the day we met?"

She turns back to me, confused. "I don't think that has anything to do with—"

"Please, Rachel." I stop her. "I'm trying to understand your...relationship with him and why he keeps coming up between us."

She flinches at my use of the word *us*, and my resolve falters. What if I'm wasting my time? It's entirely possible that she really wants nothing to do with me.

"I don't think it makes any difference..." She meets my gaze and sighs. "He told me he was engaged."

He broke her heart. "You were in love with him."

She doesn't reply.

"Tell me what happened between you two."

Her brow furrows. "I met him when I went to work at *Gilt*. We started seeing each other, stopped after about two months, but we stayed friends."

"Why did you stop seeing each other?"

"We didn't want the same things."

"You're being deliberately vague."

"I told him I was in love with him." I see the hurt in her eyes just before she faces away from me again. "He didn't feel the same way."

And she stayed in love with him for two years after that.

She'll always be his, Landon.

I can't...won't accept that.

"You told me you were completely over Weyland," I push on. "Were you being honest?"

She pulls in a deep breath. "There's really no point in talking about Jack."

Except I need to know for sure how she feels.

"Are you still in love with him?"

For a long time, she says nothing, and it looks as if I have the answer I feared all along.

"No." Her voice, when it comes, is a whisper. "I was never in love with him. For a while, I thought I was, but I was mistaken."

I let out a breath I didn't know I was holding.

She's over him. She doesn't love him. There's no reason we can't be together.

I lean my body close to hers. "Then why?"

She raises confused eyes to mine. "Why what?"

I take her hand in mine. She's trembling and I can feel it. I feel shaky, too—hopeful.

I want you to be mine, Rachel.

"Why do you keep pushing me away?"

Her eyes roam my face, unfocused then decisive. "Because I don't want this," she says in a low whisper. "I don't want to be with you. I meant it when I said you can't give me what I want."

The words are like a thunderclap in my head. An unfamiliar pain spreads in my insides. I release her hand, letting her go. The car inches forward, and as soon as we reach her building, she reaches for the door handle.

She can't wait to leave.

"I..." Her voice falters. "Thanks for the ride."

I let out a bitter chuckle that mirrors exactly how I feel inside. "I should thank you for making it clear to me, without any doubt, that I can't always get what I want."

She flinches at my words. Her green eyes are large in her beautiful face. One moment, they're fixed on my face, almost as if she never wants to stop looking at me, and then without a word, she's gone.

CHAPTER 18

There's a copy of the latest *Gilt Travel* on my desk when I get to the office. I turn to Rachel's feature about the Gold Dust and read it over and over. It's not surprising to me how well she writes. I didn't lie about reading her prior work.

Forget about her, Landon. She doesn't want to be with you.

Still, I leave the office to make the trip to a florist, choosing a bright bouquet of purple lilies and yellow orchids then sending them with a note that simply says Great article.

I want her to see the flowers and think of me. I want her to know somewhere in the same city, I am thinking about her.

It's almost pathetic.

You can't give me what I want.

Let her go, Landon.
But I can't. Not yet. I can't.

I HAVE DINNER WITH A BUSINESS ASSOCIATE, AND after, I have a drink alone in my apartment. Everything seems so empty without Rachel. I'm unable to stop imagining her out with Weyland, and it makes my solitude even worse.

When I can't bear it anymore, I call her phone, like a drunk-dialing ex-lover in a sad love song. I watch her name on the screen and listen to the electronic ringing on her side.

I just want to ask if she got the flowers.

I'm not calling to interrupt her date.

I just want to hear her voice.

Pathetic.

After two calls go straight to voicemail, all I can think about is her in bed with fucking Weyland.

I don't plan to drive over to her place, but I find myself there, waiting in my car, feeling like a fool, not even sure what I'd say to her.

I park outside her building and notice that her bedroom window light is off.

Go home, Landon.

Don't be a stalker.

She's probably still with him.

Fucking Weyland.

It takes a few meditative breaths before I feel like I can drive back to my place. I'm about to pull into the street when a cab stops in front of the building and Rachel emerges, alone.

A group of guys walk past her, and my jaw tightens when one of them whistles in her direction. She ignores him and heads for her door.

Then she stops and looks across the street to where I'm parked, a small frown on her face.

I give her a moment to wonder before I step out of the car. She looks at me, only for a second or two, then turns on her heel and walks hurriedly toward the doors.

Go home, Landon.

I can't.

"Rachel."

She ignores me, but I catch up to her before she reaches the entrance to her building. Her eyes meet mine, searching for something, dark with an emotion I recognize. I'm not the only one who wishes things were different, but why is she pushing me away?

"For God's sake, Rachel. Why are you running?"

Her chin goes up. "Maybe because you seem to be stalking me."

Her tone is stern with reproach, and for some reason, it makes me smile.

Something tender flashes in her eyes, but it

quickly disappears. "Landon," she mumbles, "you should leave."

"Why?"

She doesn't reply.

No explanation then. "How was your *date*?" The words taste bitter on my tongue.

"You came all the way over here to ask me that?" She shakes her head in disbelief. "Or did you come to make sure I didn't end up in Jack's bed? That's why you called earlier, isn't it? To make sure even though I was with him, I wouldn't forget about you. Because you're what, jealous?"

I don't bother to deny it. "Of course I am."

I take a step closer and her eyes flutter closed. "Go away."

"No."

She makes an exasperated sound and reaches for the door. I hold it open for her, following her inside the small vestibule. She tries to unlock the inner door, but her hands are shaking. I reach for her hand and take the keys. I unlock the door and follow her into the lobby.

"I'm not going anywhere," I tell her. "Not until you stop lying to me."

She snatches her keys from my hand. "I don't know what you want to hear," she snaps, heading up the stairs. I follow behind. At the door to her apartment, she stops and turns to face me, watching me as I close the distance between us.

"I got your flowers," she says.

It sounds like an olive branch, one I don't hesitate to grasp. "Did you like them?"

She nods.

"I liked the article."

She swallows. "I'm glad."

We're both silent.

"Landon..."

Whatever she plans to say, I don't let her. I reach for her, pulling her to me with one hand on the small of her back. Hungrily, I cover her lips with mine.

She melts into me with a small moan, reminding me of every intimacy we've shared. Her fingers twine in my hair and her tongue tangles with mine.

She wants me.

She's missed this as much as I have.

I brace one hand on the door, groaning when she grinds her hips against mine.

Jesus I want her.

Suddenly, she's pushing away from me, tearing her mouth from mine with a low moan. Her chest rises and falls, and she steps as far away from me as the door behind her will allow.

"You should leave," she whispers. "Please leave."

"Why?" I'm beginning to feel like I'm being tossed around in an unfamiliar sea. I don't understand what the hell is going on. She's not in love with Weyland. She wants me. So, what's the problem? "Rachel, you want this."

She shakes her head, denying the truth I can see.

I don't understand.

"Rachel." I keep my voice calm and reasonable. "I want you, and I know you want me. I'm not going to walk away from this." She doesn't reply, and I run a hand through my hair, frustrated beyond words. "Just tell me what you want from me."

She shakes her head. "You keep saying you want me, Landon—for what, exactly? Just sex? Indefinitely?"

"This means a lot more than sex and you know it." She starts to shake her head again but I touch a finger to her cheek, stilling the movement. "As long as we both want each other this much, why does it have to end?"

She pulls in a shaky breath. "I don't want you."

I know she's lying, but why?

"I already said I won't go anywhere until you stop lying to me." I search her face. "Rachel, this thing we have..."

"Landon," she interrupts. "I don't want a *thing*. I don't."

"So, you want something more serious? Some sort of commitment? A relationship?" I'll take any arrangement that makes it so I can be with her.

"Rachel, that's fine. We can have that if it's what you want, but it's crazy to keep thinking of excuses why we shouldn't be together."

"A relationship?" She studies my face. "And that's all?"

I'm being tossed around that unfamiliar sea again. I hold up my hands. "What else is there?"

She glares at me. "You're willing to let me be a small part of your life, to go out with you once in a while and be seen with you. That's what you call a relationship, isn't it? Then when you've had enough of the sex—which is what this is really all about—that will be the end, won't it?"

I stare at her, not even close to comprehending. "God! I don't understand you. What the fuck do you want?"

"I can't do this," she says, her voice odd and shaky. "I can't... Just go away, Landon. Just leave me alone."

I'm more confused than I've ever been in my life, and the reason for my confusion looks as if I'm the one causing her pain.

Go home, Landon.

I turn on my heel and stalk away, leaving her standing there, watching me go.

CHAPTER 19

I'm going to forget all about her.

There's work to be done, a company to run. I will not spend my time obsessing about someone who, for reasons she chooses not to share, has decided she's better off without me.

I spend a day in San Francisco, and when I return, I attend one of the rehearsals for Aidan's play. Afterward, he joins me for dinner.

"Are you going to tell me what's going on with Rachel?" he asks midway through our meal.

"What makes you think there's anything going on?" I grumble.

"You're grumpy, for one."

Just go away, Landon. Just leave me alone.

She's crazy.

She's infuriating.

She's confusing.

And yet, I can't stop thinking about her.

"What's going on with you and Liz?" I ask, changing the subject.

Aidan goes quiet. "She doesn't need issues like mine," he says finally.

I study him, trying to see any signs of strain in his features. He looks fine, a little pensive, but fine. "Ditto with Rachel," I tell him. "Maybe she's better off without having to deal with my issues."

"Did she decide that or did you?"

"She decided she doesn't want me."

Aidan laughs. "Somehow, I find that hard to believe."

Well, too bad it's true.

"So she's done with you? Like...no longer interested?" He shakes his head. "Did you make no effort at all? Did you lose your charm? I thought *the* Landon Court was irresistible."

"Shut up."

"I think you didn't try hard enough to make her feel like she meant something to you."

I shake my head. "It's not that. I don't know what it is, and I've given up trying."

"And now you're grumpy and miserable."

"I don't need relationship advice from my little brother," I tell him with a bad-tempered scowl.

He shrugs. "If you say so."

I glower at the food on my plate. *What does she want?* "Come with me to an event on Thursday," I tell Aidan. "It's an art thing. We're donating a couple of paintings from Grandpa's collection." I give him a placating smile. "You might like it."

He considers for a moment. "Fine. It's not like I don't need a break."

After I drop Aidan off at his place, I return to my office. The building is practically empty, and alone at my desk, it's easy to bury myself in reading reports and drawing up plans.

I won't think about her.

If she wants me to leave her alone, I will.

Does she think I don't care about her? Why would I have considered a relationship if I didn't?

Stop thinking about her.

In the apartment above my office, there's a treadmill. I change and run until I'm too exhausted to take another step. When I shower and drop into bed, my dreams are hellish, and there, like a Valkyrie fighting to calm the torture in my mind, is Rachel.

"THEY'VE BEEN SENDING OUT THE INVITES FOR THE grand opening." Tony is in my office the next day, bringing me up to date on my itinerary for the next few days.

He shows me a list, and I glance through the pages. Some names I picked, but many others are from our publicity department. They will all be there, however. Nobody would willingly miss the opening of a new Swanson Court.

At the bottom of the page, I see Rachel's name. As my date, she wouldn't need an invitation, and I hadn't considered that the publicity department would add her to the press contingent.

Just leave me alone.

I point to her name. "Has this one been sent?"

"Yes. This morning."

"Hmm." What will her reaction will be when she receives it? I assume I'll find out soon enough.

I have another meeting, and when it's over, I'm not surprised to see a missed call from Rachel on my phone. She didn't leave a message, but I know what it's about.

I'm almost too eager to call her back.

Pathetic.

"Hello." Her voice is flat and emotionless, as if she doesn't care what I have to say, doesn't care about me...but I can still remember her soft moans when I kissed her outside her apartment. I know she's not as indifferent as she's pretending to be.

Just go away, Landon. Just leave me alone.

Fuck.

"Rachel."

She's quiet.

"Rachel," I say her name again, waiting for a response.

"I received an invitation to the opening of the Gold Dust. I'm assuming it's a mistake."

I was right to assume she'd be pissed. I should tell her it had nothing to do with me, but where's the fun in that?

"Why would you assume that?"

"Because," she says tightly, "there's no reason for me to be there."

She could have RSVPed to decline. She didn't have to call me to communicate her displeasure.

Maybe she's not ready to let go either.

"I want you there," I tell her, my voice low, "with me."

"Why?"

Oh Rachel! "Do I have to tell you?" I sigh. "I want you by my side, and not just at the opening. In fact, forget the invite, Rachel. Just tell me what I have to do. Let me know what you want from me." I'm begging again, but I don't care.

"I don't want anything from you."

"You're lying. I can hear it in your voice."

"No. I'm not." Her voice hardens. "It's over, Landon. It should have been over the moment I left your apartment that first night. You should never have tried to find me, and I should never have accepted your ridiculous proposal. That's the truth. What did you think? You'd ask me to fly across the country with you and suddenly I'd forget—" She stops abruptly.

"Forget what?"

"That I've moved on." She exhales. "Because I have moved on, Landon—and you should too."

There's more she's not saying, and I intend to find out what it is. I'm done feeling like I'm throwing myself at a brick wall. She will tell me why she's pushing me away, but not over the phone, not like this.

"I have a meeting," I tell her. "We'll finish this conversation later."

I don't wait for her to respond before ending the call.

IT'S EARLY IN THE EVENING WHEN I HEAD OVER TO Rachel's place. A neighbor lets me in, and when I knock on Rachel's door, Laurie opens it.

For a minute, I forget about myself. Faced with Laurie's obvious misery, I want to find Brett and ask him what the hell is the matter with him.

"Hey, Landon." She smiles wanly. "Come on in."

I follow her inside, closing the door behind me as she curls up on the couch. "Where's Rachel?"

"Downstairs. Ice cream."

I chuckle. "Ice cream never fails."

"Yeah." She makes a face. "Sit, sit. Rachel will be mad that I let you in."

I lower myself onto an armchair. "I just want to talk to her."

She shrugs. "I won't help you if she decides to toss you out of the window."

"And I won't hold you responsible, don't worry."

Her laughter erases some of the pain from her face. Just then, the door opens behind me and Rachel enters the apartment carrying a shopping bag. Her gaze falls on me, and for a moment, I think she'll turn around and leave.

"Hello, Rachel."

She turns her fiery glare from me to Laurie. "You're obviously feeling better," she snaps. "Maybe I shouldn't have bothered with these."

Laurie, undaunted, rises from the couch and takes the shopping bag. "You're a lifesaver," she says to Rachel, totally ignoring her cousin's annoyance.

She disappears in the direction of the kitchen, and Rachel turns her glare back at me. "What are you doing here?"

I rise from the armchair. "What do you think I'm doing?"

"You need to leave."

"You have to start saying that like you mean it, but we both know you don't."

Laurie returns from the kitchen with ice cream and wine. She inclines her head toward her room. "I'm just gonna..." She grins at me. "It was nice to see you again, Landon."

I return her smile. "Likewise."

The door closes behind her and I turn back to Rachel.

"So you've moved on?"

She takes a step back. "Is that why you came here? You couldn't bear the thought that there's one woman in the whole world who isn't beside herself with joy at the thought that you want a *relationship* with her?"

"Jesus! Rachel." She says the word like it disgusts her. I've never had my intentions so misunderstood, questioned, and misinterpreted by a woman. It's almost as if she's messing with me, deliberately trying to drive me crazy. I take a step toward her and she backs away. I follow her, not stopping until she reaches the door and I'm standing right in front of her.

I search her face, wanting nothing more than to kiss her. Her lips part, making the temptation more acute.

"I'm at my wits' end," I say in a low voice. "I'm helpless, bewitched. You're my every waking thought and sleeping dream." She draws in a breath and I continue. "You want me and I'm going crazy. Stop lying to me. Tell me what I have to do."

"I don't—"

I can't stand for her to lie to me again, so I stop whatever she plans to say with a kiss. For an instant, she melts, but then she's pushing me away.

"Stop it," she says breathlessly.

"I can't! You owe me an explanation. You're driving me insane with trying to understand what the fuck's going on. I acted like a jackass on Sunday. I was jealous. The thought of you spending any time with your ex...it made me unreasonable. I'm sorry."

She says nothing.

"I need you." I bring my lips close to her skin but not quite touching. She smells like peaches and spring, like everything I want. "Stop pushing me away."

I'm itching to touch her, to kiss her, to claim her as mine. My fingers skim lightly down her side in a soft caress. Her chest rises and falls. I want her so much I can barely think.

"I want you. I want all of you, and I'm going crazy with the need to touch you. I want to bury myself so deep inside you it would be impossible to tell where you end and I begin. I want to hear you scream when you come. I can hardly think of anything else."

Her eyes flutter closed, and I breathe in the scent of her heated skin, of her arousal.

"I remember everything," I whisper urgently. "The sounds you make in your throat, the exquisite taste of your pussy, the way you cry out when you come, the perfect curve of your breast in my hand. I remember what it's like to sleep with you in my arms, Rachel, and sometimes I don't know what I want more—to fuck you or just to hold you."

Her skin is flushed, and her breath is a soft pant that tells me what I already know.

She wants me.

Her eyes are tightly shut. "Please," she whimpers.

I'm so confident about how well I know her body, the only thing I expect is capitulation. "Please...what?"

"Please." Her voice breaks and she gives me a look that breaks my heart. "Please leave."

The fight deserts me, and I straighten, stepping away from her. The worst thing is that she looks like she's the one in pain, and even though my insides are tearing up, I have to take the blame for that too. I take a deep breath and motion for her to step away from the door. She does.

I want to say something, but I don't even know what.

"I'm..." Words fail me. I have a sudden urge to laugh. "God! I'm sorry." And I am. She was right. I should have left things after the first night we slept together. Pursuing her has only opened a new door of pain, one I'm not sure will go away soon.

When the door closes behind me, I tell myself it's over and I'm done.

Because regardless of what I told myself before, that's what she wants.

CHAPTER 20

I'm in a bad mood when I pick Aidan up on the way to the Remington House, a private art gallery on Fifth Avenue that houses the impressive Remington collection. Today, I'm donating—or returning—two paintings my grandfather famously won from Shelby Remington in a bet.

Aidan is excited about an innovative set design and spends the drive describing technical aspects of scene changes while I answer in monosyllables.

Please leave.

I've decided to stop thinking about Rachel. At the Remington House, an old Beaux-Arts mansion, the director meets us at the entrance, and Aidan goes ahead to the ballroom where the event is taking place.

"We here at the Remington collection deeply appreciate what you're doing tonight," the director says effusively. He's a plump, balding man who looks as if he'd rather be anywhere else than hosting a glamorous art event.

Donating a few works of art worth a couple million dollars is not a big deal to me considering I have no sentimental attachment to the paintings, but I do my best to be gracious. "Supporting the arts is our collective responsibility, isn't it?"

He grins. "Exactly!"

He's passionate about the collection and starts wearing my ears off about plans for future expansions while I study the program idly. Lynn Foster's name jumps out at me from the list of speakers. Rachel's mom. I look toward the door to the ballroom, wondering if, by any chance, Rachel will be here.

And what if she is?

She has made it abundantly clear that she wants nothing to do with me, and I've accepted that.

No matter how much it kills me inside.

"If you're ready..." The director is waiting for me to follow him inside.

I push Rachel from my mind. "Of course."

Still, my eyes somehow find her as soon as I walk into the ballroom, and it feels as if I've been punched right in the solar plexus. The ache of longing grips me, enveloping me in a confused, miserable fog.

Why is she pushing me away?

She's with her parents and Laurie, wearing a knee-length dress and high heels. Her hair falls around her shoulders in soft waves, gleaming in the soft lights of the room.

My Rachel.

Though she was never mine.

Her eyes are closed, and there's a worried frown on her brow.

What could she possibly be worried about? I'm the one who has had to deal with her rejection.

I'm still staring when she opens her eyes and looks toward the entrance. Her gaze lands on me, and there's no surprise there, only...sadness.

I'm drawn toward her as if by a magnet. Abandoning the man beside me, I stride in her direction, stopping only when I hear my name.

The blasted speech.

I head to the podium, my mind still on Rachel.

Stop thinking about her, Landon.

I wish I could.

My speech is humorous. A few anecdotes about my grandfather get the room laughing. I avoid looking at Rachel, and after a few more words about the importance of visual art, I descend into the crowd.

Other speakers mount the podium, and I have to bear the attention of every single non-profit director who pounces on their chance to talk to me, but through it all, I'm acutely aware of Rachel across the room.

I finally extricate myself from an enthusiastic gallery owner and head toward Rachel.

When I'm only a few feet away, she says something to Laurie and hurries out of the room.

Suppressing a bitter smile, I continue forward.

What did I expect? That she'd want to talk to me?

If she wants to be a coward about us, it's her prerogative.

"Hey, Landon!" Laurie gives me a friendly hug. "You guys remember Landon?"

"Of course." Trent Foster takes my hand. "We were just talking to your brother."

Chuckling, I spare a glance toward the bar, where Aidan is fielding the attention of a determined socialite. "Great speech," I tell Lynn.

She responds with a smile that's very like Rachel's. "It's generous of you to return the paintings."

I shrug. "They'll be more appreciated here, I'm sure." I look around, wondering if Rachel will come back.

Deep down, I know better.

"She's gone to the ladies'," Laurie says, taking pity on me.

"Yeah." I nod, smiling at Trent and Lynn. "It was

nice to see you. I'll be leaving soon." I start to walk away then turn back to Laurie. "Say hello to her for me."

I leave alone, after Aidan insists he doesn't need to be rescued, and doesn't need a ride home either. As I walk down the hallway toward the main entrance, I keep feeling as if I'm being pulled back.

It's wrong to leave like this.

I've got to keep trying.

And keep getting rejected.

At the doors, I stop and turn around. I'm not surprised to see Rachel a few feet behind me, at the entrance to the ballroom. She's watching me go, her face showing regret and anguish that mirrors what I feel.

Frustration lances through me and I want to scream at her, to demand answers.

Why are you doing this?

What the fuck do you want?

Without a word, I turn back toward the exit. I will not keep trying when she won't even do me the courtesy of being straight with me.

It pains me to walk away, but it hurts more when she tells me again and again that she wants nothing to do with me.

It's dark outside, and I take a gulp of the cold night air. The limo stops in front of me and I stride to the door, pulling it open.

"Landon, wait."

I freeze.

God knows I should keep going.

God knows.

I turn around and face her, and she's standing in front of the doors. She approaches me, and I can barely stop myself from taking her in my arms.

I should take her somewhere private and unreachable by anyone else...back in time, maybe, to an era of cavemen who took the women they wanted and never let them go.

Just go away, Landon. Just leave me alone.

I swallow, watching as she stops at the edge of the sidewalk. "Landon..." The uncertainty in her voice tells me her mind still isn't made up, that she's still confused, but I can't bring myself to care. Not when I'm hopelessly consumed with wanting her, and I know she feels the same way.

I'm barely aware of closing the distance between us. I take her in my arms, drowning whatever she planned to say in a kiss I need more than life itself.

She kisses me back, hungrily. Her eyes close and she clutches at my jacket, moaning, her body pressed against mine.

Please leave.

I release her, for my own sanity. Any moment now, she'll tell me again that she's done with me.

"Fuck!" My tone is much harsher than I intended.

"What are you trying to do to me? What do you want from me?"

Her eyes rake my face. "I want you," she whispers.

I feel like a puppet on a string, a piece of cork bobbing in ocean waves—helpless and out of control. "Stop playing games with me," I warn. "Go back inside and join your family...or you can come with me, Rachel, and just so you know, I'm not going to stop until I've fucked you senseless."

Her chest rises, her eyes holding mine in a silent agreement. "Let's go."

The words galvanize me into action. For now, at least, she's mine, and I'm too desperate to question it. I hold the car door open for her before going around to join her in the back.

"The Swanson Court?" the driver asks.

"Just drive," I instruct him, my voice lacking any patience. I have no intention of waiting long enough to reach my apartment. I raise the opaque and soundproof partition then turn to face Rachel.

She's watching me, waiting. I reach for her, unable to stop myself from touching her, devouring her.

"God, I want you."

She licks her lips and I'm lost. I cover her mouth with mine, tasting her, filling my nose with her scent. Her body presses eagerly against mine. I can feel all her curves, but I want more. Her clothes are in the way, and impatiently, I push her dress up around her thighs, reaching under it to stroke her through her panties.

Her moan is eager and uninhibited. How many times have I remembered this? Imagined this?

I shove the lacy material of her panties aside, inserting my thumb inside her wet center. She makes a tortured sound of pleasure and I pull back so I can see the reaction on her face.

"You want me."

"Yes," she agrees, her hips undulating as she rubs herself on my fingers.

I pull out my thumb and stroke it over her clit, sliding two fingers into her at the same time. She shudders.

"Say it," I demand.

"I want you," she whispers. "I want you so much."

A part of me wants to torture her, to arouse her body to a fever pitch until she's begging me to fuck her, but I want her too much to hold back. Her hips move, her body clenching around my fingers, making me even more desperate to be inside her.

Grabbing her by the hips, I position her to straddle me. She cooperates eagerly, undoing my pants. I push her dress up to her waist and rip her panties out of the way. She frees my cock, moaning as she takes me in her hands.

"Oh, Landon." Her voice is thick with desire.

She sets her hips over me, bearing down enough

for me to feel her heat around the head of my cock. I grab her waist, holding her in place.

"Are you ready?"

"Yes," she moans. "Yes, Landon. Please."

Satisfied, I push inside her, and she grips me tightly all the way in. *Sweet Jesus.* Air escapes my lungs in a weakening rush.

She's moaning my name, and I repeat hers like a prayer, my fingers digging into her soft flesh. I want all of her. I want everything.

Bracing her hands on the seat behind me, she rides me up and down, gripping me with her insides and driving me to the edge of madness.

My hands circle her waist. I hold her in place and take over our movements, thrusting my hips to meet hers and drinking in the low moans that escape her lips.

I know when she's about to come. Her legs stiffen and her arms tighten around me. I quicken my pace, pushing her over the edge. Then I roll over and set her down on the leather seats, burying myself deeper inside her with each thrust. Right now, I don't care about anything apart from this. The world could end. The sun could die, and as long as I had this moment, I'd be satisfied.

She moans my name over and over, meeting me thrust for thrust. Pleasure builds to a shuddering peak, and this time, we climax together, her wild scream filling the confines of the limo as I groan my release.

After I catch my breath, I pull out of her, smoothing her dress before adjusting my clothes. Then, because I can't stop myself, I kiss her again, slowly this time. "You okay?"

She releases a soft breath and smiles. "Yes, I'm fine."

Her hair is mussed, and I smooth it gently. Sighing, she lays her face in my hand, her eyes closed. I take a deep breath. How soon before she tells me again that this means nothing and she doesn't want to be with me?

There's a futile sort of despair in my chest as I instruct the driver to take us to my apartment.

"My parents will be wondering where I am," she says, her voice soft.

"You're in no condition to go back there," I say, referring to her clothes. "Call them. Tell them you decided to leave."

She doesn't argue. "What about Aidan?"

I shrug. "I was already leaving when you saw me. Aidan has plans to indulge in the free champagne. He told me he doesn't mind walking home." I turn her face up to mine. "I'm not letting you go tonight."

She doesn't reply, but she doesn't argue either. At the Swanson Court, she takes my hand and allows me to lead her up to my apartment.

CHAPTER 21

It's the first time she has been at my place since that first night. She walks through the living room, looking around while I take off my jacket and toss it on a chair.

"Drink?"

She declines with a small shake of her head.

What is she thinking?

I go to her and take her hands in mine. "I'm glad you're here."

She gives me a tender look that warms my insides. "Me too."

"Come on then." I lead her up to my bedroom. A part of me still can't believe she's here with me, that I can kiss her and touch her. "I've imagined you here so many times, it's hard to believe you actually are." I touch a finger to her cheek, just to make sure. "I've missed you."

She places her head on my chest. "I've missed you too."

My heart expands. *Say you'll stay.* "I can't stop looking at you. You have no idea how it's been for me with you across town, so close and yet...so unwilling to have anything to do with me."

"I wasn't unwilling," she says softly. She lifts her eyes to mine, There's something luminous in their green depths. "I just...I didn't want things to get irreversibly complicated."

Irreversibly complicated? I laugh. "It's too late for that."

She puts her arms around me, her eyes closed.
Don't leave me.

"You sure you don't want anything?"

"Maybe some water?"

I show her the bathroom then go to get the water. Back in the bedroom, I can hear her taking a shower. I consider joining her but my phone rings.

It's Aidan. "You home?"

"Yes," I reply. "You?"

"Mhmm." He pauses. "I forgot to ask earlier if you saw Rachel. She was there with her family."

"I saw her."

"And..."

"She's here."

"Oookay." There's a smile in his voice. "Then I guess I better get my ass off the phone, huh?"

I chuckle. "You guess right." I unbutton my shirt, turning to see Rachel standing at the door to the bathroom, wearing one of my t-shirts, which, I have to admit, looks incredibly sexy on her. I pour water into a glass and hand it to her.

"Good night," I tell Aidan.

"Good night," he says in a singsong voice. "Have fun."

"That was Aidan," I tell Rachel, smiling at Aidan's parting words. "He managed to get home without falling down drunk somewhere."

"He's lucky to have you," she tells me. There's a tender expression on her face.

I smile. "And I'm lucky to have you here." I take the empty glass from her and set it on the nightstand. "Nice t-shirt, by the way. Looks very sexy on you." I trail my fingers down her arm and she sucks in a breath. "Can you guess what will look even better?"

"What?" she asks.

"The owner."

She bursts into peals of laughter, and it's the most beautiful sound.

Stay with me and I'll make you laugh every day.

"I'm going to take a shower," I tell her. "Don't fall asleep."

"I won't."

When I return, she's under the covers but still awake. There's a small frown on her face, and I wonder what she's thinking now. At the sight of me, the frown disappears.

Her eyes skim my chest appreciatively. "Your workouts must be intense."

I follow her gaze to my pecs. Neither my looks nor my body make the list of things I'm very proud of, but if she appreciates them, I don't mind at all. "I lift a few weights and do some martial arts training when I have the time."

"Yeah, me too." She's laughing again. "Totally when I have the time. Brett tried to get me and Laurie interested in working out when he started the gym." She shudders. "I'm just destined to be fat and unhealthy."

Laurie and Brett. "How are they?"

Rachel sighs. "It's very complicated right now."

When isn't it? "Emotions always get complicated. Some people make it work, but sometimes it just ends badly." What was the phrase she used? Irreversibly complicated—but we can be more than that. We can make this work.

I join her under the covers and take her in my arms. I can't bear for her to walk away again, and I want her to know that.

"You know I'll give you anything you want?" I whisper. "You know that, right?"

Her voice is tinged with sadness. "You don't have everything."

I don't, but I can try. "Don't walk away again." I'm begging. "Don't."

It takes so long for her to reply, it feels like forever.

"I won't," she whispers. "I won't."

I SLEEP THROUGH THE NIGHT AND WAKE UP WITH Rachel cradled in my arms. She's sleeping like a baby, cute as a button in my overlarge t-shirt.

I watch her for a long time. Then, since I don't have the heart to wake her, I leave her in bed and get ready for work.

She's still asleep when I return from the closet, fastening my cufflinks. As I watch, she opens her eyes and stretches like a cat before giving me a happy grin. "Good morning."

I'm already smiling, just from watching her. "I was trying to decide if I had the heart to wake you. You looked like you were having a good time."

"I was." She stretches again then grabs her phone and glances at the screen. "Christ! I'm going to be late! I have to get home to change."

I already took care of that. "Don't worry. Joe already got your clothes. Laurie was very helpful."

She stops and gives me a warm look. "Really? What are you, some sort of super-boyfriend?"

I hold her gaze. "I'd settle for boyfriend."

She doesn't reply. I want her to be mine. I don't want to spend the next days or weeks wondering if she will decide to walk away again. I need her to give me something, even if it's just a title. "You never told me what it is you want that I can't give."

"It's not..." She stops, as if she can't find the words.

I swallow. "I know I have a lot of baggage...and all the other issues you know about."

She makes a dismissive sound. "I don't care about any of that."

Then what does she want? "Every other woman wanted something from me...commitment, some sort of relationship...but I've offered you that, Rachel. I didn't even have to try, because it's what I want, more than anything, to know I can be sure you're mine."

Her eyes dig into mine, searching. "And you...will you be mine?"

If only she knew. I stroke her arm lightly and she pulls in a sharp breath. "I'm already yours." It's true. I am hers.

She turns her face away. "It's just sex, Landon. We're still practically strangers."

"So, we'll get to know each other."

When she lifts her eyes to mine again, there's a

sadness there that I don't understand. I wish she would explain it to me, but she doesn't. Instead, she rises to her knees and threads her fingers through my hair before pressing her lips to mine.

She's pushing our conversation away, unresolved. She's choosing instead to focus on sex, the one thing we have that's unquestionable. Despair settles in my stomach.

She kisses me deeply, her hands exploring, moving from my hair to my chest. I can't fight my reaction, the helpless arousal and need that pushes every other reservation from my mind.

"I need you," she whispers, her warm breath fanning the skin at my throat.

My breath shudders out of my lungs. For now, she's mine. Saving my questions for later, I pull the t-shirt over her head. Her naked body is like an invitation to worship. I reach for her, cupping her breasts then squeezing them just the way she likes, watching the pleasure suffuse her face.

She strokes the hard ridge in my pants then undoes my zipper, freeing me from my clothes.

In her hand, I have no thoughts at all, no desire beyond the two of us, together. She lowers herself slowly, her eyes holding mine as she continues to stroke me. Then she takes me in her mouth and pleasure rises like a wave.

She sucks me hard, and after only a few moments,

I can't take it anymore. I pull her off me, pushing her back on the bed so she's on her back. She's gazing up at me with unconcealed desire. I spread her legs, pulling her hips toward me until I'm positioned right at the entrance to her body. With a rolling movement of her hips, she urges me inside, letting out a moan when I fill her.

Her eyes fix on mine, so tender it makes me ache. She moves her hips in a slow grind, creating a delightfully tortuous friction. "Please, Landon," she moans. "Fuck me now."

My chest swells. She's so tight, so sweet. I move slowly, wanting to feel everything. Her hips rise to meet mine, and I stroke her thighs, aching to feel more of her skin. Still buried deep inside her, I find her clit, rubbing it in slow, gentle strokes.

She's saying my name, over and over, with a helpless desire that sounds like music in my ears.

"You like it." My voice is rough. "You like it when I fuck you like this."

Her muscles tighten. "Yes," she cries. "Yes."

I thrust in deep and her legs stiffen. "Come for me, baby," I urge. "Let it go."

She screams, clutching the sheets as her body convulses, sucking my climax out of me.

"God!" I fall back on the bed beside her, breathing deeply. "Oh God."

She turns to me, flushed, her beautiful lips curved in a satisfied grin.

"You should wipe that smile off your face if you have any plans of getting to work today," I warn. "I could do this all day."

"Who's stopping you?"

I drop a kiss on her nose. "You're insatiable." Leaving her in bed, I head for the bathroom. "I'm going to repair the damage you've caused," I say, pointing to my clothes. "And I think I'll definitely need a big breakfast after this."

She falls back on the bed, still smiling.

I breathe. *I'll give you whatever you want, Rachel.*

Just don't leave.

Please.

CHAPTER 22

"What are you doing this weekend?" I ask Rachel later, after we have breakfast together. I have a work trip planned, but I'm not planning to be separated from her if I can help it.

She grins wickedly, her eyes dancing. "You, if I'm lucky."

"If *I'm* lucky," I correct with a laugh. "I have to work this weekend. I'm going to Newport to look at a property."

Her face falls. "So you'll be gone the entire weekend?"

I nod. "I want you to come with me."

"Oh." She doesn't look as excited as I hoped she'd be. "But you'll be working."

"Not the whole time," I say meaningfully.

She raises her brow. "And when you are, what will I be doing with myself?"

I flick a spot of sauce from her lips. "You'll be waiting, naked, in bed." It's a particularly arousing fantasy.

One she doesn't find so appealing. Her lips purse. "I don't think so."

"How can I convince you?" I try to paint a seductive picture. "Just me and you, alone, on the beach, the sound of the sea, the gorgeous sunsets..."

She rolls her eyes, but I can see she's coming around. "What's in it for me?"

"Rest and relaxation? And some poor schmuck who can't look at you without getting a hard-on?"

She bursts into a fit of giggles. "Fine. I'll come."

"Good. Now we'd better go before I give in to my baser instincts and do what's on my mind."

"What's that?" she asks, raising her eyebrows as she rises to her feet.

I smile. "Something that'll result in neither of us leaving for work any time soon."

She blushes fiercely, and it's satisfying to know she probably wouldn't mind at all.

IT'S LATE AT NIGHT WHEN WE ARRIVE AT THE BEACH

house in Rhode Island after a long drive. Rachel is asleep with her head on my shoulder.

"We're here," I murmur in her ear.

She stirs and stretches slowly. "How long have we been on the road?"

"Four hours, and you've been asleep about two of them." She smooths her hair while I watch. "You ready?"

She nods, and I open my door, stepping out of the car as Joe opens the door on her side. She joins me on the driveway, taking in the beach cottage, which is close enough to the water that we can hear the surf break on the shore.

Rachel turns to look at me. "Do you own this too?"

"No, it belongs to a friend. He loaned it to me for the weekend." It's Alex's house for when he wants or needs to escape my Draconian demands at work.

"You have friends?" She's laughing at me. "And here I thought you were a robot."

My face conveys my hurt. "You met Cameron."

"I knew you'd play that card," she says, still laughing. "One friend—that's pathetic."

I gesture toward the house. "This makes two."

"Still not healthy," she declares, not giving an inch. "How's Cameron, by the way? And Jules?"

"Still heavily pregnant."

Inside, the cottage is simply designed with

polished wood floors, a stone fireplace, and, through a set of sliding doors, a wooden deck that overlooks the ocean.

Rachel loves it, and that's all I need.

"Your friend is lucky," she tells me. "I'd live here and pretend to be writing a book just so nobody would ask why I never leave home."

"You'd miss your job."

She raises her eyebrows. "I wouldn't have to deal with arrogant billionaires nudging my boss into sending me on assignments just so they can seduce me."

Ah well. "One day you'll forgive me for that."

She flutters her lashes dramatically. "What makes you think I'm talking about you?"

I feel something close to a heart attack. "If anybody else tried to pull a stunt like that with you, I'd probably..." I shake my head. "I don't even want to think about it."

She laughs and holds out a hand to me. "Let's go to bed. I'm tired."

She doesn't need to ask me twice.

I DREAM ABOUT HAPPIER TIMES: VACATIONS WITH my parents, Aidan squealing and running around on the beach.

I wake up with a feeling of deep, inexorable sadness. Rachel is still asleep, and I drop a kiss on her cheek. She smiles in her sleep, and something expands in my chest. I want to stay and watch her but don't want to risk waking her up, so I pull on a pair of pajama bottoms and go out to the deck. There, I spend hours watching the water in its centuries-old journey to the beach.

The sun is already up when Rachel comes up behind me and wraps her arms around me.

"Aren't you cold?"

"Not anymore," I reply, smiling as my body relaxes into her touch. "Good morning."

She places her cheek on my back and her arms tighten around me. I take a deep breath. It feels heavenly. She feels heavenly.

"Hey," she says suddenly. "How did you sleep?"

I turn around so we're face to face. "Perfectly."

She smiles and places a soft kiss on my lips. Grabbing her by the waist, I deepen the kiss until all my senses are filled with her.

When I finally release her, we're both breathing deeply. She grins up at me, her gaze tender.

What is she thinking?

"You must be hungry," I say quietly, leading her back inside the house. "Let's eat."

In the kitchen, I do the cooking while Rachel watches and lays out dishes. After we eat, she gives me a satisfied smile. "I'm going to get used to you making me breakfast."

"Why not? You have my skills at your disposal, babe—all my skills."

Her lips part invitingly, and I'm sorely tempted to take her back to bed, but I have urgent work to do, people waiting on the other end of phone lines.

"I have to get to work now," I tell her with regret. "I have a phone call with my lawyer and some proposals to look over before I visit the property."

"Oh..." She hides her disappointment. "All right."

I give her the number for the caretaker in case she wants anything then spend the morning out on the deck with my laptop and phone.

After a few hours, I'm done with the last of my phone calls. I find Rachel on the front porch, working. Of course she'd bring her work along. She's not the type to wait around, idle.

She looks up to see me watching her and raises her arms in a delicate stretch. "Hey."

My eyes follow her movements. "How's it going?"

"So-so."

"I'm about to leave," I tell her. "Why don't you come with me so you can tell me what you think?"

"Me?" She makes a face. "I'm not a real estate analyzer."

I chuckle. "You don't have to be." I want her to come with me, and not just because I'd rather have

255

her by my side than alone here. "I'd like to know what you think."

She looks unconvinced. "If you insist. What is it, anyway?"

"An old ocean-front hotel. It has historical value and, I suppose, sentimental value to the owners. They proposed a partnership."

She frowns. "But you own your properties outright, don't you?"

I nod. "Usually, yes."

"So, are you going to partner with them?"

"That's what I'm going to decide today. If I'm going to pour money into the place, I want to be sure it has a chance, and that it's going to be run like any other Swanson Court establishment."

She considers it. "When are we leaving?"

My eyes drop to her robe. "I was going to take a shower, and I wondered if you would join me."

"Oh, well..." She sighs theatrically, making me laugh. "If you insist."

We make love in the shower. After, I dress her, zipping up her dress and getting on my knees to slide her feet into her sandals. She returns the favor by buttoning up my shirt and tucking it into my pants.

It's silly and beautiful and intimate.

I watch her brush her hair, satisfied just to look at her. "You're beautiful."

Her eyes meet mine and she smiles. "Thank you."

Crossing the room, I go to take her hand. My chest is full of so many things I feel, and I wish I had the words to explain. "We'd better go," I say instead.

In the garage, Alex's Maserati is waiting. I can't help grinning when I see it. Alex loves that car more than his own life, which gives me a double amount of pleasure to be driving it.

"What?" Rachel is looking at me, curious.

"Alex—the guy who owns this place—he thinks the world of this car. He's probably having a heart attack at the thought of anybody else driving it."

"Then why did he agree to let you?"

I give her a teasing smirk. "Because I can be persuasive."

She chuckles. "Don't I know it."

The car drives like a dream, and soon we're at our destination, the Regency Grace. It's a three-story structure along the beach with a history that goes back to the Gilded Age.

The owners meet us at the door, Lucy McLaren, who inherited the hotel from her father, and her husband, Dave. They're both in their seventies but still active enough to oversee the daily running of the hotel.

The older woman gushes over Rachel. "What a lovely thing you are!" she exclaims. "Isn't she, Dave?"

Dave, who looks like a charmer, takes Rachel's hand. "Without a doubt." If he wasn't pushing eighty,

I'd have to challenge him to arm wrestle or something.

The hotel is undeniably well-managed. Most of the guests are families with children. Rachel goes on a tour of the property with Dave while I follow Lucy to her office to talk terms. I'm still on the fence about going into business with them, not because I don't think it will be profitable, but because of how attached they are to the property. I always want to have the final say in managing my hotels, and I'm not quite convinced I should put my money somewhere I would have to take a step back.

Even my people are divided on the purchase. Alex likes it, but others on my team do not.

I listen to Lucy's proposal again, giving no commitment, and then we all have lunch on the deck.

On the drive back, I put on soft music, and Rachel is quiet, reclining on her seat with her eyes closed, her hair lying around her shoulders like a curtain made of the sunset. I resist the urge to stretch an arm out and touch the strands.

"What did you think?" I ask.

Her eyes open as she considers her response. "It has a lot of potential, but it feels so old...like they've tried their best, but they don't really know how to bring it up to date."

It's almost as if she read my thoughts. "You're right. That's the impression I got too."

"So...what will you do? Will you invest in it?"

"Not if they want to keep running the place. It's admirable that they've held on for so long because corporations own everything else out there. That's why I decided to see for myself, even though my team had already put up a red flag."

"Oh." She looks sad, and I know she's thinking about the hope on the McLarens' faces.

"If I'm going to put the Swanson Court name on the hotel and inject my money into it, they're going to need new management, new ideas, and thorough refurbishment to make it less ancient and more..."

"Classic."

I smile. "Exactly."

"It's going to need more than a popular restaurant to get people interested. The décor needs changing, and we could tie in sponsorship of local events. Add a more upscale restaurant?" The more plans I consider, the more exciting it becomes. "A few private cabins along the beach...I could make something out of it."

Rachel is gazing at me. "You're so sexy when you talk shop."

I'm not sure if I should be flattered or amused. "Who knew? I'll have to do more of that when I'm with you." I squeeze her hand. "Thanks for coming today."

"I didn't mind."

"But I'm glad you were there, and that I can talk about my work with you."

She sticks out her tongue, making me laugh. "I'm glad you're glad."

"I'm going to make you dinner," I offer. "What would you like?"

"I'd eat anything you prepare," she says with a smile.

I surprise her by stopping at a popular chain store to buy groceries. Inside, she follows me around, teasing me mercilessly from the moment I park the car.

Back at the house, I make dinner and we eat out on the rear deck with the ocean just a few feet away. Later, I find a blanket and we lie on the porch swing, looking up at the stars. I try to show her the patterns of the constellations, but she insists she can't see anything, only random stars. She soon falls asleep, and I wait until she's breathing deeply before carrying her inside the house.

CHAPTER 23

I *know I can get her out of the car. I know it.*

The smoke is getting thicker as the fire spreads. I just need to get to the door and pull her out.

Mom!

"*There's nothing you can do.*"

The voice is thick and distorted, the voice of a monster —a monster with strong arms, holding me back as the flames take over the car.

Let me go!

Let me go!

"*Landon!*"

"Landon, wake up. You're dreaming."

Rachel's voice comes from far away, and the other images disappear. I'm asleep, drifting slowly awake. I open my eyes and see Rachel's are filled with alarm and concern.

I can barely remember the dream, or if I was even dreaming, but her expression worries me.

"What's wrong?"

She shakes her head. "Nothing."

I know myself well enough to know it's not nothing.

"I woke you up with the nightmares, didn't I?"

She sighs. "Yes."

Frustrated, I get off the bed.

Her voice stops me. "Where're you going?"

"I have some reports to read. Go back to sleep."

"You don't have to go, Landon. We can talk about it if you want."

Talk about my mother burning to death while I watched helplessly? "I don't think so."

"Don't you?" There's a well of accusation in her eyes. "Or maybe you still think it's none of my business?"

I don't think that. I wish I could explain to her how my nightmares rob me of my desire to forget, how my desire to forget fills me with guilt. It's my pain, not hers.

"Landon," she urges gently. "Talk to me."

Everything inside me tells me I can't, that she doesn't need to share those memories.

Still, I go to sit on the bed and take her hand. "You already know what the dreams are about. The accident. I watched my mother burn in that car, and

I couldn't do anything. Everything changed when she died. My whole family fell apart, my father became a shell, and my brother wouldn't say a word. In my dreams, I want to save her. I want to save her so badly, and it feels like it would be possible if only I could get away from the person holding me back."

She squeezes my hand. It's such a simple gesture, but it soothes me more than I can explain.

"Tell me about her," she whispers. "Your mother."

The memories are almost like a dream. My mother laughing, playing with Aidan, dancing with me, then with my dad, dressed up to go out, looking like a goddess.

I sigh. "She was the most beautiful woman in the world, at least to the nine-year-old boy I was. She used to practice at home sometimes, and watching her dance was like watching an angel. She had the softest, gentlest voice, and she liked to laugh."

Rachel is still holding my hand, and I smile at her.

"She loved Aidan, and she would play with him for hours, no matter what kind of silly game he wanted to play. She loved to read, too. My earliest memory is of her reading to me. I guess she also had a temper, especially when she fought with my dad, but he always knew what to say to her, how to remind her she was the most important person in the world to him."

Her eyes glisten. "They sound like lovely people."

The last years of my father's life were a tragedy, especially compared to what he was in his prime. I take a deep breath. "They were. Then the accident happened."

She strokes my back. "Landon, there's no shame in the fact that it haunts you. Most people would never forget if something like that happened to them. You survived. You saved your brother. You were strong for him. It's something to be proud of."

But I'm not proud. I close my eyes, remembering that day in the car. My mother, convinced my father was cheating, leaving him. Me in the back with Aidan, wanting more than anything to go back home.

"I wanted to go back." The words open a well of pain. "I didn't want to leave. I prayed so hard for anything to happen, anything to make us go back, at least until my father returned. I knew once he arrived, he'd make it up to her somehow. I didn't know what I was asking for, just any reason for us to go back home and wait for my dad." My lips twist. "Then something happened. We crashed."

She puts her arms around me, somehow knowing this is the part that really haunts me, the part I've carried alone for twenty years.

I always get what I want.

And sometimes the world falls apart to give it to me.

"Landon." She rises from the mattress and puts her arms around me. "You were a child."

"Don't you think I know that?" I close my eyes. "But it didn't stop me from torturing myself for years."

I feel her lips on my shoulder then she's on the floor in front of me, on her knees.

"Look at me," she urges. "I'm glad you told me, but it wasn't your fault. You didn't wish the accident to happen. You were just a child afraid of his parents separating. I'm sure you made a thousand more wishes that didn't come true. It wasn't your wish that caused the crash. It was an accident." When I nod, she continues. "Whenever you start thinking like that nine-year-old boy again, just remember how much you loved your mom, how no wish you made could have caused her any harm."

She's so intense, it makes me smile. "Yes ma'am."

"I'm not joking,"

"Neither am I." I pull her up and draw her onto my lap. "You're incredible. An angel."

She smiles. "You need to get back in bed. Get some sleep."

I set her down on the bed and roll on top of her. "I know what I need, and it's not sleep."

"You're insatiable."

"You're irresistible."

She cups my face in her hands, gazing up at me with a tender expression, then she presses her lips to mine. I roll onto my back so she's straddling me. Her lips stay on mine, the weight of her body just perfect.

When she pulls away, I reach up to touch her face, grateful for her existence, and for the fact that she's mine. "You're like a drug, Rachel. You make me forget everything, everything but you."

Her eyes close. "When I'm with you, I feel like nothing is missing." In her eyes, I can see a hint of tears. "It's like everything finally fell into place."

I draw her down so I can kiss her again. She tastes like home, like forever.

Don't leave me.

Her tongue meets mine, tasting and caressing, needing. She moves her hips, grazing my cock, which is already hard. I suck on her bottom lip and she lets out a soft moan.

I need to be inside her.

As if she can read my thoughts, she pulls her lips from mine, shifting her weight down to my thighs so she can wrap her fingers around my rigid erection. She strokes me slowly, tortuously, until I can't bear it for one more moment, then she brings her hips to hover over me and slowly guides my cock inside her.

She's warm, tight, and indescribably beautiful. I breathe her name. "Rachel."

She responds by riding me hard, up and down, her body tight around me as she takes the pleasure she wants. I can't take my eyes off her. I'm mesmerized by her beautiful body, her breasts, her hair. Her eyes are closed, her skin flushed as she takes me deeper each time. I rise from the bed, gripping her hips and taking a nipple in my mouth as she continues to ride me. I come with an intense explosion at the same time she shatters in my arms.

She collapses on top of me, her eyes still closed. Soon, her breathing deepens, and only after she's asleep do I notice the tears on her cheeks.

THE NEXT MORNING, I WAKE UP TO THE SMELL OF breakfast. After showering, I find Rachel in the kitchen with freshly made French toast and a nice arrangement of chopped fruits. I'm on a call, so I make myself a plate and pour a cup of coffee, kissing her before I go out to the back patio.

I can tell she's not happy. She comes out to the patio and gives me her characteristic scowl when she finds I'm still on the phone. With an apologetic smile, I blow her a kiss.

It's not enough. She pouts and stalks inside the house. After working for a few hours, I go to search for her and find her lying in bed, reading, and wearing sheer lingerie.

The lace and satin ensemble barely conceals anything beneath, and my reaction is understandably potent. Feeling almost like a randy teenage boy, I can barely stop myself from pouncing on her.

Keeping my lust in check, I join her on the bed, chuckling when she pointedly ignores me.

"What're you reading?"

She gives me a side-eye. "Are you done working?"

"Yes."

"Well, now I'm busy," she says dismissively, going back to her book.

"I can see that." I massage her feet. "Are you mad at me?"

"Why would I be?" She shrugs. "You told me you would be working. Now, if you don't mind, someone has a guild of evil magicians to challenge and defeat."

"Sounds critical." I continue massaging her toes. "I wouldn't dare to interfere with something of that magnitude, something with such potentially far-reaching consequences."

"What're you doing?" She looks suspicious.

"Nothing." I keep my expression innocent. "Go on, defeat those evil magicians. Though..." I pause. "I don't think you're suitably dressed for something so important."

She chuckles. "Really?"

"Yes," I reply. "For one, you wouldn't have just this thin lace covering your breasts. Your nipples are visible, tempting...an explicit invitation to suck on them."

She makes a dismissive sound but doesn't go back to reading. Instead her eyes stay on me, and through the lace, I see her nipples tighten and peak.

"And your thighs," I continue, moving my hands from her feet, trailing them upward.

"What about them?" Her voice is a little huskier than before.

"They're barely covered, just a little lace. Who can look at them without thinking about sex?" Cupping her through the material, I can feel the dampness of her arousal. "You're not reading anymore?"

Stubbornly, she turns back to the screen of her device. Hooking my fingers in the crotch of her panties, I move them aside. She's watching me again, her lips parted, waiting.

"You can't stop reading now," I remind her. "Think of those evil magicians."

She glares at me and turns back to her screen. I lower my head and touch my lips to her sex.

Her body shudders as I stroke her with my tongue. I suck on her clit then find her cleft and push my tongue inside her. I hear the e-reader clatter as it drops, and her fingers are in my hair.

My lips curve in triumph, but I stay focused on the task at hand, giving her pleasure. I bring her to climax after climax, intent on making up for ignoring her earlier. I make her come until she's begging me to stop, then I finally release her shaking body.

"Let's go for a walk," I tell her, loving the taste of her on my lips. She is weak and spent, her eyes barely open as she looks up at me. "We can't leave without exploring the beach."

$\mathcal{W}$e leave later in the evening, taking the plane back to New York. Rachel's brother Dylan is waiting at her apartment and she's excited about seeing him, but I just hate that our weekend is over.

Soon I'll be in San Francisco, more time I'll be spending away from her. "Will you change your mind about coming to San Francisco for the opening of the new hotel?"

She smiles at my hopeful expression. "Of course I'll come."

That's a relief considering how she reacted to the invitation before.

"I'll leave town sometime this week, but I want to see you every day before I leave."

Her eyes dance. "Every day?"

"Is that too much?"

She gives me a teasing grin. "I'll consider it."

I chuckle. "Let's have dinner tomorrow. When you're not working, I want you to be with me."

"Yes, boss."

She makes me laugh without even trying to be funny. I want to take her home with me and never let her go, because everything about her is just perfect. Perfect for me.

And I want to be perfect for her.

At her apartment, I follow her upstairs, hesitant to say goodbye. I don't want to barge into her reunion with her brother, so I drag myself away.

My apartment feels empty without her, and not just my apartment, my life. When I consider my life before and after her, the difference is like night and day.

Does she feel even close to the same?

It's just sex, Landon. We're still practically strangers.

For her, maybe, but not for me. I feel like I've always needed her in my life, and it scares me, because I don't know that she needs me even nearly as much.

She wants me. She's attracted to me.

But does she need me?

I push the thoughts away and have an early night. I'm having breakfast alone the next morning when I get a call from Alex.

Early-morning calls from lawyers are never good news.

"I've been on the phone with Claude regarding an incident at the hotel," he tells me, proving the aphorism right. "A druggie tried to break in and set fire to furniture."

What the fuck? "Why?"

There's a silence. "According to Claude, he seemed really out of it. I'm not sure he knows."

I tap my fingers on the table. "You think someone put him up to it?"

"Someone like Evans Sinclair?"

"It's possible."

Alex sighs. "Have you spoken to Ava recently?"

Not since Geneva. "No, I haven't."

"Maybe find out what she knows. If he's behind this, we might need to let the authorities handle him."

"Not yet. Let's see what we can find out first." The truth is, I'd rather not do anything that would attract attention, especially from the press, not so close to the opening of the new hotel, anyway.

After the call, I mull over what to do about Evans Sinclair. His personal vendetta against me is ridiculous and pointless. He should know that, and if he doesn't, someone needs to tell him.

Ava answers her phone as soon as the electronic ringing starts on my side.

"Darling," she drawls. "Something special must have happened for you to call me."

I cut to the chase. "Do you know where your brother is?"

She sighs. "Has it come to this? Don't we have anything to talk about besides my brother?"

I roll my eyes but indulge her a bit. "How are you?"

"Fabulous, Landon. How are you?"

My mind goes to Rachel. "I'm fine."

"How's the girlfriend?"

"She's wonderful. When did you last speak to your brother?"

"I don't know...a few days ago." She sighs. "Landon, you know he's harmless. His bark is worse than his bite. As soon as he gets used to the fact that he's lost this one, he'll get over it."

"There was an attempted arson at the hotel last night."

She's quiet. "You know he wouldn't go that far."

"Do I?"

"Landon." There's a plea in her voice. "Just let me talk to him...before you do anything."

I don't reply.

"Please?"

"Okay." I exhale slowly.

I hear the relief in her voice. "I'll be in New York

tonight. I want to talk to you about The Shelter Project. Will you make time for me?"

We've both worked with the charity foundation for years. There's even a fundraiser planned for them at the opening night of the Gold Dust. I'm sure other people on my staff can handle whatever she wants to discuss, but I don't see the advantage in refusing to see her.

"Come by the office in the evening."

"The office?" She doesn't sound happy about that. When I don't reply, she sighs. "Okay. I'll be there."

After the connection ends, I dial Rachel's number.

"Good morning." She sounds cheerful and happy, and the feeling somehow permeates into my consciousness from the phone, buoying me.

"Did you have a good night?"

"Mmmhmm."

"Dream of me?"

I can almost hear her playful smile.

"What do you think?"

I exhale. "Your brother still around?"

"Yeah. He's leaving today."

The loud blaring of a car horn almost drowns out her reply.

"Where are you?" My worried frown spills into my voice.

"On my way to work," she tells me. "I'm a few blocks from the office."

I imagine her shouldering her way through crowds of hurrying New Yorkers. "You're walking?"

"Yeah." She laughs nonchalantly. "It's the only way to keep my weight from catching up to my IQ."

I don't find it funny. "You and Laurie walk together?"

There's a pause. "Sometimes. Other times she leaves earlier than me."

"I'm not convinced it's safe."

"Well, it is." She laughs again. "I've been doing this for two years."

"When are you leaving the office?"

She tells me.

"Joe will pick you up. Just let me know when you're about to leave."

She protests, like I knew she would, but I'm determined not to budge.

"Landon, it's not necessary."

"I think it is." Trying to sound gentler and convincing, I soldier on. "Your safety is important to me. The more people know who you are to me, the more unreasonable it becomes for you to traipse around with no security at all."

"It's not like we're taking out an announcement or anything like that."

"We won't need one." Not when my life is gossip

fodder. "Just let Joe pick you up," I urge. "I'm having enough nightmares about how porous your apartment building is as it is."

She sighs. "Fine."

"I'll send you Joe's number so you can call whenever you need him." She doesn't answer, and I know she's pissed. "I'm probably going to work a little later than I planned tonight, but I'll call you."

"Sure. See you whenever."

Definitely pissed.

"Where are you now?"

"Almost there."

"Good." I wait until the sounds of traffic become muted and I know she's in the building. "I'll see you soon."

AFTER SPENDING MOST OF THE DAY IN CONFERENCE calls and missing lunch, I'm famished when Ava arrives late in the evening.

She walks into the office, painstakingly flawless in a silky ensemble that looks like it just came off a runway in Paris. Tony is practically gawking at her, slack-jawed.

"Thank you, Tony." I dismiss him before he makes a fool of himself.

He drags himself away, and Ava comes over to my desk to give me kisses on both cheeks.

"You look good, Landon."

"So do you."

"You know me—I always take the best life has to offer." She pauses. "How's Aidan?"

I almost laugh. Aidan hates her guts, and she knows that. "He's working on the play."

"Hmm." She gives me a questioning look. "Has he met her?"

"Rachel?"

"So that's her name."

I raise an eyebrow. I'm willing to bet she already knows everything it's possible to know about Rachel.

"Yes, they've met, and they hit it off."

"Oh." Her lips curve downward, but the expression only lasts about a second. "We were going to talk about The Shelter Project.

I nod. "But let's do it over dinner. I'm starving."

Her eyes light up. "I'd love that."

At dinner, we talk about the fundraiser, and she gracefully sidesteps all talk of her brother. Her attitude toward him is one of endless optimism, and she's not willing to change it. Finally, I drop her off at her hotel and go home to my empty apartment.

It's already late, and I hate that I ended up not talking to Rachel on the phone. It's hard not to hold a grudge against all the other claims to my time.

After working out, I take a shower and try to go to sleep.

I'll see her tomorrow.

I need to see her now.

Finally, I get dressed and drive over to her place. She doesn't pick up her phone when I call, but Laurie answers hers and lets me in.

"Hey you." She's grinning, most of her face taken over by large glasses with thick lenses. From the papers scattered all over the living room floor, it's clear she's working.

I glance at all the stacks of documents. "Is someone in trouble? A lawyer working this hard is always bad news for someone."

"It's just old contracts," she replies, laughing. I want to ask her how things are going with Brett, but I don't want to risk ruining her good mood.

"Rachel's gone to bed," she tells me.

I nod. "I guessed, but I was hoping to see her anyway."

"Hmmm. All right!" She waves me toward Rachel's room with a dramatic flick of her wrist. "Let it not be said that I, Laurie Foster, ever stood in the way of passion."

I'm still chuckling when I enter Rachel's bedroom and find her fast asleep in bed. Her t-shirt leaves her legs bare, sprawled carelessly across the bed.

She's sleeping beauty, and me...I'm definitely not anyone's prince.

The thought is sobering.

I undress and join her in bed, and her eyes flutter open. She reaches for me and I take her in my arms, breathing in her sweet, warm scent.

"Hi," she whispers.

"Hi." I kiss her on the lips, and she responds like she has been waiting for me all night.

"I missed you today."

She pouts. "When you weren't bossing me around."

She's still pissed about this morning. I kiss her forehead. My stubborn darling.

"You're the only boss in the room," I whisper, kissing her soft skin and covering her body with mine. I'm not lying. I would do anything for her. She helps me pull the t-shirt over her head, exposing her breasts. Her nipples are pink and hard. I take one sweet nub in my mouth while teasing the other with my thumb, and she moans her pleasure, opening her body to me.

Moving one hand between her thighs, I stroke her gently. Her hips move, grinding into my touch.

Hmmm. "Did you think about this while you were at work?"

"Every minute," she replies breathily.

I push her panties aside and stroke her soft, slick

flesh. She responds eagerly, moving with my touch and urging me on. I slide my fingers inside her, and she makes a strangled sound, her hips rolling with uncloaked desire.

Massaging her inner walls with leisurely strokes of my fingers, I drink in the look on her face as her pleasure increases. Her hands fist around my cock and she moans. "You're so hard."

"Because I've been waiting all day for this."

"Me too," she admits with a sigh, "and I can't wait anymore. I want you inside me."

It would be my pleasure. I slide her panties off then get on my knees and draw her up to the same position, facing me. I hold her tight while I position my cock between her spread legs, she buries her face in my neck, and then I slide her down slowly until I'm buried inside her.

She feels so good, almost too good to be real. I'm almost afraid to move, afraid I won't last more than a few moments. She rolls her hips, her body demanding more movement, more friction, but I hold her still, kissing her face, her lips, her throat, telling her just how much she means to me.

Her lips are parted, letting out soft moans. Her muscles tighten around me, squeezing and demanding. I slide one hand down over her butt, cupping the soft round flesh before sliding between her cheeks, teasing the tight rim for a few moments before pushing gently inside.

She lets out a sweet, tortured groan. Her hips grind, urging me to move.

"You're so sweet," I whisper in her ear. "I love being buried so deep in your hot pussy."

"Oh God! Landon." Her voice is weak, desperate. I watch her fall to pieces, devouring every minute, every expression on her face. "Please Landon, fuck me now, fuck me hard...oh God!"

I give her what she wants, still holding her tight, her knees tight around my hips. I push deep inside her, keeping her off balance, thrusting deeper each time I enter her until she cries out again and again. I don't stop until she's too weak even to moan, only then do I let go and drive her over the edge one last time, taking her with me.

She soon falls asleep, and I hold her for a long time, unwilling—unable to let go. My soul feels like it's a part of her. I want things to stay like this.

It's just sex.

Is it?

I watch her, wondering what she's dreaming about when she smiles in her sleep. Finally, I leave her in bed and let myself out of the apartment.

CHAPTER 25

The next morning, outside Rachel's apartment, I watch from the car as she leaves her building and walks the few steps to the car. She's expecting Joe to be alone, so when she opens the door and finds me waiting in the back, her face lights up with pleasant surprise.

"Hi, sexy," she drawls, grinning widely.

I resist the urge to kiss her senseless. "Good morning."

She leans close to me. "I dreamed about you last night," she whispers, running a finger over my tie. "It seemed very, very real."

I raise an eyebrow. "If you thought for a moment that was a dream, I'll have to work harder next time and make sure you're really awake."

She inhales. "Are you going to make a habit of slipping into my bed?"

"I'm going to make a habit of going to bed with you every night." She doesn't reject the idea, and I continue. "Let's have dinner at my place tonight."

She considers for a moment. "Okay."

"Will you spend the night?"

She grins. "Yes, of course."

Now I wish it were evening already. "Come over straight from work. Don't bring anything."

"Why not?"

"You'll see." I've been working on a surprise for her, and if she likes it, we'll probably spend more time together. As the car edges through the traffic, I hand her a keycard for my apartment at the Swanson Court. "We added some security measures at the hotel, but this will allow you to access my apartment whenever you want."

She reaches for it, slower than I would have liked. What is she thinking? Does she think it's too soon? She slips it into her purse and looks up at me, her face unreadable. "Thank you."

I wish I knew what was going on in her mind. "I'll leave for San Francisco on Thursday morning. A plane will be here for you Saturday morning, and I'll have someone take you to the airport."

"I'm looking forward to it."

I raise an eyebrow. "To me being gone?"

"No!" She laughs softly. "To joining you on Saturday."

Happiness unfurls in my chest as I look at her, along with a feeling I can't explain or identify. I squeeze her hand. "Can you go out tomorrow night?"

"Yeah. What's happening?"

"A friend of mine..." I stop and smile when she gives me a teasing look. *I have friends, Rachel.* "A friend of mine is launching a new product for the American market, some new European champagne brand. There's a mixer, and I want you to come with me." *As my date.*

"Of course." Her dimple dances on her cheek. "I'd love to." The car stops in front of her office and she places a quick kiss on my lips. "Enjoy your day." She reaches for the door handle.

"Wait."

She stops and I pull her back for a proper kiss. She responds with a familiar urgency, her tongue twining with mine in a dance that brings my cock to life. "I'll see you tonight," I whisper.

She nods in agreement then she's gone, leaving my world just a little less bright.

I work late, and it's torture knowing Rachel

is waiting for me. When I can't take it anymore, I end the last conference call and head home.

At the hotel, the doorman looks like he wants to say something to me but then changes his mind. My thoughts are focused on Rachel, so I barely notice.

Inside the apartment, I see that she ordered dinner. Her jacket is on the sofa in the living room. Upstairs, I find her purse in my bedroom, but she's not in the apartment.

Alarm bells start in my head.

Where is she?

Her phone rings and rings but she doesn't answer. I try again and it goes straight to voicemail.

"I'll find out from the doorman," Joe assures me when I call him. He calls back a few moments later.

"What happened?" I bark into the phone.

"She left about half an hour ago."

Left where?

"Did she take a cab?"

"No."

A dark thought crosses my mind. "Was she alone?"

There is a pause from Joe. "As far as he could see, yes."

"Bring the car to the front."

"Already waiting."

I call Laurie on my way downstairs.

"Is Rachel with you?"

"No." A worried tone creeps into her voice. "I thought she was with you."

"No." I sigh. "She left before I got home. Are you at home?"

"Yes, and she's not here. Hold on, I'll call her."

I shake my head. "She turned her phone off."

Laurie is quiet. "Did you two fight?"

"No. No." I pause. "Did she tell you anything... about..." I don't even want to think about it. "Someone else...maybe?"

"Oh no, Landon. No. Nothing like that."

I breathe. "Just wait there. I'm on my way...and let me know as soon as she gets home."

"Okay."

The drive to her apartment is excruciating. Knowing she could be heading some other place makes it all the more frustrating. I don't want to think she could be in danger, but even if she's only walking home, it's late, and anything could happen to her on the dark streets.

At Rachel's apartment building, I tell Joe to drive back along an alternate route and be on the lookout for her. Laurie comes to join me downstairs.

"She still hasn't called?"

"Nope." Laurie frowns. "What happened?"

I push a frustrated hand through my hair. "I have no idea. She was at my place, waiting like we planned, then she left."

Laurie looks around the street, shivering as a cold breeze hits her. "I'm sure she'll turn up soon." Her voice is tinged with worry.

"Why don't you go inside? I'll wait out here."

Laurie does as I say, and I pace the sidewalk, waiting, unable to calm the worry building inside me.

It feels like hours later when I see Rachel turn the corner. She's walking slowly, and when she sees me, she stops. Too relieved to wonder why, I'm by her side in seconds.

"What happened?" Her only response is a soft sniff, and I rub the cold from her shoulders and arms. "What happened?"

Her eyes fill with tears, and a tight rage builds inside me. If anything happened to her, God knows I will not hesitate to hurt anyone who harmed her in any way.

Drawing her closer, I wipe her face with a handkerchief. "I got home, and you'd left, but your things were there." She sniffs again. "What's wrong?"

"I..." Her words falter.

Jesus! If anyone so much as laid a finger on her... "Are you all right?"

"I'm fine." She pushes away from me, putting some distance between us. Then she's accusing me with tear-stained eyes. "Where were you? Where were you last night?"

I don't understand the words, or what she's getting at. "Where was I?"

"You told me you had meetings, but I saw a picture of you having dinner with some woman."

It takes a moment for me to understand that she's accusing me of something. "You what?"

"I saw you," she repeats in a shaky voice. "I saw you with your dinner date, and you looked like you were having a good time."

"And you left?" She saw some gossip somewhere, and that's why she's been out on the street alone? That's why she put herself in danger? My anger turns to frustration. "You didn't think you needed to ask me about it before walking away?"

"You lied to me about where you were last night. Maybe I didn't want to wait to be lied to again."

She was leaving.

Suddenly, I'm laughing, and there's no humor in the sound because inside, I feel like crap. "I didn't lie to you. I had meetings. I had a meeting with her, just like I had meetings with other people over the course of the day. I decided to conclude our meeting over dinner to save time. Are you satisfied, or would you like a fucking list of every single person I spoke to yesterday?"

She flinches at my tone, but I'm too angry to care. "I'm not supposed to care that you were out with someone else when you told me you'd be working?

I'm not supposed to care that you didn't think to mention it to me until I saw it online?" She shrugs. "Fine then. I don't care."

I don't bother to reply. I'm too pissed to say anything to her. I will not stand here and lecture her about the worry she caused everyone over...what? Some gossip?

I pull out my phone and call Joe. "You can come back now." Then I call Laurie. "She's here."

"Did anything... Is she...?"

"No. She's okay."

I end the call and glance up the street, looking for Joe. I don't trust myself to say anything without losing my cool.

Of all the stupid, childish, dangerous things she could have done.

"Do you realize I had my driver searching the streets for you? Do you realize your cousin was worried about you? You preferred to take a walk across the city, at this time, alone, because you saw a picture online. For fuck's sake, Rachel! Do you know what could have happened? How would I ever fucking forgive myself if anything happened to you?"

My words do something to her. The accusation melts away, giving way to a sheen of tears in her eyes. I fight the urge to comfort her. *No.* This one is on her.

"Landon." She covers her face with her hands. "I didn't think..."

"No, you didn't," I interrupt. "You were too eager to indict me."

Because she's still looking for a reason to leave.

The realization hurts like hell.

"Are we still at this stage, Rachel? Are you still looking for excuses to walk away?"

She doesn't reply. Out of the corner of my eye, I see Joe drive up the street. He comes to park right next to where we're standing.

"You can go up now," I tell her, heading for the car. "I'll send your things later tonight."

"Wait." Her voice shatters my anger. "Please, Landon." When I face her, her eyes are glistening with tears. *Fuck!*

"I'm sorry," she whispers.

A lone tear rolls down her cheek.

"Dammit, Rachel." I take her in my arms and wipe the tear away. "You're going to drive me crazy," I whisper, knowing she already has.

She buries her face in my chest. "I'm sorry."

My arms tighten. God, I don't want to let her go. "Are you sure you won't go up? Laurie was very worried."

She shakes her head. "No. I want to come with you."

In the car, she switches on her phone and replies

to her messages. I try not to torture myself with images of what could have happened. I try not to connect my fears to what happened to my family twenty years ago.

Why didn't she wait for me?

It's just sex, Landon.

She still doesn't trust me. She still wouldn't hesitate before walking away. Where does that leave me?

Am I fooling myself by thinking we have a chance when she's looking for any excuse to end things?

At my place, I go to change then lay out dinner. She disappears to the bedroom for a while, and when she returns, I see she has discovered the additions to the closet. I commissioned a couple of personal shoppers to stock the wardrobe with two weeks' worth of clothes and accessories for her. It was meant to be a pleasant surprise, but now I'm not sure what it is.

She's wearing a pair of sleeping shorts and a tank top. I chose them personally, because of how similar they are to a pair she already owns.

"I hope you don't mind," I say quietly, barely looking at her. "I thought having a few things here..."

"I don't mind," she replies in a small voice. "They're all perfect."

"I'm glad you like them. The shoppers came highly recommended, but in case there's anything else you want or something you wish to exchange, I'll make sure you have their contact details."

"Okay."

We have dinner in front of the TV, watching a show. After, we finish a bottle of wine together. We talk little, and we don't talk at all about what happened.

When the show is over, she reaches over and takes my hand. "I'm sorry," she says again.

I take her hand in mine. "You don't have any reason to be jealous, Rachel. You have to believe me when I tell you that."

"I don't know what I was thinking." Her eyes close. "I wasn't thinking at all."

I can understand that—not thinking, acting on emotions alone. Before her, that would have been foreign to me, but now, I understand. "No matter what happens, don't run. I want this to work, and I want to be sure you want the same thing."

Her voice is firm. "I do."

I draw her into my arms, and she lays her head on my chest while I stroke her hair. I want to take all her doubts away, and mine too, but I don't know how.

"I was so worried. When your phone went off..." I close my eyes. "I don't think I've ever been so afraid in my life."

Her only response is a soft sigh. She's exhausted, and after a few minutes, she falls asleep on my chest.

CHAPTER 26

The next day, when I arrive at Rachel's apartment to pick her up for the cocktail mixer, she meets me at the door. As usual, she looks stunning.

For a few moments, I just stare, thanking all the stars that aligned to bring her to my apartment on the night we met.

I take her hand. "Rachel, I'll never get used to how beautiful you are."

"Thank you." She's blushing, and it's almost too cute. "You look fab, as usual."

I'm more interested in touching her than in enjoying her compliments. I trail my fingers down her arm, wishing we didn't have to go anywhere.

"Are you ready?"

She sighs. "Yes."

On the drive, I can barely take my eyes off her, and she notices.

"You look like you're about to jump my bones."

"I'm trying not to," I admit shamelessly. "We're leaving as early as we can manage. I'm not spending valuable time at a party when I'd rather be with you."

She wets her lips. "Now I don't want to go at all."

Careful not to mess with her hair and makeup, I pull her into my arms. "I'm going to have a hard time surviving two days without you. What have you done to me?"

She grins. "I bewitched you."

"You certainly did."

Her eyes close and she touches her forehead to mine. I listen to her breaths, caught up in the unexpected intimacy of the moment. After a while, she pulls back then smiles naughtily. "Just so you know, I'll be having fun while you're gone. I'll be out clubbing all night Friday, so I won't miss you too much."

"I'll be suffering alone." I chuckle and place one hand on my chest. "I think you just broke my heart."

She takes a deep breath. "I'll miss you too," she says quietly. "Every single minute."

We take pictures outside the venue then walk in together. The host, Steven Yeagar, soon joins us. He's an old friend from college and a serial entrepreneur.

"I'm glad you could make it," he tells me before turning to Rachel. "Landon, who is this angel?"

"She's Rachel Foster." I hold her gaze as I speak. "My girlfriend."

A spot of color stains her cheeks and her eyes soften. Then Steven is talking to her, almost gushing, and though I can't hear what he tells her, I love the way her face lights up.

The evening progresses. Many of the guests are young and hip. Steven likes to roll with a fashionable crowd. They're not exactly interesting to me, and I'm thinking of leaving when I hear a familiar voice.

"Landon!"

Rachel and I both turn toward the voice. Ava is walking toward me, a lazy smile on her face. Trust her to make a late and dramatic entrance.

She hugs me, smiling brilliantly.

"I didn't know you were coming," I tell her, pulling back.

"Steven invited me," she replies, turning to Rachel.

I wonder if Rachel recognizes her from the pictures. I can't tell from her face as I introduce them.

"How nice to meet you," Ava drawls.

"It's good to meet you too." Rachel's voice is calm and impersonal. "I've met your brother," she continues. "Evans Sinclair?" She smiles. "It was a very...memorable meeting."

Ava doesn't reply. It's not the answer she expected, obviously, and Evans is a sore spot.

"I thought you'd returned to San Francisco."

Ava shakes her head. "Not yet. I had a few things to take care of." She takes my hand. "I want to say hello to Steven. It's been ages. Why don't you come?"

I'm not looking to prolong my stay at the party, not when Rachel and I have plans.

"We already saw him." My eyes are on Rachel, and I barely notice as Ava lets go of my hand.

"All right then." She does a small, quick wave before walking away.

We leave soon after that. After spending all night trying to keep my hands off Rachel, I'm more focused on getting her alone than on anything else. As soon as we're alone in my apartment, I do what I've been aching to do all night.

By the time we fall asleep, exhausted, Ava is the furthest thing from my mind.

"A LITTLE BIRDIE TELLS ME YOU'RE SMITTEN WITH the writer from *Gilt*," Alex tells me after a meeting. It's my second day in San Francisco, and even though I have a mountain of work to get through, I've been spending as much time as I can on the phone with Rachel.

"Tell your little birdie to mind their own business."

He laughs. "Okay. I just never thought I'd see the day."

I glare at him.

"My little birdie also told me you had dinner with Ava last night?"

"Why doesn't your little birdie work for me?"

"Don't we all?"

"She wanted to talk about Evans," I say with a shrug. "She's worried about him."

"Have they considered rehab?"

"Many times. He doesn't exactly have a cooperative personality."

"So, no progress."

"She thinks if we ignore him, he'll go away."

He makes a face. "She could have told you that over the phone."

"She could have," I admit. Alex is another person in my life who can't stand Ava Sinclair.

His gaze turns more serious. "Do you think he'll go away? We're having to field questions about unlawful acquisition of properties, coercion, and bullying. How long before the rumors become ammunition for a more powerful enemy? We'll survive any investigation of course—we're clean—but at what cost?"

I shake my head. If we go after him now, that will be the story, and I promised Ava I'd let her take care of him, for now. "He's a failure with a substance abuse problem," I tell Alex. "Nobody will listen to him."

Alex looks unconvinced. "Well, once you decide you want to go after him, we can bury him."

"I don't doubt it."

The next day, there's a round of last-minute preparations and meetings, and of course, Rachel's arrival. I can't wait for her to see how the hotel has turned out.

I message her as soon as my watch tells me she should have landed.

Tell me you've arrived.

I have.

I can't wait to see you.

Me neither.

I have no choice but trust her to Tony and Claude as I'm still swamped with meetings, but I call her as soon as I have a moment.

"Are you settled in?"

"Yes. The hotel is beautiful, Landon."

"I'm glad you think so."

She sighs. "Where are you?"

"Downstairs." But I can't go to her right now, as

much as I'd like to. "Do you have everything you need?"

"Yes!" She laughs. "Everybody keeps asking me that."

Her laughter makes me smile. "I want to see you. I have the press conference in about half an hour. After that, I'm coming to you."

"Are you sure you have the time?"

"I'll make it," I tell her in a low voice. "I'm so fucking hot for you. I'm going to fuck you so hard you'll feel it for days."

Her response is a little breathless. "You have a hotel to open and homeless people to raise money for—are you sure you should be thinking about sex at a time like this?"

"Can you blame me? I have a hard-on just from the knowledge that you're here, and it's not going anywhere until you take me inside your hot, delicious pussy."

I know she loves it when I talk dirty, and I'm not disappointed. She sighs. "You're making me so hot."

"Stay that way. I'll be with you as soon as I can manage it."

The press conference goes smoothly for the first half-hour. I answer questions and try to be charming, though I would rather be anywhere else.

"How are you dealing with the rumors about your unlawful acquisition of property?"

The question annoys me. It's the first time I've had to address Evans Sinclair's malicious rumors publicly, and the truth is, I'd rather not, especially not today.

Without abandoning my smile, I address the reporter. "I should clarify that the rumors are not about the unlawful acquisition of property. They are merely speculation, driven by gossip, about the reasons why people feel confident enough to entrust their properties to the Swanson Court brand. If you take a look at the Gold Dust, today. Ms..."

"Hader."

"Ms. Hader." I pause. "Compared to the Gold Dust of say, two years ago, the reason should be obvious."

More questions follow that, and none of them mention the rumors again. Soon, the hour ends and it's time to go to Rachel.

Tony hurries over to go over my itinerary for the rest of the day.

"Just email it," I tell him.

"I already have."

I check my phone. The itinerary is there, along with a few other emails, one of them from a management address at Insomnia Lounge.

An amateur photographer was shopping for buyers for photos and videos he took around the club yesterday. One of our people saw this. I thought you might want to know.

It's from Duane, who manages the club, and it's a short video of Rachel and Jack outside my club, kissing.

For a moment, I'm totally frozen, unable to do anything but stare at the image. Then white-hot jealousy twists inside me.

Containing my thoughts, I type a quick reply. *Thanks, but there was no need. Just make sure he loses the video.*

I don't wait for him to reply. I go back to watching it, dying slowing each time I see Weyland pushing his tongue into her mouth.

I watch it until my insides are burning with bitterness.

Why did she come to me after being with him?

Why the fuck is she here?

Up in the suite, Rachel is on the sofa, watching my press conference on TV.

"Hey." She draws out the word, smiling softly. Why does she look so happy to see me if she'd rather be with him?

I want to confront her, but I'm afraid to. I'm afraid she'll confirm my fears.

I shove the phone into my pocket and glare at the screen. "I hate press conferences."

"You handled that one well enough."

"I had to."

"I read about the rumors," she says with concern. "Is it a problem?"

No, but you kissing Weyland is.

"Not really." I shrug. "I know who's behind them, and he's bound by contract not to slander me directly, so he's planting the gossip with the help of his social circle. They have gotten out of hand, but they only damage public perception. The banks and investors don't care. Most businesspeople would rather cut off their ears than stop doing business with me."

There's an edge to my voice I can't control, and I'm sure she notices. I toss my jacket aside and head to one end of the room, where a glass wall provides a spectacular view of the city and the bay.

Tell me what happened.

She doesn't.

She comes to join me at the wall. Why can't I stop thinking about her with Weyland? Why can't I trust that there's a good explanation? Why do I want to demand answers?

Focus on right now.

Right now, she's here.

I stroke her cheek and she leans into my touch, sighing. "Are you worried?" she asks softly.

"No." I shake my head. "Have you had anything to eat?"

"I'm not hungry," she whispers. "Not for food anyway."

It's just sex, Landon.

Taking her face in my hands, I rest my forehead on hers, breathing in her sweet scent.

It's just sex, Landon.

I draw in a breath and release her long enough to pull off my tie. Reaching for her, I curve my hand around the back of her neck and pull her in, claiming her lips in a hungry kiss.

Does she wish it was him right now?

If she did, she wouldn't be here.

I wish I could shut off the thoughts, but I can't. I release her, and she frowns, sensing that there's something wrong.

She places gentle hands on my chest. "You said something about fucking me so hard I would feel it for days," she reminds me.

"Yes." I let out a chuckle. "I remember."

She trails one hand down to the front of my pants, where it's obvious how much I want her. My mind might be in chaos, but my body can't resist her.

"I'm so ready," she whispers.

For me.

I lift her off her feet, touching her back to the glass before setting her down and claiming her lips again. She moans into my mouth, and I lift her dress, slipping my fingers into her panties, where she's already slick.

Does she respond to him like this?

I push the question from my mind. "You're so wet."

"I told you I was ready," she replies, breathless.

I pull her dress over her head. Through the lace of her bra, I can see her nipples, pink and swollen. I take one between my teeth and she makes a breathy sound. With one hand, she strokes the length of my cock, making it impossible for me to think.

Finally.

I take her lips again. Her hands are busy, undoing my pants and freeing me, then she pushes me back and gets down on her knees, taking me in her mouth.

It's torture and pleasure at the same time, and it's almost unbearable. I pull out of her mouth with a sigh and drop to my knees, joining her on the carpeted floor. I nudge her head back to my cock, and she takes me eagerly, sucking me deep.

My chest rises and falls. I'm almost breathless. My hands rove over her back, memorizing every contour, every smooth inch of her skin. I reach as far as I can, cupping her ass, sliding my fingers into her from behind.

"I love your mouth," I rasp, straightening to watch her head bobbing up and down. I thread my fingers in her hair. "So hot..."

She moans, and with her lips around me, the vibration feels like heaven.

I nudge her away from my cock and up to her

feet. "I want to come inside you," I tell her. Still on my knees, I tug off her panties. I taste her hungrily, kissing her soft lips and sucking on her clit.

She loses her balance, but I hold her steady. She whispers my name, grinding her hips as I slip my fingers inside her. Unable to wait, I rise and steer her back toward the wall.

As soon as I lift her off her feet, she wraps her legs around my waist and braces her back on the wall. I drive deep into her and she grips me tight, her muscles squeezing me as if she'll never let go.

God, she feels good.

Her nipples poke through the lace of her bra, and I free them from the sheer constraint, taking one in my mouth and sucking hard.

Rachel is moaning, whispering my name, telling me how much she loves what I'm doing. Soon she's shaking, coming hard. When her orgasm subsides, I let her legs drop to the floor and turn her around to face the glass. I pull her hips toward me and enter her from behind.

She cries out, meeting me thrust for thrust. I want to touch her everywhere. I have a feral need to leave a mark on her somehow. I feel desperate and needy, almost afraid.

She cries out, shaking as her body explodes, clenching hard around me. I'm not far behind, whispering her name as I come.

I wait a few moments to catch my breath before I pull out of her and turn her around to face me. She wraps her arms around me as I lay kisses on her face, her cheeks, her lips.

Her smile is tender. "You really did miss me."

I adjust her bra and pick the rest of her discarded clothes from the floor. "You haven't seen anything yet,"

She laughs. "I can't wait." There's a pause. "I missed you so much."

And yet you couldn't wait to lock lips with your ex.

I push the thought away, but not quickly enough. She catches the momentary change in my mood.

"What's the matter?" Her tone is full of worry. "Is something wrong?"

I shake my head. "You should get dressed. There's nothing wrong."

She doesn't believe me. "Tell me what's wrong." This time, it's a demand.

I exhale then take her chin in my hand, lifting her face to mine. "I don't like to share what's mine. Not now, not ever. Do you understand?"

She backs away from me with a suspicious frown. "What are you talking about?"

"I'm talking about Jack Weyland."

Her face clouds with hurt and disappointment. "Is that why you have Rafael driving me around? So you can spy on me?"

"I didn't need to spy on you. You kissed him in front of my club. I didn't need Rafael to tell me about that."

"You could have asked me what happened instead of jumping to conclusions."

"Oh, really," I snort dismissively. That's rich, coming from her.

"Yes, really." She glares at me. "For your information, he kissed me. I neither wanted it nor invited it, and you know what? I don't like to share what's mine either, so the next time you decide to enjoy Ava Sinclair's company, you can keep that in mind."

With those words, she stalks away, heading to the bedroom. I follow her, because I'm not done.

"I thought we had this conversation about Ava."

She whirls to face me. "I thought we had the conversation about Jack! Why were you with her yesterday? Why didn't you tell me you used to sleep with her when I saw that picture of you two?"

"I've never asked you for an inventory of everyone you ever slept with," I reply evenly. "Do you think I should punctuate everything I say about her with a statement about how, a long time ago, we used to fuck?"

"Maybe it would have been fair for you to give me that information seeing as everywhere I look, the two of you are being photographed together." She stares at me, her eyes burning with hurt. "Was it also a business meeting yesterday?" She laughs. "Did you decide to *save time* by concluding your business over dinner?"

"You're one to talk," I toss back. "I'm supposed to endure an inquisition whenever you see and totally misconstrue a picture. Meanwhile, it's perfectly okay for you to spend as much time as you like with your precious Jack."

She makes a sound of disbelief. "My precious Jack?" Her eyes close, and she sighs. "You know what? I have no idea why we're arguing. We both know why we're still together, so we might as well forget the things we can't agree about and you know, maybe fuck... That's obviously the only area where we work well together."

She heads for the bathroom, but I stop her. "You're right," I growl, pulling her to me. "Maybe we should do just that."

She pulls her arm from my grip. "Just as long as you know I'm not Ava."

I laugh bitterly. "And you know I'm not Jack."

"God!" She stamps her foot. "How can you be so—"

"So what?" I interrupt, furious beyond reason. "So jealous? But you know exactly how that feels, don't you?" I'm crazy with a need to possess all of her, and it's killing me. I want to beg her to forgive me, to accept all of me, to forget anyone else but me, but I keep seeing that kiss in my head. I crush her body to mine and slide one hand between her legs. "This is mine," I tell her. "You are mine, and your body knows it."

At my touch, her breath hitches. "Landon..." she says, and it comes out like a moan.

"It's what you want, isn't it?" I continue. "It's the only reason you ever agreed to be with me." I carry her over to the bed and lay her on her back, her legs spread. "You like how it feels when my cock is deep inside you." I kneel between her legs and undo my pants. "That's what you want."

At first, she looks as if she'll argue, but her eyes meet mine and fill with a stubborn challenge.

"Yes," she sneers. "It's what I want."

Why does it hurt so much?

It's just sex, Landon.

Well she can have it. All of it. As long as she wants.

It's over very fast. It's pleasure and punishment for the both of us. She comes with a moan just as I climax. I pull out of her and lie beside her on the bed, ashamed and desperate.

I can sense her sadness like a solid wall between us. I watch her rise from the bed and, contrite, I take her hand, urging her back to sit beside me.

"I should have told you about Ava," I say gently.

It's not enough. Even I know that whatever I say cannot mend the situation between us, not right now at least. "I'm sorry. I didn't think it mattered. I was wrong."

She responds with a shrug. "It's okay."

It's not.

"I tried not to care about you and Jack," I continue. "You told me you no longer have feelings for him, and I tried to concentrate on that. I...I just couldn't."

She exhales. "I know how the kiss with Jack would have seemed to you, but it wasn't what it looked like."

She doesn't offer anything else, and I let her go. I hear the shower running. I know I've pushed her further away, and I have no idea what I can do about it.

CHAPTER 27

*A*fter her shower, we have a late lunch together. The conversation is awkward. There's so much I want to say, but I don't know how. Finally, I give up and leave her alone, heading back downstairs to see how things are going.

When I return, Rachel is getting her makeup done. I take a quick shower and get dressed. With only my jacket left to go, I go out to the balcony.

Outside, the view is lovely as the sun sets, but everything inside me is chaos. I almost don't recognize myself. I used to have a better handle on my emotions. I used to be in control, but with Rachel, I'm uncertain, confused.

She's had me unsure of myself from day one.

And now it's getting worse. I only know how

desperately I want her, how I dread the thought of losing her.

When I return inside the suite, the makeup people are gone. In the dressing room, I pull on my jacket and fix my tie. As I button the jacket, I see Rachel in the mirror, standing at the door to the bathroom, watching me.

Her beauty is unearthly. Her makeup is perfect, and the deep blue stones at her ears set off the blue-green accents around her eyes. Her hair is swept to one side in an elaborate curl. She's wearing only underwear, but I can't imagine anything more gorgeous than how she already looks.

I should fall on my knees and worship at her feet. She deserves that, and more.

A hundred years should go to praise thine eyes and on thy forehead gaze.

"You look incredible."

Her lips curve in a wry smile. "Thanks. I'll just put on my dress and then I'm ready."

There's something about the tone of her voice that tells me everything has changed between us. I follow her to the bedroom and watch her slip on her dress, a pale blue vision that looks as light as gossamer.

I help her zip it up and she turns around to face me, that wry half-smile still on her face.

"I..." I search for a word that can do her justice. "I'm speechless."

"Thank you."

Lowering myself to my knees, I take each shoe from a box on the floor and carefully slip them on her feet.

"I'll be waiting outside," I tell her when I'm done.

She doesn't reply, but I can feel her eyes on me as I walk away.

She joins me a few minutes later, and we go down together. We take pictures at the red carpet and she stays by my side as I welcome the guests.

In the ballroom, the theme is *A Midsummer Night's Dream*, and soft lights hang from the ceiling, making it look like a moonlit night. The waiters are dressed like sprites and fairies, and there are plants and flowers gleaming with faux fireflies.

"It's very beautiful," Rachel whispers.

She is more beautiful. I squeeze her hand. "Thank you."

I spend the next half-hour talking to guests and acknowledging congratulations. When Aidan arrives, I'm relieved to see his roguish face.

"Took you long enough to get here," I scold.

He laughs, shaking my hand vigorously before giving me a hug.

"God! It is lovely," he exclaims, taking it all in. "You did it again...and I'm sorry I'm late."

I smile. "I'm just glad you're here."

"Last-minute issues with the play." He turns his attention to Rachel. "Didn't hurt that he had a plane waiting for me." He hugs her lightly and kisses her cheek. "It's good to see you, Rachel."

"Same here," she replies. "You look good."

"Desperate damage control before leaving the plane." He grins. "You should have seen me escaping New York and those horrible rehearsals. I looked like a fugitive."

I watch them laughing, realizing just then that they are the two most important people to me in the world. Rachel catches me watching her and gives me a questioning look.

How do I tell her she means the world to me?

A guest approaches me to gush about the hotel, forcing my attention away.

Rachel and Aidan are still talking when Ava joins us. She takes my hand and almost blinds me with her smile.

"Always so sexy in a tux," she whispers in my ear.

There's a quick flash as someone takes a picture. I back away from her, wondering how much she's had to drink.

"Ava Sinclair." Aidan's dislike is evident in his voice. "I never thought I'd see this face again."

Ava gives him a look that mirrors his. "It's been

ages, hasn't it?" She turns to Rachel. "How d'you do, Rachel?"

"Wonderful, thank you." Rachel is smiling. "You look great."

"Well, so do you."

"I was just thinking it's such an enchanting event you all put together," Rachel says, still smiling.

Ava preens even though she only organized a small part of the fundraising event. "Were you? We did have a great time arranging it all." She bats her eyelashes at me then saunters away. Rachel watches her go, a strange look on her face.

I place my hand around her waist. "They should announce dinner any minute."

"And then after the boring speeches, some dancing." Aidan grins at Rachel. "I'm looking forward to seeing what you can do."

"Game on."

Their conversation continues throughout dinner, and I try not to let it bother me. She seems determined to focus her attention on Aidan, who is blissfully unaware that she's deliberately ignoring me.

I can't wait for the evening to be over, to have another chance for us to talk and maybe get past whatever this is. I felt like I was losing her before. Now, it feels like I already have.

I go through the motions of conversations, giving

a speech and announcing the auction for The Shelter Project, but I only have eyes for Rachel.

After the auction, when I finally escape from the multitudes of people who want to talk to me, I return to our table. Rachel isn't there, and I see her dancing with Aidan. They're having fun, and it makes me smile just to watch them.

"How long do you think it'll last?"

Ava is standing beside me, a glass of champagne in her hand.

"Still keeping tabs on me?"

She shrugs and lowers herself on a chair. "Why don't you sit for a while? She's having fun. Let her."

I pull out my chair and join her. "I think we've established by now that my relationship isn't your concern."

She chuckles. "If I were placing bets, I'd say it's already over. She seems a little shaky already. Not everyone can keep up with you, after all. Remember when you told me you wished your father had died along with your mother instead of lingering for a decade after? So dark, Landon. Do you share things like that with her?"

"It's none of your business what I share with her." I scowl, annoyed by the reference to things I shared with her in the past. "Why do you care, anyway? Have you run out of playboys and princes to marry and discard?"

She is quiet. "What if I have?"

I lean close to her. "I'd say...I really don't care. Stay out of my personal life, Ava. I'm serious. And for your information, I have absolutely no interest in yours."

I leave her at the table and go over to where Rachel and Aidan are still dancing.

"May I?"

Aidan raises an eyebrow at Rachel, and she nods. He hands her over to me then saunters off.

The song is slow, and I hold Rachel close, barely moving to the mellow music.

"Are you enjoying yourself?"

She shrugs. "Aidan has been excellent company."

Meaning I haven't. The small dig makes me smile. "I'm glad you two like each other."

"What's not to like? You know I think he's great."

The music continues, and I can feel the distance between us like a widening fissure. "Rachel..."

Her eyes meet mine, and I continue.

"What happened earlier in the suite—"

She stops me. "Not now, Landon."

"No, I...I haven't stopped thinking about it. You being here means a lot to me, Rachel. I hate the idea that I hurt you. I don't... I'm sorry for not trusting you about Jack."

She doesn't look at me. "You already said that."

I exhale. "I want us to work," I tell her. "I want—"

"Landon. We don't work." Her eyes fix on mine, wide, green, and almost luminous. "We just don't work."

I feel as if I've been kicked in the gut. Anybody else and I would walk away, but here, now, with her, I want to beg, to plead.

My voice is miraculously even. "You're wrong."

"Am I?" She searches my face. I can hear all the words she's not saying, the jealousy and suspicion. She's rejecting me, the man she no longer wants.

"Don't do this again." I'm begging now. "For God's sake, don't do this again."

"Why not? What does it even mean to you that I stay? It's just sex, Landon. Apart from that, we have nothing."

It's just sex, Landon.

"We talked about this, and you said you wouldn't walk away."

"I'm not walking away. I'm trying to make you see that we don't have a chance." She sighs. "You don't trust me. I don't trust you. We don't have anything to build a relationship on. Maybe it's best if we both walk away."

Please. The word is on the tip of my tongue.

Don't be pathetic, a voice says in my head.

Then Ava's voice. *If I were placing bets, I'd say it's already over.*

I pull in a breath. "Tony will arrange for your transport. You can go any time you want.

She steps back and her hands drop from my shoulders. "Landon—"

"No." I cup her face in my hands and smile down at her. My face feels tight with the effort. "Whatever it is you're looking for, Rachel, I hope you fucking find it."

The rest of the evening passes in a blur. I don't register anything else that happens.

We don't work. We just don't work.

Well, fine.

I will not keep chasing a dream that doesn't belong to me.

Ava pulls me to the dance floor, and I can barely hear what she says while we dance. All I know is that Rachel is leaving, and I'm not good enough for her.

CHAPTER 28

I know exactly when Rachel leaves the room. I feel the emptiness inside me intensify until it's unbearable.

I won't go after her.

"Where's your mind?" Ava teases. She stops a passing nymph with a champagne tray. "Here, have a drink."

I wave the waiter away. "I'm fine."

"Lovers' quarrel?"

"Mind your business."

"You are my business."

I stop moving. "Ava, I don't know what kind of game you're playing, but you have to know there's no point to this...whatever it is you're doing."

She pouts. "Next you'll be telling me you're in love."

I freeze at the word. She's watching me, smiling, waiting for a reply. Without saying anything else, I leave her on the dance floor and stalk out of the room. The party is still ongoing, but I don't care. I go up to my suite and find Rachel in a robe, her face scrubbed clean of makeup. Her suitcase lies open on the bed.

Seeing for myself that she's serious about leaving causes another wave of pain.

"You're actually leaving." I feel stupid for stating the obvious. Only she would make me feel like a fool.

She sighs. "Yes."

I won't beg. "When do you want to go? Tonight? Have you called Tony?"

She shakes her head.

"I'll let him know you want to leave. He'll have a plane waiting for you for whenever you're ready."

She doesn't reply.

I'm trying my best not to feel anything, but I'm dying inside. "Do you want me to go? I can arrange for another suite if you'd rather not have me around."

She shakes her head again. "No...don't. You don't have to go."

I stalk to the bar in the living room to pour myself a drink before tearing off my jacket and going out to the balcony. I can't breathe. Out there in the cold, the night air feels like lashes on my skin.

Soon, she'll be gone.

I send Tony a message telling him to arrange for a ride for Rachel.

Soon, she'll be gone.

"Landon." The sound of her voice is like a shot of adrenaline to my senses. I whirl, hope squashing every pain inside me then dying when I see the look on her face.

Soon, she'll be gone.

I turn back to face the city, taking a long swill from my glass and welcoming the burning in my throat. "What do you want?"

"I have..." She stops. "I wanted to talk."

My laugh is bitter. "You've already said it all. We don't work." I face her again, hating to see how fragile she looks, how hurt.

Don't leave.

My lips curl and I set my glass down on top of the balustrade. "What else is there to say?"

"Landon—"

"Stop, Rachel. Just stop it." I hold up one hand. "I'm done. I'm sick of the mixed messages, the drama..." I shrug and laugh again. "You always have an excuse to walk away, no matter what I do. I get the message now. You've proven beyond any doubt that you're out of my reach."

Her eyes fill with tears and I hate myself—for not deserving her, for not being good enough for her, for not being what she wants. "You really should leave," I say with a sigh. "I intend to get well and truly drunk tonight." I reach for my drink again.

"I love you." The words stop me in my tracks, and I freeze. Slowly, I turn back to face her.

"I love you," she says again. "I'm in love with you." Her eyes fall away from mine. "I have since that first week we spent together. I...I didn't want to fall in love with you, and I didn't plan to, and it has hurt...It has hurt every day knowing you don't feel the same way."

I'm staring at her, hearing her speak but not quite sure I understand what she's saying.

"I just...I thought it would be easier if I let you go." The words are spilling out of her, faster than I can comprehend. "I didn't want something that, at best, was just a prolonged hookup, and now I don't want a relationship that has no chance of becoming something more, because I won't be able to bear it."

She loves me.

"You don't have to say anything," she continues. "I'm not asking for anything from you. I already know how you feel about commitment. I just wanted you to know the truth. I love you. That's the only reason why I ever walked away. I knew it was the only way I would have a chance to get over you."

She loves me, and that's why she's leaving.

"Rachel..." I take a step toward her. "Don't go."

Her body is trembling. "Landon..."

"Don't go," I repeat. "Please."

She comes to me and puts her arms around me. "I love you," she says again. "Nothing is ever going to change that."

I close my eyes. She loves me.

She has loved me...all this time, and she never told me.

I had no idea.

I feel exultant, yet strangely sad. "You have no idea how afraid I am of hurting you."

She lifts her face to mine and places a kiss on my lips. "You won't."

I hug her close, feeling her body tremble in my arms. I have no plan for this. I had no expectation of this. I feel undone.

Love.

For so long, that word has meant only pain to me.

And now...

Her eyes rove my face. "I love you," she says again. Then she reaches up to kiss me. I kiss her back, tasting her desire, her love. Her fingers tangle in my hair as my tongue strokes hers.

When I release her, she smiles up at me, I wonder if she can see the fear in my eyes.

"Stop thinking," she urges, her voice soft. When I don't say anything, she kisses me again. I kiss her back, clinging to what I know, what I understand.

She unbuttons my shirt and slides her hands over my chest.

She loves me.

I tear my lips from hers. "Rachel..."

She shakes her head. "Don't stop."

I take her lips again, undoing the tie of her robe. She shrugs it off and presses her body to mine.

Carrying her inside the suite, I set her down on the soft carpet, and she looks up at me with eyes soft with desire...and love.

I take a deep breath and cover her body with mine, kissing her again, trailing soft kisses from her face to her chest. I want to shower every inch of her with care and attention. I want to take the pain away from her eyes. Lowering my head to her breast, I draw a nipple into my mouth and suck in deeply through her lace bra. Her body arches and I slide my hand between her legs, stroking her gently.

Her eyes flutter closed, and she makes a sound of pleasure. I reach behind her and undo her bra then my hand is back between her legs, sliding inside her panties.

Still stroking her, I drag my lips from her breasts back to her throat, kissing the tender spot under her ear. Impatiently, she grabs my face and thrusts her tongue in my mouth.

I groan, tearing my lips from hers. Her hips move to the slow thrum of my fingers, her slick flesh demanding more. I slide two fingers inside her, and she lets out a breath.

"What do you want me to do?" I'm more uncertain than I've ever been in my life. "What should I do?"

She breathes. "Don't stop touching me."

I bring her to a climax with my fingers, watching her body shudder and tremble. I kiss the moans from her lips, tasting her pleasure.

She dozes off in my arms, and I slide her robe back around her, leaving her only to close the doors to the balcony. When I'm done, I carry her to the bedroom and remove the robe before tucking her under the covers. I undress and join her in bed, pulling her into my arms.

"Don't leave."

She doesn't hear me.

∽

I'M WATCHING THE CAR FILL WITH SMOKE.

"There's nothing you can do."

I can see my mother's face, unconscious as the smoke fills the car, but this time, the face looks different.

Because it's not my mother. It's Rachel.

"Please," I scream. "Please."

"There's nothing you can do."

I wake up to Rachel's voice in my ear. She's

whispering soft soothing words. I open my eyes, the tension in my body draining away.

"You're here."

She smiles. "I am."

I draw her into my arms, and her body relaxes into mine.

"You were crying," she says. "Was it worse than usual?"

When I don't reply, she lifts her face to mine, waiting for an answer.

"It was you," I whisper.

She frowns. "I don't understand."

"It's always my mother in the accident," I explain. "This time, it was you, and I couldn't save you."

"There's no accident, Landon. I'm fine. I don't need saving."

I want to argue, but before I can say a word, she rises from the bed and takes my face in her hands. "Stop torturing yourself," she says firmly. "You're not going to hurt me. I'm going to be fine."

But she's already hurt. She's been hurting these past weeks, and I didn't know.

I take her hands in mine. "I already have." More than I had a right to.

She shakes her head. "Don't think about that."

She loves me.

"Say it again." It's selfish, but I want to hear her

tell me she loves me. I want to hear it until I believe it without a doubt, until I feel like I deserve it.

"I love you," she whispers.

I bury my face in the crook of her neck, inhaling the sweet scent of her skin. She settles over me, and I lay gentle kisses on her neck and her shoulder.

She closes her eyes and I roll over so she's lying beneath me. I continue to lavish kisses all over her, letting my touch say all the words I can't bring myself to say.

"I had no idea."

She smiles. "I know."

I kiss her everywhere, from her face to her toes. My lips find the heat between her legs and she spreads herself for me. I kiss her down there, tasting her desire, the sweetness of her body. I don't stop until she's crying out, breathless as she climaxes with my name on her lips.

I rise to my knees and she urges me forward. I settle between her legs and lift them to my waist, pulling her forward as I enter her.

Her eyes hold mine, glistening with a wetness that wrecks my heart. Still, she reaches up to touch my chest, stroking me languidly.

My chest rises. "You feel so good. So good."

In response, she grips my ass, urging me deeper. I peel her hands off and pin them to the bed, hovering above her. Bracing my elbows on the mattress, I push into her, my eyes never leaving her face.

I love you.

When she comes, her whole body rocks off the bed. I hold her tight, thrusting deep as I reach my release. I fall asleep holding her, and when I wake up hours later, she's gone.

CHAPTER 29

*S*he's gone.

I don't wonder where. I know as soon as I wake up she's left for New York.

Tony confirms it when I call him. "She left very early, with Aidan."

I call my brother as soon as I figure they've landed.

Aidan sounds like he's pissed at me. "I was just going to call you," he says reproachfully.

"Where is Rachel?"

"Why don't you ask her?"

"I'm asking you."

He sighs. "At her apartment. We dropped her off a few minutes ago."

"Okay."

"Landon, if there's something—"

I stop him. "Everything's fine. I just wanted to know she was home."

After that, I deal with the silence from her.

I love you.

The pleasure of hearing those words from her lips is quickly drowned by the realization that she'd rather end things than be with me right now.

And why wouldn't she?

Almost from the first night we met, I pushed her, hounded her, ignored any resistance from her, and gave her almost no choice but to be with me the way I wanted.

I told myself I was ready to give her the world, but I never considered giving her myself.

Because you don't consider yourself worthy to give.

My inner voice is right, yet also wrong, because despite everything, she loves me.

You don't need to do anything.

Oh, but I want to. I want to confront her, demand she comes back where she belongs—with me. I want to convince her she's mine.

I want to tell her I love her too, more than I can explain or articulate.

I always get everything I want.

But not this time.

This time, it must be her choosing to be with me,

not me pushing forcefully through the distance she has put between us.

No matter how colorless my life is without her.

No matter how much I miss her.

The next few days are busy, both in San Francisco and when I return to New York. I push myself hard, refusing to think, because when I don't think, I don't feel like I'm dying inside.

I close a few deals, travel, and attend a party in Europe, seeing Rachel's face everywhere I look.

I love you.

WHEN I GET BACK IN TOWN, I FIND REASONS TO BE around the Gilt building in the mornings. When I see her, it makes my loneliness more bearable.

One such morning, I notice she's walking instead of in the car with Joe.

"What's happening?" I demand on the phone.

"She refused to get in," Joe tells me. "She says she doesn't need the ride anymore."

I knew this was coming. She's cutting away our connections, and soon they'll all be gone.

"Maybe she'll change her mind," I tell Joe, even though I know she won't. "Stay available, in case she needs you."

He doesn't reply.

~

"ARE YOU REALLY GOING TO LET HER GO?"

I give Aidan a look to remind him I'm not open to talking about Rachel, not with my little brother.

He's not cowed. He meets my gaze with a stubborn one of his. We're having dinner together at a restaurant close to the theater. He's exhausted, as usual, but in a passably good mood.

"Opening night is only a few weeks away," I say, trying to change the subject. "Are you ready?"

"As ready as we'll ever be." He shakes his head. "But we were talking about you and Rachel."

"Leave it," I warn.

"Look, I know you think I don't know anything about love and relationships."

"I don't think anything of the sort."

"But I can tell you're tearing yourself apart right now. If you want to be with her, why aren't you?"

Because she left!

"Maybe she's better off without me. Maybe she doesn't want to be with me."

His expression tells me he thinks I'm being ridiculous. "Did she tell you that?"

I shake my head. "She loves me."

His face fills with understanding. "She told you that?"

"Yes."

"And what? You pushed her away?" He chuckles bitterly. "Wow! How did we both become so..." He sighs. "What are you going to do?"

"Nothing." I smile tightly. "It's all in her hands."

"Did you tell her how you feel?"

I don't reply.

"Then it's not fair to wait for her to come to you. You need to let her know you feel the same way."

"When did you become a therapist?"

He sighs. "Maybe I'm in the same position."

"Aidan..."

"Don't ask." He laughs. "It's not nearly as fixable as what you have with Rachel."

Fixable.

If only.

STILL, WHEN THE WEEKEND COMES, I DRIVE OVER to her place. I'm not sure what I'll do or say to her when I get there.

On an impulse, I buy a bunch of roses from a roadside florist. Then, after waiting in the car for far too long, I finally call her number.

She doesn't answer. I try again, and it's the same thing.

I take a deep breath. She doesn't want to talk to me.

I call Laurie.

"Hey, Landon," she says warmly. There's laughter in her voice. She sounds happy, and it cheers me a little.

"Hey," I reply. In the background, I can hear voices and music. "Is this a bad time?"

She giggles. "No, not really."

"Okay." I pause. "I was trying to reach Rachel…"

"I guessed." She pauses. "She's here."

"Where? At your parents'?"

"Yes. It's my engagement party."

I'm only slightly taken aback. "Congratulations to you and Brett."

She laughs again, and the sound is filled with a happiness that makes me both glad and envious. "I didn't say it was Brett."

I chuckle. "You didn't have to. I can hear it in your voice."

There's a pause. "You should come," she says suddenly. "If you want to, anyway."

"Is she…" I'm not sure what I want to ask. "I'd love to come."

"So…do that?" She switches to her no-nonsense voice. "I think it's time you two talked, anyway."

After ending the call, she texts me the address. I stare at the words on my screen. Am I ready to do this?

Is Rachel ready?

I don't know.

But I can't keep waiting, because I'm no longer sure what I'm waiting for.

All I know is that I love her.

I have loved her for a long time, even when I didn't know the words to say it.

The drive takes almost an hour, and by the time I get to Laurie's parents' place, I've almost talked myself into going back.

It's an outdoor party with tents and flowers and music. I get out of the car then realize I've forgotten the flowers. I reach for the bunch, but then decide on just one, a single rose. Carefully, I place it inside my jacket before walking down the drive.

Laurie is dancing with Brett, laughing happily. She doesn't see me, and I stay at the edge of the party, happy for her, and for Brett.

"Landon?"

I turn around to see Lynn Foster. She clearly wasn't expecting me and doesn't look thrilled to see me either. Beside her is Laurie's mom, Jacie.

"Hi." I try a smile. "I was looking for Rachel."

"Did you call?" It's Jacie, sounding protective.

"I...I spoke to Laurie."

"So, Rachel doesn't know you're here?" Lynn asks.

"I don't think so."

Jacie studies me for a long moment. "She's in the garden."

"Jacie..." Lynn raises her brows.

Jacie meets her gaze and Lynn sighs. "You'll find her in the gazebo. That way." She points toward the back of the house.

I smile my thanks at the two of them. "I'll go find her."

Lynn is still giving me a pursed-lip look as I walk away, and for a moment, I envy Rachel her protective family...even when I'm the person from whom they're protecting her.

I find the gazebo easily. It's a small white structure set in the middle of the garden. Around it, shrubs and flowers bloom in a perfect arrangement. Inside, on a white bench, Rachel is seated quietly.

For a while, I say nothing. I watch her without moving. She looks so beautiful, and yet so delicate. As I stand there, a breeze rustles the surrounding leaves, and with a soft sigh, she hugs herself.

I say her name.

At first, nothing happens. I can't even be sure she heard me. The music from the party continues, muted from the distance.

"Your mother told me you'd be back here," I continue, praying she'll at least turn around.

Slowly, she faces me, and it breaks my heart to see a lone tear on her cheek.

"Landon?"

"Hi." I try to smile, but I'm too nervous. "I hope you don't mind if I join you."

Her eyes flutter closed, and when she opens them again, there's a brightness there that wasn't present before. "No," she whispers. "No, I don't."

CHAPTER 30

I join her on the bench. She's as nervous as I am, I can feel it. Her fingers grip the edge of the bench. Is she glad I'm here? Does she want me to leave?

I reach into my jacket and hand her the rose.

She accepts it and studies the petals silently. "I didn't know you were coming."

"I wasn't... I tried to call you. You weren't picking up. Laurie told me about the party, and that you were here."

"My phone's in the house," she tells me.

"I guessed."

She sets the rose down on the bench. "Why did you come?"

How could I not?

I can barely put all my feelings into words. I take her hand. "Rachel."

She pulls her fingers from mine and jerks away, rising from the bench. "Don't touch me."

"Rachel—"

"Two weeks, Landon." Her voice is heavy with accusation. "I waited for you..."

"Rachel." There's a plea in my voice. "Come back."

She shakes her head. "I told you I was in love with you and you let me stew in your silence for two fucking weeks. Do you have any idea how hard it was for me to open up to you about my feelings?"

I get up and face her squarely. "You left." How was I supposed to be certain what she wanted when she left me after I begged her not to?

Her eyes close. "Yes, and I'm sorry. I'm sorry I walked away when I said I wouldn't. It hurt me to leave you, Landon, but I had to. It was clear that even though I told you how I felt, you were still holding back."

"So, as usual, you decided to walk away." I can't keep the accusation from my voice.

"I couldn't wait around for you to decide you didn't want me!"

I take a deep breath. "Please come back. Sit. Let's talk."

She stares at me, eyes wary. "I don't think—"

"Rachel, for God's sake! For once, will you stop fighting me?"

She comes back to the bench and I lower myself beside her.

"Look at me."

She does as I say, and suddenly her eyes are filling with tears. I dab them away with a handkerchief before taking her hands in mine.

"These past two weeks," I start. "I've been...I don't know what I've been doing." I take a breath. "I didn't know. I didn't know why you walked away before. I didn't know how you felt. I didn't know you thought you needed to get away from me. I didn't know your feelings made you believe you needed to get over me, or that my behavior—pursuing you relentlessly, ignoring your requests for me to leave you alone—took away the space you needed to do that. I understand now. I get it. I get why you walked away that first time."

She doesn't reply.

"I've been trying...I've been trying to stop thinking about you," I continue. "When I woke up and you had gone, I...I wanted to come after you, Rachel. You have no idea what it took to stay back and let you have the space I didn't give you in the past."

Her small hand is soft in mine. My fingers flex around hers.

"There were so many times I wanted to come to you. There were so many things I could have said, but Rachel, the last thing I wanted was for you to think I was telling you what you wanted to hear just to get you to stay."

Her voice is tight. "I didn't tell you I was in love with you because I wanted you to say some meaningless words back to me. I told you because it was the truth. If you don't feel the same way, I totally understand. I really do."

"Will you let me finish?" I say in a low voice. She stops talking and I continue. "I've been trying to make sense of a lot of things, my feelings, yours...I was trying to make the best decision for both of us, trying to determine the right course of action. I didn't want to pester you as I had in the past, so I decided to wait a while, but then you told Joe you didn't want him picking you up anymore, and I thought... I didn't know what to think."

She pulls in a breath. "I didn't want to be reminded..."

"Of me?"

She nods. "Yes. Joe's presence reminded me every day that even though you knew how I felt, you chose to stay away."

"I'm here now," I tell her.

I can feel her tremble, and inside, I'm trembling too.

"Why?" she whispers.

"Because I couldn't wait anymore. I'm crazy about you, Rachel. I've always known that much. I've always known I wanted to be with you, that I'd protect you, give you anything you wanted, that I could never let you go."

She tries to pull her hands from mine, but I can't let her go.

"I knew all that, but I've never allowed myself to think about love, being in love. I've never wanted it. I never thought it was for me. I grew up in the devastation that kind of emotion can cause, and so I..." I stop talking for a moment. "Then you told me how you felt, and it took me by surprise. I wasted so much time being jealous of your ex, being insecure about why you wanted to be with me, why you always walked away. I never thought it was possible that you had those kinds of feelings for me."

She stares at me, almost like she can't comprehend my blindness. "And after I told you?"

I chuckle. "I was shocked, but more than that, I was so fucking scared of doing something wrong and hurting you. The fact that you felt that way about me...I can't begin to explain how it made me feel— happy, humbled, elated, afraid. That night, I could have responded and told you I felt the same way, and now I know it wouldn't have been a lie. At the time, I was afraid you would leave, and I didn't want to say those words just to make you stay."

Her throat works as she swallows. "What about now?"

"I've been trying to take control of my feelings, trying to define them, to escape the...the vulnerability that comes with knowing I'd give up everything else to make you stay, but the truth is, deep down, I've always known in a part of me that there would never be anyone else for me."

Her eyes close, and I wish I could know what she's thinking.

"I think I've been a fool for a very long time," I whisper, smoothing a stray strand of her hair. "I've been in love with you for a while now...a long while."

I hear her breathe. "Tell me," she whispers.

I know exactly how she feels, because I've felt it too.

"I don't want to be without you," I tell her, saying the words I should have said two weeks ago. "I want us to make this work. I love you, Rachel. I'm helplessly, hopelessly in love with you."

She's crying again, but this time, she's happy, not sad. Her face lights up, and it's the most beautiful thing I've ever seen.

"I love you," I repeat. Then I put an arm around her and draw her close to me. "I love you."

She touches her lips to mine in a soft kiss.

"Just so you know, I hate you for leaving me adrift these past two weeks."

I smile. "But?"

"But I love you, Landon."

I kiss her again, and it feels like heaven. My chest feels light and achy with happiness. It's not a feeling I'm familiar with, but I could get used to it.

"I'm glad you came," she whispers.

"I couldn't have stayed away." I close my eyes and touch my forehead to hers. "I've seen you every day I've been in town, and if you knew how hard it was for me not to reach out to you, you'd know I'm never going a day without you by my side."

She raises her brows. "You've been stalking me."

Laughing softly, I shake my head. "It's not such a large city, and I wouldn't call it stalking...just taking longer detours to work so I can see you at least once every day."

"Stalking," she insists, but she leans into me, sighing with contentment. I kiss her hair and her face. I stroke her back gently. I could stay with her like this forever, and I would love every minute.

We sit together for a long time, and then she glances toward the front of the house where the party is still lively.

"You can't come all this way to a party and not get to dance," she tells me.

I follow her gaze. Now that I have something to

celebrate, dancing sounds like the best thing in the world. "Well, come on then." I get up and take her hand, and we join the rest of the guests.

THE HARDEST THING IS LEAVING HER AND DRIVING back to the city alone, but she's spending the night at her parents' place and won't let me steal her away.

I call her as soon as I get home, not yet willing to let the magic of the night end—the magic of dancing with her under the stars, kissing her goodnight, hearing her say she loves me.

"Are you home?" she asks.

"Yes, just got here. Are you in bed?"

"Yes."

I glance at my empty bed.

"You should have come with me. Say you will and I'll come right back to get you."

She laughs. "You waited two weeks—what's one more day?"

I sigh. "I'll make you forget about those two weeks. I promise you that."

"Knowing your methods, can I just say I'm looking forward to that?"

"Say anything, baby." I'm laughing, happy. "When I get you here tomorrow, the only thing you'll be saying is my name."

"Maybe I'll run away."

"I'll find you. No matter where you go."

She sighs. "I love you."

My heart fills. I'm happier than I've ever been in my life. "I love you too."

CHAPTER 31

*S*he loves me.

She's mine.

And I love her too, more than life itself.

The next few weeks, I can barely let her out of my sight. I'm the happiest man in the world and it's all because of her.

Not long after her engagement party, Laurie announces her plans to move out of their apartment to be with Brett. Rachel is heartbroken, but I finally convince her to move in with me.

That's not the only big move in her life. She leaves *Gilt Travel* and moves to its more respected sister publication, *Gilt Review*, where she has always wanted to build a career.

But I am the lucky one. I'm the one who gets to

wake up beside her every morning and fall asleep with her in my arms.

She loves me.

"How was your farewell party?" I ask her. We're on our way to the theater for Aidan's opening night, and she is breathtaking in a black dress and her signature barely there makeup.

I love you, Rachel.

"I shed a few tears," she says with a sad smile. "But I consoled myself with the thought that I'm moving on to bigger and better things."

I chuckle. I know leaving *Gilt Travel* and all her friends is bound to be hard for her, but she'll be in the same building, close to them, so it's not that bad. "I love how happy you look at the prospect of editing short stories. It's charming."

"Oh, shut up." She punches my arm, laughing. "We can't all build hotels all over the world. This is my equivalent, if you really want to know. It's what I've always wanted to do...well, after I changed my mind from undercover agent and racecar driver."

"You're an excellent *under the covers* agent," I concede.

She tries to maintain a disapproving expression, but she can't help the smile tugging at her lips. "I...I have no idea what to say to that."

"What?" I'm laughing. "It's a compliment! When I was little, I wanted to be Superman."

"You and every other little boy."

"Well, after a while, I decided I wanted to be a pilot. I distinctly remember that. And not just any pilot, one of those World War II Navy pilots." I chuckle, remembering my short-lived childhood. The darker memories soon follow. "Then I just wanted Aidan to start talking again."

Rachel places a soft kiss on my lips. "You've been an awesome big brother."

"I know." I laugh softly, thinking of Aidan. "These days I can't get him to shut up."

Outside the theater, Aidan's name is prominently placed on the playbills, and I can't hide my pride. It's been a long journey to this point, and now, more than ever, I'm convinced we can both make it past all the darkness.

Inside, there's a press junket and a red carpet in the circulation area. After we take pictures and meet a few people, I'm relieved when Wilson and Betsy Hayes join us, and we go to our seats.

I've already seen the play a couple of times, but like all theater productions, there are always a few changes from the last performance. Still, it's the kind of play that doesn't get old no matter how many times it's seen.

You did it, Aidan.

We did it.

Beside me, Rachel watches with rapt attention,

and when the final curtain drops, she leaps to her feet, taking part in the loud applause.

Back outside, the excitement is palpable. There are congratulations and handshakes and talks of Tony nominations. McKay is practically bursting with happiness, and I don't blame him. His daughter has cemented her position among the stars, and I have an idea how that feels.

Betsy and Wilson leave early, and amid all the conversations with people who want to talk to me, even Ava shows up for a moment.

If I were placing bets, I'd say it's already over.

Well, she was wrong, as I'm sure she already knows, guessing from her lack of surprise at seeing me with Rachel.

I'm much too happy to gloat, and she doesn't say much to me, or to Rachel.

"Time to go congratulate Aidan," I tell Rachel, leading her to the chaos backstage. Actors and theater staff are running all over the place, and there are flowers everywhere, especially in front of the door marked with Liz McKay's name. An assistant stands there like a guard, accepting new deliveries and sending people away.

At the end of the hall, Aidan's small office is empty. I pull out my phone to call him just as the door to Liz's room opens, and he emerges, almost stumbling over the flowers and the beleaguered assistant. I don't have to guess what he's been up to. It's obvious in his disheveled hair and rumpled clothes.

Still, he hurries over and hugs Rachel.

"The play was marvelous," she tells him. "You must be so proud."

He grins. "I'm not going to pretend I'm not ecstatic, because I am. Though, I'm disappointed my brother is no longer duty-bound to get me drunk and procure the services of a couple of hardworking women." He chuckles self-mockingly. "That was going to be my consolation if the play bombed."

I let my eyes drift over his disheveled clothes. "I believe you've consoled yourself fairly well," I say with a smirk.

His smile slips, but only for a moment.

"I think it's great that you worked out your differences with Elizabeth," Rachel declares. "You'll be working with her for a while, obviously."

He makes a sound that could be agreement then glances back at the rapidly increasing offerings of flowers. "Yes. It's great." He unlocks the door to his office. "Dennis McKay is hosting a party tonight to celebrate the opening," he tells us, cheerful again. "Do you guys want to come?"

I shake my head. My association with the theater crowd is limited to Aidan and a few others. "Since I no longer have to get you drunk, I'm only here to applaud you. Go to your party and enjoy your success. You'll be the toast of the evening."

With no warning, he puts his arms around me. "Thank you," he whispers.

I close my eyes and hug him back, silent.

After handing him my gift, a watch my grandfather gave my father when he started running the hotels, I leave with Rachel.

"What are you thinking about?" she asks me in the car on our way back home.

I shake my head. "Just Aidan." I sigh. "The direction his career is going to go now..."

She frowns. "It's going to get bigger from what I can see. I'm sure you're very proud."

"Oh I am, but I'm also worried. The pressure on him will be so much. He has to follow success with success."

"But you have faith in him?"

"Yes, but..." I search for words to explain my fears. "Aidan is very prone to depression. He's struggled with it since...almost his whole life."

Rachel is silent. "Success makes some people depressed, Landon, but not all of them. I'm sure Aidan can handle it." She squeezes my hand. "Tonight, you should be celebrating, not thinking about the past."

I touch her cheek, wondering what I did to deserve my personal angel. "You're right."

She searches my face. "How can I take your mind off it?"

I'm instantly at attention. "You know how."

Her eyes light up with mischief, and with a chuckle, she hikes up her dress and comes up to straddle me, her knees on either side of my thighs. She places her hands on my shoulders and smiles down at me. "Tell me what you want."

I pull in a breath, and her scent fills my senses. "First, I want you to stay right where you are."

"Done." She grinds against the front of my pants, rubbing on my already rigid erection. I exhale.

"The drive's not long enough for what I want to do to you."

"I know." She grins. "I'm just teasing you."

Temptress. I stroke my hands over her ribs then cup her breasts over her clothes. She leans forward to kiss me and I seize her lips eagerly, stroking my tongue against hers until she's moaning into my mouth.

Under her dress, I find the damp crotch of her panties and press my fingers over the soft fabric. She sighs and arches, inviting me to touch her some more. I move the barrier of her underwear aside and my fingers slip over her wet folds, teasing her gently before sliding inside her.

I love that I'm the one who gets to touch her like this, who gets to make her moan with pleasure. She moves her hips, urging my fingers deeper. Just then, the limo stops. I hear Joe step out of the car, and with a sigh, she scrambles off me and fixes her dress.

Outside the car, I take her hand as we walk to the elevator. She's flushed and beautiful, and I can barely wait until we're alone to show her the plans I've made for her pleasure tonight. As the elevator goes up, I hold her gaze then raise my fingertips to my lips and lick them.

She lets out a moan.

"What?" My smile is innocent.

"Stop driving me crazy."

I step over to where she's standing and bring her flush against my body so she can feel just how much I want her. "Never."

As soon as the elevator stops and the doors open, I lift her into my arms and carry her upstairs to our bedroom, where a bottle of champagne is chilling in a bucket along with covered dishes.

I lay her on the bed, and she props herself up on her elbows on the soft mattress, looking around before giving me a quizzical look. "We're celebrating?"

"Yes." I shrug off my jacket then dim the lights and turn on music from hidden speakers. The low sound of vintage jazz fills the room and her lips curve.

"Aidan's success?"

I nod. "And you and me." I pop the champagne

and pour out two glasses. Joining her on the bed, I hand her one, clinking mine against it in a toast. "To you and me. To us."

"Us," she echoes softly.

I feed her in between kisses, undressing her as we eat. Soon, we're both naked, and I nudge her back on the bed. I have one more surprise for her tonight.

She watches, curious as I retrieve a box from a drawer in the nightstand.

"What's that?"

"Shhh." I kiss her again then, taking both her hands, I stretch them over her head. "Do you trust me?"

"Yes."

Good, because I plan to give her pleasure like she's never felt before. "Close your eyes."

She does as I say, staying silent as I bind her wrists lightly, then her legs.

"Can I open my eyes now?" Her voice is breathy.

I position myself between her legs. "Yes."

Her eyes open and land on me. A soft moan escapes her lips.

"How do you feel?"

She sighs. "Expectant?"

We haven't even started. I reach back into the box for a special toy, fastening it so the small velvety nub is directly over her clit. Then I turn it on, and she gasps.

"Oh my God!"

"Do you like it?"

She moans again, her legs stretching and tightening as the vibrations intensify.

"Tell me you like it."

"I love it," she murmurs.

Smiling, I cover her body with mine and take her lips then trail downward, giving attention to her nipples while drawing one hand down between her legs so I can slip a finger inside her wet core.

Her body is shaking. "Landon…"

"You're perfect," I tell her. So fucking perfect. I drop a kiss on her smooth belly and withdraw my finger from inside her. She moans, and I shush her gently, reaching inside the box again. Retrieving the small lubricated and vibrating tube from inside, I slide it between the curves of her ass and inside the tight opening between her cheeks.

She cries out. "Landon!"

"Hmm." I drink in her pleasure. "How does it feel?"

"So good." A shudder rocks her body and she moans. "I'm going to come. I'm coming."

I slip my finger back inside her and she cries out, shaking helplessly as pleasure takes over. I cover her mouth with mine, taking her moans and her cries. Long after her body stops shuddering, she's still moaning, her arms and legs straining against the bonds. Her eyes follow me as I settle on my knees between her legs.

"I want you inside me," she says breathlessly. "Please fuck me."

She doesn't have to ask me twice. I feel her pleasure the moment I surge into her. She's wet and hot, soft as petals, and so tight, so welcoming.

I want to stay inside her forever.

She screams my name over and over while I make love to her. Her body shudders as she comes again and again. When I can no longer hold back, I follow, losing my senses as I surrender all of myself.

Later, she lies plaint while I untie her and remove the toys. She curls against my side, and I place tender kisses all over her face and hair. Soon, she is asleep, breathing softly as exhaustion takes over.

"I love you," I whisper in her ear. "I love you forever."

CHAPTER 32

"We were at the theater earlier and Aidan showed us around. Things are not as crazy as they were the week before the play, so we got to meet most of the people in the production." Betsy smiles across the table at Rachel and me. "That Liz Mckay is such a charming girl. I can see why Aidan is crazy about her."

"At least he admits it now." I chuckle. "I can't tell you how many times I had to listen to him complain about how hard it was to work with her."

Wilson laughs. "Typical Aidan."

"Sometimes attraction can get mistaken for dislike," Betsy says.

"That's what I said." Rachel is smiling as she meets my eyes. She guessed right the first night she saw Aidan and Liz at the preview. I squeeze her hand under the table.

There's a lot to talk about, and it's relaxing to take my mind off work and be with the people I love.

We're having dessert when I look across the restaurant and, from a few tables away, see Evans Sinclair glaring at me.

To tell the truth, I couldn't care less about Evans. I'm more concerned about his dinner companion, Devlin Barkely, the chairman of a hotel conglomerate. He's also Sinclair's godfather. The older man follows Sinclair's gaze to mine and bares his teeth at me in what is supposed to be a smile.

Beside me, Rachel has noticed Sinclair, and she gives me a worried frown.

I smile. "More wine?"

She nods and I refill her glass.

Determined not to let thoughts of Sinclair ruin my mood, I focus on my companions, answering Wilson's questions about the Newport hotel. We're still talking when Barkely approaches our table.

"Landon Court." His smile is all charm as he offers his hand first to me, and then to Wilson. "It's been ages." He turns his smile to Rachel before nodding in Betsy's direction. "I'm Devlin Barkely," he announces.

"Rachel Foster, my girlfriend," I say drily. "And Betsy Hayes, Wilson's wife."

"I'm charmed," he tells Betsy. "I tried to hire your husband away from the Courts a long time ago. He wouldn't give me the time of day."

"He was happy where he was," Betsy replies.

Barkely's smile doesn't waver as he turns back to me. "I stopped to congratulate you on your accomplishment with the Gold Dust. I have every confidence in your continued success."

I study him for a moment. I know how to fight for what's mine, but I don't court enemies, and I know certain people are formidable enemies to have. Barkely isn't just the head of a powerful conglomerate with the means to bully, blackmail, and arm-twist other organizations, he's also a shrewd businessman.

Shrugging, I keep my voice level. "Your choice of dinner companion doesn't give me much confidence in your words."

He chuckles and glances back at the table he just left, where Sinclair is glowering in our direction like the little goblin he is. "Evans is my godson. I owe him a fair hearing, but I owe it to myself to make sound judgments." He smiles. "Have a good evening."

He leaves us, and after a few moments, Sinclair follows toward the exit, swaying from too much wine and whatever else he has imbibed. He flips me off as he goes, but I ignore him.

"Who was the other guy?" Rachel asks once they're gone.

"He's the chairman of a conglomerate that acquires and manages hotel chains," I explain.

Her brow furrows. "Acquires? Like takeovers?"

"Yes." Wilson's voice is grave. "They take the soul out of hotels and kill them with so-called efficiency. Sinclair there was probably trying to get him to try to acquire Swanson Court International from under Landon's feet."

"If he can." Betsy's voice is dismissive, and her confidence in me is bolstering.

Rachel is still frowning. I give her a reassuring smile. "It doesn't matter. He doesn't matter." I squeeze her hand. "Swanson Court International is a very strong institution. I've dedicated my life to ensuring that. Even if Evans got a few people to sympathize with him, they'd be on a fool's errand trying to hurt me."

That seems to placate her, and she relaxes. We move to other topics and finish our dessert.

After dinner, we head outside. A car is already waiting at the entrance for Wilson and Betsy, and after we say our goodbyes, they leave.

Soon after, Joe pulls up, and I open the door for Rachel, waiting for her to settle inside before going to the other side.

I have my hand on the door handle when I hear the loud sound of an engine revving.

At first, it doesn't register. It takes me a moment

to realize the car is coming in my direction, fast.

Everything slows. The car moving toward me, the sounds...and in my mind all I can see is Rachel's face. I pull the door handle in my hand and leap inside the car, shutting the door just as a black sedan zooms past, right over where I was standing, so close it almost scrapes the side of my car. The sedan comes to a screeching halt a few feet away.

Even before I push the door open and follow Joe as he approaches the other car, I already know who the driver is, and when Evans climbs out, grinning and weaving on his feet, I can barely control the urge to punch him.

By the time I get to where he's standing, Joe has him in a viselike grip.

"Are you insane?" I can barely keep the anger from my voice.

"Come on!" he slurs, his eyes going from my face to Joe's. "It was an accident. I lost control of my car for a moment."

He's lying, and he knows we know it.

"You're a disgrace," I retort. He flinches and I continue. "Look at yourself, for God's sake, and try to take responsibility for once."

"Fuck you, Landon. You think you're better than me? Fuck you." He sneers. "You've always thought too much of yourself. You think you can go around taking anything you want. I'll show you."

"Take him home," I tell Joe, ignoring Sinclair's outburst. I hear him spit at me as I walk away, but I don't bother to respond. He's a drunken fool and I will not waste my time with him.

Rachel is standing beside our car, watching me with worried eyes.

"Are you all right?"

She nods then glances in Evans' direction. "He tried to kill you."

"He's stupid and drunk." I open the passenger door and wait for her to climb in, then I go around the hood, getting in the driver's seat. "Joe will drive him home and make sure he doesn't hurt himself, or someone else."

"Shouldn't you call the police or something?" She's staring at me, her eyes still wide with fear. "He could have hurt you."

I don't want to think about it. "Let's go home."

She's silent throughout the drive, and I can't even imagine how she must have felt seeing that car come toward me. In the apartment, I can barely let go of her hand. The adrenaline recedes and I'm suddenly aware of how real the danger was.

Rachel is shaking, and when we get into bed, she clutches me tight.

"I'm fine," I whisper, over and over. "I'm fine."

Nothing will take me away from you.

I'm up early, especially since I spent the night unable to sleep. In my study, I make a few calls. When I dial Ava's number, her voice tells me she's not surprised to hear from me.

"I heard about what happened, Landon. I'm so sorry."

I can't keep the impatience out of my voice. "You know that doesn't cut it."

She makes a sound. "He's crazy."

"And dangerous."

"Landon...I don't know what to do. I'm worried about how all this could end."

The uncertainty in her voice gets to me. I've spent the last few months pushing her away without caring if she had any other support. Now, it makes me feel slightly guilty.

I sigh. "I would have called last night, but I didn't want to wake you. He's your brother, and he's out of control. It's time to stop talking and do something about him."

"But I don't know what to do! I'm worried, about him, about you...what he could do. He's barely functioning, and the drugs aren't helping."

She's crying now.

"Ava..." I don't know what to say. She has to take care of him, or I will. "Try rehab or a sanatorium. The next time he tries anything like what he did last night, I won't be so easy on him."

"What will you do?"

"Nothing, for now. Get him under control. Stage an intervention or something. Convince him he still has a lot going for him and hating me will get him nowhere."

She sighs. "That's easy for you to say."

"He's not my responsibility, Ava."

"Yes, I understand...and obviously neither am I."

I don't argue. I have other priorities now, and making sure Rachel has nothing to worry about is more important to me than Ava's feelings.

Later, I find Rachel in the kitchen drinking coffee.

"Good morning." I peer at her face. "Are you okay?"

She gives me a tight smile and a shrug. "I'm fine. Good morning."

I can see she's not fine. I order breakfast and watch Rachel pick at her food.

"So what's going to happen with Evans?" she asks.

"Don't worry about it."

She makes an exasperated sound. "Of course I'm worried. I was there yesterday. If you hadn't moved out of the way so quickly..."

I wish she would stop thinking about it. "He's unstable and struggling with substance abuse problems. He's blaming everyone but himself for everything that's wrong with his life...but forget about him. He won't be causing any trouble anymore."

"Is Ava going to get him into rehab?" she asks. Then, meeting my eyes, she continues. "I was looking for you earlier. I heard part of your conversation with her." She sighs. "The thing is, no matter how easily you brush last night away...I was afraid, Landon. I still am."

"Rachel—"

"No, let me finish. It's not just the physical danger to you. It's more than that. I don't like feeling that you let Evans off because of what his sister still means to you."

"Rachel," I say gently, "I won't deny that I tried to be considerate of Ava—not because of what she means to me, but because I would have done the same for anyone else, especially someone I've had both a business and a personal relationship with."

Her throat works, but she stays silent.

"Evans is obviously battling personal issues...and I'm familiar enough with those to have some compassion for him."

Her eyes flash with barely suppressed anger. "You can't seriously compare what he's going through to what you went through. You witnessed an accident and blamed yourself when you shouldn't have. Evans is a spoiled playboy who is acting out his dissatisfaction in a dangerous way."

I know she's right. "Well, he will go to rehab, or he'll go to jail. Those are the options I will give him. Either way, he won't be bothering us again."

Her eyes close. "Okay," she concedes. "If you're sure."

CHAPTER 33

*R*achel spends most of the next week getting ready to go to Barbados for Laurie and Brett's wedding.

Even with the last-minute shopping and work deadlines, it's a quiet week for the both of us. We don't talk much about the incident with Evans, or about Ava. I only tell her that Evans has checked into a facility.

I don't tell her that only a few days after checking in, he assaulted an orderly and left. His whereabouts are unknown, but the last thing I want is for her to worry about him when she should be enjoying the days leading up to Laurie's wedding.

Now, on the way to the airport, even though I hate to let Rachel out of my sight even for a few days,

I'm relieved she won't be beside me if he tries anything again.

Joe is driving, and in the front passenger seat is another man, one of the new security additions to my staff. I've assured Rachel his presence means nothing. It's a necessary lie. I don't want her to be apprehensive about my safety.

Except, it doesn't work. As the car moves through the busy streets, she's studying me, her eyes tinged with concern.

"What are you worrying about now?" I ask, smiling to put her at ease.

She smiles back. "Am I so transparent?"

"No, but I've made it my business to memorize your every expression."

She sighs softly. "Stop saying lovely stuff to me. It's hard enough to leave you as it is."

"Then don't go." For all my relief about her being out of Evan's reach, it's still killing me that we'll be apart for a week. "I want to turn the car around, take you somewhere, and hide you away." I chuckle wryly. "I love Laurie and I know she's your family, but I'd rather steal you away than lose you for a week."

"You're not losing me. I'm just going to be halfway across the globe." She laughs softly. "Does it help that I feel the same way you do?"

"No. That just gives me more incentive to want to steal you away." The tender expression in her eyes makes me catch my breath. "I know I'm being selfish."

"You're not selfish. I'll miss you too, terribly. It's just...however tempting it is, we can't lock ourselves away forever."

"Why not?"

"You know why not."

Her laughter soothes me. "I don't want to go a day without you, not ever, if it can be helped at all."

The car stops. Not far away on the tarmac is the jet I provided to take her family to Barbados.

"I love you," she whispers. Her eyes go to the front passenger seat and her face falls. She looks at me. "I need you to be safe."

"I will be."

She sighs. "Landon..." Her eyes are on mine. "Will you at least think of talking to someone about your nightmares? Whatever you're afraid of..."

I swallow. My nightmares have been getting worse —another thing we haven't discussed.

"The only thing I'm afraid of is losing you."

"You won't."

"How about you start thinking about the kind of welcome you're going to give me when I do get to Barbados."

"I'll give you the tourist treatment, show you the sights."

I grin. "I know the sights I want to see, and I don't have to fly miles and miles to see them."

"You have a one-track mind."

"You make me unable to think of anything else."

She sighs. "I hate that I have to go now."

I nuzzle her lips, memorizing the feel and taste of her. "I hate that I have to let you."

Her phone rings, interrupting us. It's her mother.

"I love you," Rachel says, pressing another kiss to my lips.

I grab her arms and kiss her properly. "I love you too. Call me when you land."

AS A PREVIEW OF WHAT MY LIFE WOULD BE LIKE without Rachel in it, the next two days are excruciatingly lonely. The silence of my apartment is no longer comforting. It just feels empty without her.

The third day of her absence, I head to San Francisco. I have a lot to discuss with the management team at the Gold Dust, and it takes up most of my morning. I spend lunchtime visiting with Cameron and Jules then arrange an early dinner with Ava.

I didn't tell Rachel I was meeting with her, but now, as I wait in my suite for Ava to arrive, I consider that I should have. But then, I'd have to tell her why.

I still don't see why I should ruin her time in Barbados with the news that Evans is walking around, probably looking for ways to hurt me.

The door opens and Ava walks into the suite, trailed by Claude. She's dressed demurely in white silk, and though perfectly made up, her eyes are filled with concern.

"Oh Landon!"

She comes in for an embrace, and I extricate myself after a quick hug.

"I'm so sorry," she continues. "I really thought he'd stay in rehab until he got better."

My smile is tight. "Obviously you were wrong." I motion for her to sit. "Claude, why don't you arrange to have dinner sent up?"

Almost reluctantly, he leaves me alone with Ava. She settles on an armchair. "Are you going to try to find him?"

"I have to know where he is, Ava."

She sniffs. "I understand how you feel. When I heard he tried to hurt you, I swear, Landon...I..." Her voice breaks.

I watch her wipe her eyes. A hotel staff member arrives, wheeling in our food, and he lays it out it in the dining room.

"Why don't we eat," I suggest. "We can talk about Evans later."

She follows me to the table. With the food and

wine, she is soon relaxed and regaling me with stories of her last trip to Europe, including running into two exes at a party. I feign interest. I think she knows where Evans is, and I need to get that information out of her.

After dinner, I refill her glass. "When was the last time you saw him?"

"Evans?" She's taken aback by the change in subject. "I...um..."

I don't take my eyes off hers. "You can't protect him forever."

"You don't understand." She pushes the glass away. "He's unstable. My uncle is suing for conservatorship —did you know that? He'll lose access to his money, his independence... His accounts are already frozen, all because of..."

"Of me?"

"I didn't say that." She sighs. "He blames you. He thinks if he hadn't lost the hotel—"

"That's bull and you know it. He'd have lost the hotel anyway."

"I know that." She rises gracefully to her feet and walks to the windows. Through the sheer curtains, the sunset paints the sky in many vibrant colors.

Rachel would love this sunset.

Rachel.

I miss her.

"I need to know where he is." I'm losing my

patience. "It's bad enough he wants to hurt me, but I can't let the people around me be in danger too."

"The people around you." She spits out the words. "It used to be me you cared about, Landon. All these years, I thought if I waited long enough..."

The words trail off, but I know what she was going to say. Her flirting, her interest in my relationships...all of it should have told me she was still deeply invested in the idea of us.

Slowly, I rise from my seat. "I'm sorry to have disappointed you, but my main concern at this point is finding out where Evans is."

She exhales. "He came to see me. He wanted some money..."

"God! Ava!"

"He said he wanted to travel," she says in a rush. "To get away from it all." Her eyes are imploring. "I couldn't say no, Landon. Without you, he's all I have."

"Ava." My voice is firm. "You never had me."

Her eyes fill with tears, but I don't move. "All those years ago, I thought...we were too young...you had so much work ahead of you... I tried not to mind that you chose your precious hotels over me, but now? Her? What does she—"

I stop her. "Don't even talk about her."

"Why? Because she's so precious to you?"

"Exactly. I love her, and if you want me to help

you find Evans and ensure he gets the treatment he needs, you won't say one more word about her."

"You can't—"

My phone trills in my pocket. It's Rachel. Relief at the interruption makes me accept the connection without thinking. Only after do I consider that it's not a good time to talk.

"I can't talk now," I say softly. "I'll call you later."

"I suppose that's the girlfriend." Ava's voice is bitter. Her lips curl. "How like her to somehow interrupt the minute I finally get a moment with you."

At my glare, she turns her sulky expression back to the window.

"Hello?" Rachel's voice comes through the phone, full of questions I can't answer right now.

"I'm here," I tell her. "I'll call you later."

"Who is that?" Her voice is thin. "Who's there with you?"

I wish I could lie. I wish it was anyone else. "Ava."

She doesn't reply. I hear the sudden beep as she ends the call.

Ava is watching me, and the wounded, sad, helpless expression is back. "Landon—" she starts.

"I'll find Evans," I tell her in a dry, dismissive tone. "I'll let you know when I do."

She pauses. "I know he's dangerous, and I know

why you feel the way you do. He's my brother, and even I'm afraid of him."

"Yet you gave him money and didn't think to let anyone know."

"I—"

"You should leave now." I don't bother to hide how pissed I am. "If you're so afraid of him, you can stay here for now. Claude will arrange a suite for you." That's the best I can offer.

She inhales.

"I'll show you out."

Her eyes register hurt and betrayal, but I don't care. I'm more concerned with what Rachel is thinking.

For the rest of the evening, Rachel doesn't take my calls. I finally give up and spend a long time on the phone with Jed, discussing what we can do to locate Evans and make sure he can't get near any of my properties. When I try to reach Rachel again, she still doesn't answer.

I finally call the hotel and ask to be transferred to her room. That works. When she takes the call, I can tell from her tone that she doesn't expect it to be me.

By then, I'm frustrated, and it shows in my voice. "Are you avoiding my calls?"

"How was Ava?" she demands without missing a beat.

"So that's it, isn't it?" I sigh tiredly. I have more to

worry about than her mistaken assumptions about Ava and me, and I wish she could see that. "You were ignoring my calls because I met with Ava? How about trying not to interpret every single situation to confirm your insecurities?"

She exhales sharply. "Why would I feel secure about the fact that you saw your former long-term girlfriend without letting me know, even though you're aware that I have an issue with your continued relationship with her?" The words tumble out of her in rapid succession. "Maybe you need her to convince her family to sell you a few more properties, or maybe she needs some comforting seeing as her asshole brother is going off the rails. And you're so considerate of her feelings, aren't you, even when your safety is at stake."

I take a deep breath. "Don't be like this."

"Why did you meet her?"

"Evans left the rehab facility, and I haven't been able to find out where he is. I thought she might know."

Her silence goes on for a few seconds. "When?"

"More than a week ago."

"More than..." She makes a frustrated sound. "You didn't tell me! I was right there with you and you didn't tell me? You let me travel..." Her voice constricts with pain. "You keep treating me like I'm some piece of candy on your arm. I ask you to see someone about your nightmares—you don't. You have a problem and you ignore my input, and the problem escalates but you choose not to share it with me."

She's right. Everything she's saying is right, and I should have seen it before now.

"I want to trust that I'm your partner," she continues. "Not just a replacement for Ava, the woman who somehow keeps popping up in your life, in our lives."

She's not a replacement for Ava. How many times do I have to tell her Ava means nothing to me and she never meant anything compared to what I feel now?

"Stop it," I reply. "You're making this much more than it is."

"Am I? Why did you have to meet with her? Why couldn't she tell you on the phone if she knew where he was? Did she ask to set a date, tell you she'd rather talk in person? I'm sure she did, and of course you couldn't say no because...Ava."

How can she be so wrong and so convinced she's right? "You're obviously not prepared to listen to me. I have a lot to deal with over here. If you want to be supportive instead of creating a scenario in your head and refusing to entertain anything else, understand that I have a lot on my mind."

"So, I'm being unreasonable," she mutters. "You

know what? I don't feel like talking anymore. I want to go to bed."

"Rachel—"

She ends the connection before I can say anything else.

I ARRIVE IN BARBADOS LATE AT NIGHT THE NEXT day. Rachel is still not taking my calls, so I leave her be, trying instead to get some sleep before the wedding the next day.

It's a beautiful ceremony right on the beach. Laurie is glowing with happiness, and Brett looks like he can't believe his luck. The sight of Rachel in her bridesmaid dress makes my heart expand, and I know right then that one day, it'll be me and her, planning to spend forever together.

If only she'll trust me.

I don't get a chance to talk to her until after all the pictures have been taken. When I walk up to her, she glances up at me, a shadow passing over her eyes. Her hair is braided with flowers, and the salty breeze ruffles them gently. She looks like a sea nymph, beautiful and sad at the same time.

"Hey," I say softly.

"Hey to you too."

"You look lovely."

She sighs. "So do you."

"But I don't have flowers in my hair."

Reaching into hers, she pulls out a flower and sticks it in my hair. I don't resist, though I'm sure it makes me look ridiculous.

Our eyes lock and I can't go one more moment without addressing our fight. "I'm sorry—"

"No," she interrupts. "I'm sorry. I said a lot of things I didn't mean."

I swallow. "We shouldn't do this here." The party is lively, and children are playing and chasing each other between the tables. "It was a beautiful ceremony."

"Yes, it was." She smiles. "When did you arrive?"

"Last night, much too late to do anything after the manager told me you weren't in your room. I had breakfast with the men in your family this morning."

"I'm glad you came."

That she would even doubt that I would come... I touch her cheek. "I wouldn't dream of missing something so important to you."

Through the rest of the ceremony, I stay by her side, meeting the members of her extended family and enjoying the happiness that permeates the air. We linger at the beach long after Brett and Laurie leave for the first stage of their honeymoon. Then we all head back to our hotel.

"I have sand everywhere," Rachel complains in her room.

"Yes, I probably need a shower too." I start to remove my shirt then remember all my clothes are in my suite a floor above. "My clothes are in my suite."

Her eyebrows go up and she gives me a naughty smile. "Do you think you'll need them?"

The teasing invitation is all I need. "Come on," I pull her into the bathroom. We're both laughing as we shed the clothes from the beach. In the shower, I finally get to kiss her as I've been longing to do all day.

"About Thursday night..." I explain when we return to the bedroom. We're sitting in bed wearing hotel robes.

Her smile disappears as she waits for me to continue.

"I love you," I say simply. At the core of everything, that is what matters the most. "I need you to know that. I need you to know I'll never do anything consciously, deliberately to hurt you. There is nothing as important to me as you are."

Her eyes fill, and I want to stop and kiss the tears away before they fall, but I have so much more to say.

"I should have told you I was going to see Ava, and I should have told you why. I was hoping I'd be able to resolve the whole situation with Evans before coming here and you'd never need to know he was missing." Now, I realize how stupid that was. "Of course, that was wrong as well."

"At least I know now," she says, reaching for my hand. Her voice is tender. "You still haven't found him?"

I shake my head, frustrated. "I have no idea what he's doing or planning, and Ava refuses to get the police involved. With his drug use, he's irrational and unpredictable, and it's been such a relief that you were here while I was trying to find him, because at least I know you're safe."

"What about you?" Her eyes close and she shudders. "There's a madman on the loose who blames you for his life choices, and I've been partying over here with no knowledge of that. It makes me feel useless."

"I understand that now, and I'm sorry I didn't think of it that way before. I didn't want to ruin the experience of your cousin's wedding for you."

"I'm not a child you protect from everything, Landon."

"I know."

"So, Ava didn't know where he was?"

I tell her what Ava told me.

Rachel searches my face. "Do you believe her?"

"Maybe, but I don't believe him."

She's deep in thought, and after a few seconds,

she shudders. I know she's thinking about Evans and what he could do.

I need to find him.

I sigh. "You understand why I had to meet with her."

She nods. "I do."

"We have something special, Rachel. I want to know you won't ever let anything like suspicion make you think of throwing it away."

She shakes her head. "I'll never walk away from you."

The words soothe the deepest parts of me. I pull her onto my lap. "I've missed you. It took a lot of control for me not to steal you away from Laurie's wedding and find some corner to fuck you senseless."

"Jeez!" Her laughter tells me we're done talking about the Sinclairs. "Well, I'm glad you didn't. Although..." She gives me a meaningful look. "You can feel free to do so now."

"I intend to." I'm already undoing her robe, and I push it off her shoulders, almost sighing at the sight of her breasts. As I watch, her nipples harden. It's beautiful to see. "I love how responsive you are to me," I tell her, parting her legs. "Your body was made for my touch."

Her smile is heavenly. "Yours was made to drive me crazy."

I slide one hand between her legs, palming her, and feeling just how wet she already is.

"God, I need to fuck you."

Her eyes close and she lets out a soft sigh. "Feel free."

I cover her lips with mine, and for the rest of the night, I remind her, with my body, just how much she means to me.

CHAPTER 34

On the flight back to New York, I try to decode the reason behind Rachel's silence and pensiveness. Is she missing her family already, still worried about Sinclair?

"Are you fretting about something again?" I ask her gently.

She smiles quickly. "No. No, I'm just thinking about work."

It's not work. I can tell. I hold out my hand to her. "No matter what you're thinking about us, you can tell me, and we'll talk about it."

Her response is a smile. She takes my hand, squeezing it gently. She keeps holding it until she dozes off, but even as she sleeps, there's a small frown on her brow.

When we land, it's still daylight. Rachel keeps her

gaze out the window, and I busy myself reading reports on my tablet. I don't notice the crowd in front of the entrance to the Swanson Court until we're almost on top of them.

They surround the car, shouting questions we can't hear from inside the car.

Joe gets the car to the entrance, and the reporters surge.

"What's going on?" Rachel asks.

I shake my head. "I don't know."

"Do you want me to go into the parking lot?" Joe suggests.

"No." I run through various scenarios in my head and come up with nothing that could have caused this. If there was any accident involving my properties or, God forbid, Aidan, I'd know about it long before the press. "Whatever it is, it's better if we don't look as if we're running away from it."

The reporters keep swarming around the car, taking pictures. "Wait here," I tell Rachel, squeezing her hand. She nods.

I open the door and noise explodes in my ears. Along with Joe, I go over to Rachel's door, waiting as a few of Jed's guys join us and make a path so she can get inside without being mobbed.

They keep screaming my name, and Ava's.

Something has happened to Ava.

I focus on getting Rachel inside the building. After that, I'll find out what the hell is going on.

Jed is waiting in the lobby.

"What happened?" I can't keep the anger out of my voice. The presence of all that commotion outside the doors is very far from what we promise our guests.

"We are working to get rid of them."

"That is not what I asked." I need to know what the disturbance is all about.

Jed looks from me to Rachel then back.

"Ava Sinclair was stabbed this morning in her suite at the Gold Dust in San Francisco."

I freeze.

"She's currently in intensive care," Jed continues, "and we know the attacker was her brother. She was expecting him. The tapes show she let him into her suite..." I can't hear the rest of what he says. My head is pounding.

I didn't find him, and he attacked her, in my hotel.

He could have killed her, and it would be my fault.

"How is she?" Rachel asks, her voice full of concern.

Something happens in my chest. If he could get into the Gold Dust, how many more people in my life can he reach, and hurt...

"She's in intensive care," Jed is saying, "but from the reports I'm getting, they're sure she'll be fine."

"And Evans?"

"They don't know where he is."

"You'll shut this down?" She gestures to the entrance, and I realize we're still in the lobby. My head is still pounding. I should take control of the situation, but I just want to be as far away from it as possible.

"Already on it," Jed says.

Rachel turns to me. "Come on. Let's go up and decide what we're going to do."

I follow her silently. Poor Ava. I was too harsh on her. I dismissed her too cruelly, and now she's hurt, maybe even close to death.

Because however long it takes, everything I touch eventually suffers.

In the apartment, Rachel hands me a drink. I take it silently, downing half the fiery liquid in one gulp.

"Please don't blame yourself." Her voice comes as if from far away. "There's already so much you feel responsible for."

She's an angel, and I don't deserve one of my own. I never have.

"But I am responsible." I close my eyes. I can feel myself slipping into a dark place. "She was meeting him, probably trying to talk him out of his insane vendetta, and he stabbed her, his own sister, because

I put her in a position where he saw her as an enemy."

Rachel is shaking her head. Her eyes hold mine, pulling me out of the darkness. "Landon, he's clearly insane. You can't blame yourself for that."

She has no idea, no idea how much pain already lives in my past and how much of it I'm responsible for.

"Can't I?" I down the drink and face her. "He wasn't insane before I bought the Gold Dust out from under him. He was happily running it into the ground, but at least he was sane."

"Landon..." Her eyes are pleading. How can she not see that under everything else, this is all I can give? Pain.

"Don't you see how messed up everybody around me is? Evans is crazy. Ava is fighting for her life. Aidan is dealing with severe depression...did you know that? Sometimes he goes off the rails and disappears for days."

She reaches for me, but I shrug her hand away.

"You already know about my mother and my father, that miserable... We might as well have killed him, you know, me and Aidan. That's why Aidan can't bear to look at himself at times. The last thing he told our father was that we would all be better off without his alcoholic, useless presence, and I stood there and said nothing, because I felt the same."

Remember when you told me you wished your father had died along with your mother instead of lingering for a decade after? So dark, Landon. Do you share things like that with her?

Ava's voice mocks me in my thoughts, and I wait for Rachel's affection to turn to judgment.

I'm not worth your love, Rachel.

Can't you see?

"Maybe I thought there was some truth in the stories that drove my mother to her death," I continue bitterly. "Maybe I was sick of watching him drink himself to death while ignoring his sons, but I stood there while Aidan shredded him, and the next morning he was dead."

"Stop this..." she whispers. Her voice is shaking, but her eyes don't waver.

She loves me.

"How long before it's you?" I can't bear the thought. "Aren't you afraid you'll end up like us?"

She takes my hands. "No, because I don't see anything wrong with you, Landon. I love you."

If I were a better man, I'd let her go. I pull my hands from hers and head to the bar. "I need another drink."

Her voice stops me. "Stop feeling sorry for yourself. This is not the time to fall apart. Think of the negative press, the questions people will ask about the security at the Gold Dust. Think of the fact that Evans is on the run, of how much he hates you. You have to pull yourself together and manage this."

I lower myself back on the sofa. She's right. Of course she's right.

"I'm going to ask Jed to call the pilot and make sure you're ready to leave in a few hours," she says. "The whole world knows she was asking for you. You have to go."

Yes. Ava will need a familiar face beside her, a friend, and I need to find her brother before he hurts anyone else.

"You're right," I admit. "Of course. I have to go."

She rises from the sofa and starts to walk away.

"Will you come with me?"

She doesn't turn around, and for a moment, I'm afraid she'll say no.

"Of course," she says finally, then she turns around and gives me an encouraging smile. "Of course I'll come.

THERE'S MORE PRESS OUTSIDE THE HOSPITAL, BUT they're far enough away from the entrance that they aren't really a problem.

An orderly lead us to Ava's ward. Outside, there are a few of her relatives, uncles and cousins I vaguely recognize. We have little to talk about, and I'm relieved when the doctor arrives.

"You're Landon Court?"

"Yes." I take the hand she offers. "How is she?"

"She's asleep right now, as you can see." She gestures toward a small window where I can vaguely see Ava hooked up to a couple of machines. "And she's healing nicely. The attacker missed any major organs, so she'll be out of here in a few days."

"She's not in pain?"

"Not right now, no, though it will take some time for her to heal completely."

I nod. Rachel is looking through the window at Ava, a look of immeasurable sadness on her face.

"She looks..." She trails off, but I know exactly what she means. It's hard to think of the woman on the bed as Ava.

"I know."

Rachel sighs, and I notice the signs of tiredness on her face. In just one day, she's spent hours in the air, taken an unplanned trip, been harassed by reporters, and endured proximity to a tragedy, because of me.

How can she still love me?

"You should go back to the hotel," I suggest, feeling almost too guilty to look her in the eye. "I'll wait and talk to her when she wakes."

"Okay." She places a soft kiss on my cheek. "I'll see you later."

I watch her leave, the smell of her fragrance lingering in my nose. I wish things were different. I wish being with me would be a source of unending pleasure for her, not of pain, and fights, and stress.

How can she still love me?

The next few hours, the rest of the Sinclairs leave, and I'm left alone waiting for Ava.

Inside her room, there are a few bouquets of flowers. I sit on a chair beside the bed and watch her breathe.

"I'm so sorry, Ava," I say quietly. "I'm so sorry this happened."

She doesn't wake up. I stay till late in the night, and then I head to the hotel.

Rachel is already fast asleep when I get there, and in the bedroom of our suite, I watch her sleep, praying I can always protect her. Finally, I take a shower and join her in bed.

She wakes up when I slide under the covers and she turns to me, whispering my name with a question in her voice.

"Shhh." Kissing her, I slide my hands down her body. She's naked, and warm. She kisses me back with something that feels almost like ferocity, matching my need for her.

We make love in the dark. "I love you." I say the

words over and over. She echoes them back to me, and for now, that is enough.

THE NEXT MORNING, I LEAVE THE SUITE EARLY TO talk to Claude. It's disappointing that Evans could get into Ava's suite and leave without being seen. Claude is distraught, but it's not really his fault. The focus of my team was watching where Ava went outside the hotel. It never occurred to them that she would bring him here.

After I review all the security footage and spend a few minutes on the phone with Jed, I return to the hospital.

Ava is asleep when I get to her room, the machines beeping around her.

"She woke up for a little while. She asked about you. She was glad to know you were here," a friendly nurse tells me.

I nod then settle in the chair. The other Sinclairs are not around today, and I can't say I regret that.

After a while, I get up and go to the window. Outside, it's a beautiful day, and somewhere out there is Evans, hateful and vengeful, eager to hurt me, willing to hurt his own sister because of how much he hates me.

I should be with Rachel. I should be protecting her.

"Landon..."

I turn to the bed.

Ava is smiling at me, her face pale. "I knew you would come."

I move closer to the bed. "How do you feel?"

She makes a sound. "A bit weak."

"Do you want the nurse?"

"No. Not yet." She holds out a hand to me. "I'm so sorry. I should never have asked him to come to the Gold Dust. He wanted more money, and I wanted to see him. I think being there, he got a little triggered, and when he found out I'd seen you in New York, he just..." Her eyes fill with tears. "I just wanted to talk to him."

"Forget about all that." I smile at her. "Focus on getting better."

"But what will happen to him?" Tears slide down the sides of her eyes. "He can't go to jail. You have to help him."

"I don't..."

"Please..." She turns tear-stained eyes to me. "I love you, Landon. I always have. It's killing me to think it's all going to end like this, with you walking away from me and Evans ending up in jail."

"Ava." I try to sound patient. "You're not well. You need to rest."

"I love you," she says again. "Does that not matter? I waited a decade for you, and now I've almost died for you. You can't just walk away from me, Landon, please."

"Stop it. This"—I gesture around the room—"it's not about us. It's about you getting better."

Her eyes flash with something like resentment. "Fuck getting better. I need you. You always came back to me before. Why can't it be the same this time?"

"Because I love someone else, Ava, more than I ever thought it was possible to love." Her lips tremble, and I can't help feeling bad for her. "I'm sorry this happened, but if you want to be in my life in any capacity, you must accept that Rachel is the only woman who'll ever mean anything to me."

She turns her face away. "So why did you come?"

"Because she asked me to."

She makes a sound. "And she's here too?"

"Yes."

"Well, you can leave." Her jaw sets. "I'll be fine."

"Ava—"

"No, don't." She smiles bitterly. "I don't want your pity. Please. I'll be fine."

She presses a button, and a nurse enters the room. I wait as she attends to Ava. In a few moments, she's asleep again.

"She'll be out for a while." The nurse smiles at me. "Maybe you can come back?"

I shake my head. "No. There's no point."

When I return to the suite, Rachel is not there. For a short moment of panic, I rush to check that her things are still in the closet. They are.

She's not leaving me. She said she wouldn't.

Though after everything, after all the things I told her before we left New York, who would blame her?

I fix myself a drink, remembering the resentment in Ava's eyes, the pain and dismissal. But no matter how sorry I feel for her, I can't give her what she wants, and I can't let Evans hurt anyone else.

The door to the suite opens and Rachel comes in. She's dressed simply, and when she sees me, her face breaks into a soft smile.

Her appearance and her smile bring me so much relief that for a few seconds, I'm speechless. "I wondered where you were."

"Claude could have told you," she says. "I went to see Jules."

I haven't even done more than speak to Cameron on the phone. "How is she?"

"Ready to pop."

I spend a moment imagine Cameron and Jules's future offspring. "Would you like something to drink?" I ask Rachel.

She refuses with a small headshake. "How is she?"

Ava.

"She's doing great. Evans is still missing, but many people are trying to find him. He wanted more money, it seems, and when he found out she met with me in New York, it drove him crazy enough to hurt her."

"What will happen when they find him?"

At this point, I don't care how much Ava blames me. "He'll never hurt anyone again."

Rachel turns away from me, leaving me wondering what I've said wrong, wondering if, maybe, she blames me too.

"When are we leaving?" she asks.

"As soon as you're ready."

She leaves the room, getting ready to go while I make the arrangements for our trip. We barely talk through the journey to the plane and during the flight. I soon succumb to exhaustion, waking up when we arrive in New York.

I know there's something wrong, but I have no idea what it is, and Rachel makes no attempt to talk to me.

After an early dinner, she goes to bed. I work for a while, and when I finally join her in bed, I dream she's somewhere beyond my reach, hurting, and I can do nothing to save her.

CHAPTER 35

The silence continues over the next few days. Rachel barely talks to me. I know I should ask her again what the matter is, but I'm afraid of hearing the answer.

I feel like I'm watching her slip away, and it's killing me.

I bury myself in work and wait for my people or the police to find Evans Sinclair. At night, my sleep is filled with nightmares.

Every night when my nightmares wake me up, the sight of the quiet pity in Rachel's eyes leaves me feeling more helpless. I start to spend the nights in my study.

I finally arrange to see a new therapist. When I tell Rachel about it over breakfast one morning, her only reply is a quiet nod. It feels like I have lost her already.

That day, I spend only a few hours at work before going to find Aidan in his office at the theater. After the opening, his role in the play is winding down, and he's already looking at other projects, trying to decide what his next job will be.

He's also in love.

"Everybody loves her." He's talking about Liz. "The reviews are out of this world. She'll be one of the biggest things Broadway has ever seen."

"I'm glad."

He gives me a puzzled look. "You sound grouchy."

"Do I?" I shake my head. "I just needed to get out of my world for a while."

"Hotels aren't doing it for you anymore?" He laughs. "I could wrangle you a bit part in a musical."

I chuckle. "I'd steal the show, you know."

He laughs again, and in his eyes I see the respect and admiration I've tried to deserve all my life. "I'm sure you could," he says.

I let out a deep breath. "I can't focus on work."

"Is it this thing with Evans?"

The *thing with Evans* affected Aidan too. He protested when I hired someone one to protect him. Even though his new bodyguard is an unobtrusive guy whose job is to keep an eye on him during his journeys to and from the theater, he still finds it humiliating, but he's accepted it for my sake.

"Some. Yes." I grimace. "It's not been the same, with Rachel...since we got back."

"Since you dragged her halfway across the country to Ava's bedside, you mean."

"I didn't..." I shake my head. "I didn't drag her... and I had to go to see Ava. She was asking for me. Rachel wanted me to go."

"Maybe." Aidan shrugs. His dislike for Ava has always been clear. "I've never liked her, nor that little gremlin she calls her brother."

"I know."

"Have you tried talking to Rachel?"

"She's just closed me off. To be truthful, I think it started even before we left Barbados."

"So, ask her what the problem is."

That's the problem—what if her answer is something I don't want to hear?

"I can't even imagine my life without her." I look at Aidan, and his face tells me he understands.

He pats my shoulder. "All the more reason to end the silence."

I have that in my mind when I return to the apartment. It's still early, and the lobby of my hotel is busy with people coming and going from a book signing.

I wonder if Rachel knows about the event. It's the sort of thing she would like.

The apartment is empty when I enter.

As soon as I enter the foyer, I can see that something is wrong. Rachel's purse in on the floor, and on the carpet close to it, there's a small red stain.

On a reflex, I hit the panic button on my phone and hurry into the living room. My eyes go to the curtains leading to the balcony. They're billowing inward, letting in the biting wind.

"Rachel." I'm already running toward the doors.

"He has a gun!" Her scream is filled with terror, and my heart stops beating. "He has a gun," she screams again just as I clear the doors.

Her hands and feet are bound. She is leaning on the balustrade, edging away from a figure dressed in black. Evans Sinclair has a gun trained on me, and that's fine with me, as long as it's not pointed at Rachel.

I keep my voice steady though I want to scream. "What do you want?"

Evans jeers at me. "What do you think?"

My eyes go to Rachel again. Her terror is tearing me apart. What has he done to her?

I turn back to Evans. "You're not going to get it."

He smiles. "I think I already have."

"Really?" I need to keep him talking until Joe gets here, hopefully with the rest of my security. "You're a wanted man. You're going to jail. You won't get your hotel back, and you won't get away with whatever you plan to do here."

He glares at me, his eyes filled with hate. "You have no idea how much I hate you, how much I've hated you all these years. I loved her, and she chose you, over and over again. Ava was perfect, and you ruined her. You made her give you all the time, all the attention she should have given me."

At first, I'm confused. It takes me a minute to realize what he means. "Your sister—"

"Yes!" he screams. "I loved her, and you took her from me, and then you stole my hotel." He goes silent and draws in a breath of cold air. "Maybe I won't get my hotel back, but then, maybe I don't want it anymore. Maybe I won't even get out of here or get away with this, but I'm going to hurt you, Landon Court, and you're never going to forget about me."

I know he's about to do something, and when he swings the gun in Rachel's direction, my vision goes black. I leap for him, my only thought is to prevent that gun from going off.

He turns back to me, as if in slow motion. His eyes widen, and I feel something hit me like a sledgehammer. I crash into him just as the recoil from the gun swings his arm backward, my weight does the rest, and we both go over.

The last thing I hear is Rachel screaming.

I love you, Rachel.
I love you.

CHAPTER 36

I watch Evans fall. I watch him hit the ground with a sickening thud as Joe pulls me back over the balustrade, onto the balcony.

Rachel is passed out on the floor.

I crawl toward her. "Rachel." My voice is hoarse desperate.

"She's passed out." Joe's voice is calm. "You're bleeding. I'm calling an ambulance."

As the adrenaline recedes, the pain in my shoulder seizes me. Joe, done with his call, pulls me off Rachel's inert body, takes care of my jacket, and starts to bind my shoulder.

My vision blurs. I hear sirens. I try to reach out to touch Rachel's face but she's too far away.

I panic. "I need to talk to her."

"You will." Joe's voice comes from far away. More

people enter the balcony. "He's lost a lot of blood," I hear him say. "She passed out."

"Rachel..." I say her name, again and again. My voice rises. I see a strange face peering at my eyes. Then, I feel a pinprick, and everything goes from blurry to black.

WHEN I WAKE UP IN THE HOSPITAL, RACHEL IS ON a chair beside my bed. I try to reach for her, and the machines around me go off. Medical personnel rush into the room, and I try to see her between their scrub-clothed bodies. They feed me some more drugs, and I'm sleeping again.

The next time I wake up, Rachel is still there. Now, she's asleep, and I watch her for as long as I can before I drift off to sleep again.

"He's stable now. As you know, the bullet barely missed a major artery. He's very lucky."

"As am I."

I open my eyes to see Rachel talking to a man in scrubs. I try to say her name, and it comes out as a croak.

"Look who's awake!" The doctor sounds too cheerful for his line of work.

"Rachel," I croak again.

She's already beside me, taking my hand, her eyes full of tears. "Landon."

I try to smile, but my mouth feels like dust. "Rachel."

"I'm here."

I squeeze her hand then go under again.

They move me home the next day, with a nurse to help change the dressing on the wound and feed me pain medication.

The pain in my shoulder is a dull thud, nothing compared to the relief I feel when I see Rachel beside my bed.

I kept her safe.

For the rest of my life, I will be grateful that I was there, to put myself between her and Evans.

I kept her safe.

This time, I didn't fail.

I wake up feeling peaceful, not sure if it's morning or night. My shoulder is aching dully, but Rachel is beside me on the bed, and I can bear any pain just for the pleasure of watching her for a few moments.

I watch her sleep for a long time, curled up on her side, facing me.

My angel.

How did I get so lucky?

I know no matter what happened, I would have gladly given my life for her, and I'd do it over and over again.

After a while, her eyes open, and she sees me watching her. She smiles softly and leans up on her elbow.

"You're awake."

"Yeah." I groan. "I feel like I've been asleep for weeks."

"A few days on and off, to give your shoulder time to heal." She studies my face. "How're you feeling?"

"Achy."

Concern shadows her features. "Would you like some water?"

"Yes."

She starts to rise, and I reach out a weak hand to stop her. "But don't go yet. I just want to look at you."

Her eyes water. "Landon..."

My eyes are stinging too, but not because I'm sad or anything. All I feel is gratitude. I'm so grateful to be here, with her.

I take her hands, and they tremble forcefully in mine.

"You're shaking."

She smiles through tears. "I know."

I close my eyes, searching for words to comfort her.

"Let me get you that water." She moves to get up again.

"Wait." I swallow. "I'm sorry. I'm so sorry about Evans, for everything you went through... If only I'd listened to you after the thing with the car..."

She shakes her head "It doesn't matter. It's over now."

"It matters to me. I..." I see her out there on the balcony again, him turning the gun toward her. "God!" I swallow. "When I saw you out there with him, I think a part of me died of fear. I would die without you, Rachel. You are my life."

Tears fall down her face. "I love you so much," she whispers. "When I saw you start to go over, I think my heart stopped beating."

"You think?" I smile. "You passed out."

The teasing works. She laughs. "Yeah, I did."

"When Joe pulled me back and I saw you lying there, for a moment I thought I had failed and he'd hit you." I grimace. "Joe had to pry me off you."

"They sedated you because you kept on screaming about me." She smiles. "They couldn't work on your wound."

Makes sense. She lies beside me for a few more moments before going to get the water. I drink as much as I can then fall back on the pillows.

"Do you want to go back to sleep?"

"No." I want to keep looking at her. "Come back."

She returns to bed.

I take a deep breath.

"The reason I was home early that day..." I take her hand and meet her gaze. "I wanted to talk to you, about San Francisco, about Ava, about the fact that I could see that I was losing you."

"You weren't..."

I shake my head. "You were here, physically, but emotionally, you were drifting away. I could feel it, and I knew it had something to do with Ava, her stabbing, how I reacted to it..."

"It doesn't matter now," she says gently. "I love you, more than anything. I don't care about Ava now."

"But at the time?"

She pulls in a shaky breath. "I was... I don't know what I was feeling. I guess I thought she still meant too much to you. I thought that was why you wouldn't get Evans locked up after he tried to hit you with his car, why you were so broken up when you heard about her stabbing... She told me, more than once, that you always came back to her, that I was only temporary. She's known you far longer than I have, and she was so confident... I tried to ignore it, but watching you so devastated about her, it all came back."

The revelation that Ava said something to her makes me realize how blind I've been. Of course Ava would not have kept her games to just me. She'd have tried to hit Rachel too.

I remember every event we attended where Ava showed up...the hotel opening, Aidan's play, Rachel's mood afterward...*of course.* I was so blind.

And Rachel suffered for my blindness.

I sigh. "*She* always came back, Rachel, after every divorce or high-profile breakup, and if I was single, as I usually was, I let her in, because she already knew, more than anyone else, that I didn't want permanence—at least I didn't before you."

Rachel's eyes mist with pain. "She made me think she was the great love of your life."

I shake my head. "You're the great love of my life, and I have a scar to prove it."

Her smile is sad. "You're already joking about it. It's going to take a while for me."

I take a deep breath. Slowly, I explain to her about my history with Ava, the shared pain that brought us together all those years ago, how I thought I deserved nothing better. Our relationship was never exclusive. She always left to gallivant with high-profile lovers, and then she'd come back, professing to miss me. I didn't realize then she was trying to make me admit I loved her. She proposed, and I refused, because even though I didn't think there was anyone else for me, a part of me refused to consider that kind of commitment. So, I chose to focus on my hotels. A week later, she was married.

"She thinks she broke your heart," Rachel tells me when I finish.

"She told you that. Trust me, she knows it's not true." I've never given Ava any reason to believe I belonged to her, and I tell Rachel that.

"She made me feel like I was just someone temporary in your life, and she was much more than that to you." Rachel sighs. "When she was hurt and you were so shaken...I was jealous and scared...and ashamed of my reaction. She was fighting for her life, and all I could think about was losing you."

My darling angel.

I want to put my arms around her, but I make do with only one.

"You're never losing me, Rachel." I hold her gaze. "As for Ava, at the hospital, she said some things that made it clear I had to let her know, very plainly, we will never be more than friends again."

She looks down at our hands, fingers entwined. I need her to believe me.

"You own me, Rachel, every part of me. Knowing you're mine is what keeps me going. It's what makes it all meaningful. Before I met you, I thought I liked being alone. I took pride in not needing anyone, but I need you, and I'd give up everything just for you to never doubt that again."

"You don't have to give up anything," she whispers. "I love you, helplessly and completely."

Hearing the words fills me with so much joy. It feels like my shoulder has healed miraculously.

"I'm exhausted," I say with a smile. "Who knew intense declarations of love could be this tiring?"

She chuckles, but then her face clouds with worry.

"I need to tell you something," she says.

I swallow my alarm. Whatever it is, I can take it, as long as I have her.

"What is it?"

She takes a deep breath.

"I'm...I'm pregnant."

At first, I'm not sure I heard right.

She continues talking before I can reply. "I found out in Barbados, and I wanted to tell you, but when I called... Well, you know what happened when I called."

I close my eyes. I knew something was wrong, and now I hate that I didn't bother to coax it out of her. Instead, I got mad at her. I should have been soothing whatever anxiety she was feeling, and instead I accused her of overreacting.

And yet she still loves me.

I don't deserve you, Rachel.

"When Evans..." She sighs. "I couldn't stop thinking about how I didn't tell you, how I'd never get a chance to."

"Stop." I won't let her punish herself for this one. "I understand how you felt...I do." There's an ache in my chest as I continue. "You know now that everything I do—work, solving the problems that have come up in the last few weeks—is so I can get them out of the way and come home to you. Meeting with Ava, trying to find Evans—it was always about making sure he could never hurt you, because I'd rather die than let anyone hurt you."

She nods. "I know."

"I hate that you felt unsure of me, and I take the blame for that. You'll never have cause to doubt me again." I hold her gaze, imploring her with my eyes. "I promise. Everything I am, everything you want, I'll give you, and if you let me, I'll give everything I have, for you, for us, and for our child."

She smiles through tears. "I only want you."

"All of me," I tell her. "You already have all of me."

EPILOGUE

"Ohhh, that feels good!" Rachel moans, her eyes closed. Her hair is in a knot on top of her head, and soft tendrils frame her face. She looks unbelievably lovely, and she is, both inside and out.

I increase the pressure of my fingers and press down on the bottoms of her feet.

She sighs. "Don't ever stop."

"Okay." I'm laughing. "I'll massage your feet forever."

Her eyes narrow in suspicion. "Are you making fun of me?"

"Never!"

She rubs at her stomach, which, at eight months and three weeks, is bigger than I ever thought possible. I'd never say that though.

"Just so you know, I can still kick your ass."

"I know," I admit.

"Really?"

"Hmm."

She looks petulant. "Now you're just humoring me."

"Have I told you how lovely you look today?" I'm not lying. She looks lovely, lush and ripe, with curves everywhere.

She groans. "Stop flattering me." She pulls her foot from my grip and rises to her feet, then stops and makes a sound of exhaustion.

I'm instantly by her side. "Are you all right?"

"Yes. I stood up too fast. I'm fine. I'm pregnant, not an invalid."

"Okay." I smile. "Can I get you something to eat?"

Her eyes light up, and she spends the next few minutes detailing everything she wants to eat and then changing her mind.

I listen patiently. I love taking care of her, especially now that in a few days, our lives will change forever.

"I thought Aidan was coming over." she says suddenly, forgetting about the food. "Is he coming?"

"Yes, later."

Her voice softens. "How is he?"

Hurt. Heartbroken. Enraged. Ever since Liz left the play and him, flying across the country to work on movie projects, he's reverted almost to his lowest point. "He's a little sore, but seeing you will cheer him up, I'm sure."

She laughs. "Because I look like a hippo."

"Because he loves you and can't wait to meet his nephew." I put my arm around her. "And...you look like a sylph."

"Liar."

"Never."

She grins then scowls. "You promised me food."

I spring into action. "I'm on it."

Esmeralda is in the kitchen, and with her help, I make up a platter for Rachel. She likes to nibble at a variety of things at the same time, and it amuses me to watch. When I return to the living room, she's standing beside the sofa, a look of horror on her face.

I drop the platter. "What? What is it?"

Horror turns to wonder. She looks at me, eyes wide. "I think my water just broke."

THE NEXT FEW HOURS ARE A BLUR. I GET THE BAGS and get her down to the car. She insists she's fine, but I don't let her hand out of mine.

At the hospital, her doctor is already waiting. I've prepared for this for months, but my nerves are shot as all the professionals do their jobs.

I make all the necessary calls, parents, Laurie, her

brother Dylan, Aidan. Soon, the waiting room is full of family.

Breathe, Landon.

Inside the delivery room, I clean up and scrub up then wait, holding Rachel's hand as the contractions come.

It's an easy birth. The hours fly by, for me at least, and when they put my baby in my arms, I'm the one doing the crying.

"He's beautiful," I blubber. My emotions are a mess.

Forceful, ruthless, single-minded...

Cold, heartless, unfeeling...

Hotel magnate.

All that is washed away the moment I hold my son in my arms.

Landon Court...Dad.

Husband, lover, dad.

That's who I am.

Rachel is looking at me, smiling through her exhaustion. "Let me see."

I put him in her arms, and he makes a satisfied sound. She touches a finger to his tiny nose and her lips quirk. "He looks like you."

I study the contented face. "I don't know."

"Hello, Preston," she whispers, saying the name we chose a long time ago. It's for my father, and for her family too. "Hello, Preston Foster Court."

He squirms and yawns.

I chuckle. "I think he likes it."

She meets my gaze and gives me an angelic smile. Even with the exhaustion in her eyes, she has never looked more beautiful.

"Yes," she agrees. "I think he does."

The End

ACKNOWLEDGMENTS

It's entirely possible that I would have procrastinated this book into oblivion were it not for the wonderful readers who never let me forget that I promised to write Landon's story. Thank you for keeping me on my toes.

Also, thanks to Caitlin at Editing by C. Marie for picking out my grammar mistakes, and awesome proofreader Cassie Hess-Dean for making sure I missed nothing.

Thanks to my readers, without whom none of this would be possible.

And my husband, for his unending support.

ABOUT SERENA GREY

I'm obsessed with books and read whenever I can—romance, fantasy, mystery, history—anything I can lay my hands on. I grew up reading Danielle Steel, Nora Roberts and many other romance authors. These days, I read Whitney Garcia Williams, Laurelin Paige, E.L James and Sylvia Day, though you're as likely to find me reading Brandon Sanderson and George R R Martin.

I'm an older millennial—made in 1985. I have a husband I love and a baby son I adore. I love wine, coffee with lots of cream, chocolate chip cookies, and my superpower is knowing how to live on the bright side of life.

To be the first to find out about my new releases, sign up for my Mailing List at www.serenagrey.com/alerts

For more information, go to www.serenagrey.com

bookbub.com/authors/serena-grey

facebook.com/authorserenagrey

twitter.com/s_greyauthor

instagram.com/theserenagrey

BOOKS BY SERENA GREY

A DANGEROUS MAN SERIES

Awakening: A Dangerous Man #1

Rebellion: A Dangerous Man #2

Claim: A Dangerous Man #3

Surrender: A Dangerous Man #4

UNDENIABLE

SWANSON COURT SERIES

Drawn to You

The Hooker

Addicted to You

Lost in You

Landon

WILD SEXY SERIES

Wild Sexy Thing

Wild Sexy Fix

Wild Sexy Hurt

Wild Sexy Love

MORE THAN ANYTHING: A CHRISTMAS
ROMANCE

~

Find at www.serenagrey.com/books

CONNECT WITH SERENA

Facebook: www.facebook.com/authorserenagrey

Twitter: @s_greyauthor

Goodreads: www.goodreads.com/serenagrey

Website: www.serenagrey.com